I0585645

Engagements with Adaptation

Engagements with Adaptation invites students both to consider adaptations on their own terms and to engage with the urgent questions they raise about literary canons; the media industry; the relations between different kinds of media; the nature of national, political, and cultural identities; and the ways in which contemporary digital and social media have complicated the roles of producers and consumers of texts.

Thomas Leitch guides students through six ways of thinking about adaptation: aesthetic, intertextual, industrial, biological, sociological, and participatory. He explores multiple media and discusses a wide range of sources, including *Frankenstein*, *Persepolis*, *Bridgerton*, and the world of DC and Marvel comics. Each of the six chapters includes a detailed discussion of Greta Gerwig's film *Barbie* to help readers compare the ways in which these six approaches can engage with a single text. The book also offers invaluable insight into copyright, censorship, critical race theory, and immigration. The questions at the end of each section embed and reinforce learning and prompt further research.

This accessible and engaging guide reveals how the "anti-discipline" of adaptation studies is adjacent to a remarkable array of disciplines, making it a much-needed resource for students interested in television studies, moving image studies, digital media studies, translation studies, performance studies, music and art history and creation, border studies, race studies, queer studies, disability studies, and ecocritical studies.

Thomas Leitch holds the Unidel Andrew B. Kirkpatrick, Jr. Chair in Writing at the University of Delaware, USA. His most recent publications include *The Scandal of Adaptation* (2023) and *The History of American Literature on Film* (2019).

Routledge Engagements with Literature

This series presents engagement as discovery. It aims to encourage ways to read seriously and to help readers hone and develop new habits of thinking critically and creatively about what they read—before, during, and after doing it. Each book in the series actively involves its readers by encouraging them to find their own insights, to develop their own judgments, and to inspire them to enter ongoing debates. Moreover, each *Engagements* volume:

- Provides essential information about its topic as well as alternative views and approaches;
- Covers the classic scholarship on its topic as well as the newest approaches and suggests new directions for study and research;
- Includes innovative "Engagements" sections that demonstrate practices for engaging with literature or that provide suggestions for further independent engagement;
- Provides an array of fresh, stimulating, and effective catalysts to reading, thinking, writing, and research.

Above all, *Engagements with Literature* shows that actively engaging with literature rewards the effort and that any reader can make new discoveries. My hope is the books in this series will help readers discover new, better, and more exciting and enjoyable ways of doing what we do when we read.

Available in this series:

Engagements with Shakespearean Drama
William Walker

Engagements with Contemporary Literary and Critical Theory
Evan Gottlieb

For more information about this series, please visit: https://www.routledge.com/Routledge-Engagements-with-Literature/book-series/EWL

Engagements with Adaptation

Thomas Leitch

Routledge
Taylor & Francis Group

LONDON AND NEW YORK

First published 2025
by Routledge
4 Park Square, Milton Park, Abingdon, Oxon OX14 4RN

and by Routledge
605 Third Avenue, New York, NY 10158

Routledge is an imprint of the Taylor & Francis Group, an informa business

© 2025 Thomas Leitch

British Library Cataloguing-in-Publication Data
A catalogue record for this book is available from the British Library

Library of Congress Cataloging-in-Publication Data
Names: Leitch, Thomas M., author.
Title: Engagements with adaptation / Thomas Leitch.
Description: Abingdon, Oxon ; New York, NY : Routledge, 2025. |
Series: Routledge engagements with literature |
Includes bibliographical references and index. |
Identifiers: LCCN 2024043713 (print) | LCCN 2024043714 (ebook) |
ISBN 9781032572314 (hardback) | ISBN 9781032572321 (paperback) |
ISBN 9781003438410 (ebook)
Subjects: LCSH: Film adaptations–History and criticism. |
LCGFT: Film criticism.
Classification: LCC PN1997.85 .L34 2025 (print) | LCC PN1997.85 (ebook) |
DDC 791.43/6–dc23/eng/20250101
LC record available at https://lccn.loc.gov/2024043713
LC ebook record available at https://lccn.loc.gov/2024043714

ISBN: 978-1-032-57231-4 (hbk)
ISBN: 978-1-032-57232-1 (pbk)
ISBN: 978-1-003-43841-0 (ebk)

DOI: 10.4324/9781003438410

Typeset in Sabon
by Newgen Publishing UK

To the students in ENGL 685: Approaches to Adaptation (Spring 2024), who did so much to bring this book to life.

Contents

Acknowledgments

It seems appropriate that in writing one of my shortest books, I have had the help of more people than ever in bringing it to completion. The list that follows is as comprehensive as I can manage; I offer my humble apologies to anyone I've forgotten to thank.

I will always be indebted to Karen Raith for first approaching me about this project, whetting an appetite for working on it that I'd never recognized, and rolling back the deadline we'd agreed on long enough for me to experiment with using a rough draft of it as an outline for a new course before submitting the manuscript. I am obliged to the three anonymous reviewers who read my proposal and gave invaluable feedback on it. Receiving a Lars Elleström Residential Fellowship from the Centre for Intermedial and Multimodal Studies (IMS) gave me a priceless opportunity to talk over the project with colleagues, friends, and students at and around Linnaeus University during Summer 2023. I'm particularly grateful to my hosts, Niklas Salmose and Jørgen Bruhn, for revising, or adapting, their initial plan to leave me in peace to write and instead, at my request, creating opportunities that would bring me into many productive conversations, formal and informal, with Nafiseh Mousavi, Piia Posti, Beate Schirrmacher, and the IMS members—Yagmur Atlar, Elliott Berggren, Matilda Davidsson, Heidrun Führer, Heidi Hart, Anna Ishchenko, Signe Kjaer Jensen, Viktor Ferdinand Kovács, Liviu Lutas, Emma Tornborg, Martin van der Linden, and Shawn Zou—who challenged me to think harder about the approaches to adaptation that I was rehearsing.

Several members of the Adaptation Today listserv (adaptation-today@ gaggle.email), the indispensable online community launched by Kristen Figgins—Jim Fleury, Tom Grochowski, Julie Grossman, Jerod Ra'Del Hollyfield, Lissette Lopez Szwydky, Kyle Meikle, Rebecca Raddatz, and Elsie Walker—generously took the trouble to suggest so many exemplary adaptations they had used successfully in their classrooms that it was impossible for me to include more than a fraction of them here. Ursula Vooght kindly read a draft chapter and offered helpful suggestions for its improvement; and friends and colleagues at the F. Scott Fitzgerald Association, the South Atlantic Modern Language Association, the Northeast Modern Language Association, the Literature Film Association, and the Association for Adaptation Studies watched my trial balloons with a critical eye and offered helpful comments of their own. Carolyn Boyle worked tactfully and tirelessly editing the manuscript to bring it into alignment with Routledge's house style and to purge many errors, and Ann-Kathrin Klein and the production staff at Routledge managed to be at once efficient, professional, and accommodating. It goes without saying (except in this sentence) that I take responsibility for any errors that remain. My deepest gratitude goes to the students in my graduate seminar in adaptation studies—Sarah Bradshaw, Summer Cardarelli, Ellie Carver, Cat Champney, Kallie Comardelle, Remy DeJoseph, Alexis Kennedy, Michael McShane, Erica Quinones, Noah Slowik, and Violet Strawderman—who agreed to take such leading roles in choosing critical texts and prooftexts and organizing discussions that I often played a supporting player to their star turns. It was a privilege to work with them, and it's an honor to dedicate this book to them.

List of illustrations

Figures

Introduction

In an increasingly and relentlessly professionalized educational environment, why would anyone invest time and energy to study adaptation? Certainly not to get a job. Although there are lots of writers, filmmakers, television producers, videographers, agents, managers, and other workers whose jobs involve adaptation, "adapter" is not a common or therefore a viable description for any of these jobs. Nor is the study of adaptation the key to landing a place in a top graduate school. Although many graduate programs offer courses in adaptation, the only dedicated graduate program in adaptation in the world is in De Montfort University in Leicester, United Kingdom. Practitioners have been studying adaptation since time immemorial. Theorists joined them over a century ago. And the subject has become ever more common in college classrooms over the past 60 years. Yet adaptation studies has made little progress in establishing itself as an academic field or discipline in its own right. That's why Jillian Saint Jacques has called it "a praxis that perpetually moves in and out of all academic fields" (Saint Jacques 12), rather than a field in itself. For better or worse, it has not followed cinema studies in becoming a discipline of its own. Instead, it remains a non-discipline, even an anti-discipline—a decidedly marginal field of study, if it is indeed really a field.

The marginalization of adaptation studies begins with the exceptional reluctance of its leading practitioners to define its subject. The two most authoritative books on adaptation studies, Linda Hutcheon's *Theory of Adaptation* and Kamilla Elliott's *Theorizing Adaptation*, define "adaptation" in highly problematic ways. Hutcheon, who suggests that we consider adaptation in three different ways—as a series of works, a process of creating those works, and a process of receiving and interpreting those works—defines a given work of adaptation as "an announced and extensive transposition of a particular work or works" (Hutcheon with O'Flynn 7)—a perfectly satisfactory definition until you lean on the words *announced, extensive, transposition*, and *particular*, all of which turn out to be disconcertingly hard to pin down. Is the screenplay for *Barbie*—whose credits describe it as "based on 'Barbie' by Mattel"—an original screenplay, fitting the category in which it was nominated for a Critics Choice Association award, which it ultimately

DOI: 10.4324/9781003438410-1

won? Or is it an adapted screenplay, as the Academy of Motion Picture Arts and Sciences held in ignoring the exception the Academy rules make for screenplays based on material originally presented in another medium? According to the Academy, if that material is "non-fiction and does not contain a narrative or is used as research material for the project," this means that "the screenplay is not an adaptation of the underlying material"—a position director Greta Gerwig, who with her partner Noah Baumbach had written its screenplay, had taken when she campaigned for a Best Original Screenplay nomination. Was the Academy acting in accord with its own rules when it rejected this position?

This question is hardly unique to *Barbie*. Is the 1995 movie *Clueless*, whose credits nowhere mention Jane Austen, an updated adaptation of Austen's novel *Emma* or not? Are short memes or TikTok videos that borrow ideas or material from earlier texts extensive enough to be called adaptations or not? Is it possible, with the best will in the world, to produce a copy of a given text that is not a transposition? Elliott's far more extensive definition, which fills a page and a half in *Theorizing Adaptation*, is introduced with a facetiously self-conscious proviso—"This adaptive definition of adaptation has been adapted from prior scholarship and is subject to further adaptation" (Elliott 198)—which preemptively qualifies rather than emphasizes its authority as a definition-in-progress.

If you are dissatisfied with these definitions, you should know that scholars have suggested many other ways to approach adaptation. Robert Stam notes that earlier writers have thought about adaptation as:

> reading, writing, critique, translation, transmutation, metamorphosis, recreation, transvocalization, resuscitation, transfiguration, actualization, transmodalization, signifying, performance, dialogization, cannibalization, reinvisioning, incarnation, or reaccentuation. (The words beginning with the prefix 'trans' emphasize the *changes* brought about in the adaptation, while those beginning with the prefix 're' emphasize the *recombinant* function of adaptation.)
>
> (Stam 25)

Julie Sanders, citing Adrian Poole, lists as possible synonyms for adaptation "borrowing, stealing, appropriating, inheriting, assimilating, ... being influenced, inspired, dependent, indebted, haunted, possessed ... homage, mimicry, travesty, echo, allusion, and intertextuality," and adds to this catalog several new alternatives: "variation, version, interpretation, imitation, proximation, supplement, increment, improvisation, prequel, sequel, continuation, addition, paratext, hypertext, palimpsest, graft, rewriting, reworking, refashioning, re-vision, re-evaluation" (Sanders 2, 3). Elliott, in preparation for her own definition, notes that earlier writers have equated adaptation at different times and in different contexts with pastiche, palimpsest, bricolage, dialogization, imitation, intertextuality, supplement, mimicry, assimilation, paratext, hypertext, prequel, sequel, transmodalization, inspiration, transformation, transfiguration, incarnation, recreation, metamorphosis, vampirism, haunting, possession, actualization, revocalization, realization, homage, inheriting, influence, echo, allusion, indebtedness, and travesty (Elliott 183).

Given such a profusion of ways to engage with adaptation, the six approaches this book has chosen—aesthetic, intertextual, industrial, biological, sociological, and participatory—are anything but exhaustive. Although they all depend on different definitions of adaptation, they are more interesting and valuable for their implications about how adaptation operates in a wide range of contexts. As the catalogs above indicate, these six approaches are only the tip of a very large iceberg. For this reason, my selection, emphasis, and analysis of them may seem frustratingly arbitrary. You may find some of them more compelling or useful than others, but I don't intend to steer you toward a preference for any of them in particular; instead, I think you'll find that they are altogether stronger as a repertory of possible approaches you can draw on as needed, and perhaps expand on your own. My discussion of them is largely chronological—not in order to imply a narrative of progress from yesterday's limited knowledge to today's more comprehensive wisdom, but in order to show the ways in which each of them grew out of the others—and out of the challenge of new, or newly discovered or emphasized, adaptations the field has needed to deal with.

Just as these six approaches are not meant to be exhaustive, they are not meant to be monolithic or mutually exclusive either. Although many scholars have become identified with a single approach to adaptation, others have shifted their ground or incorporated multiple perspectives over their careers, and you should feel free to do the same, even within a given essay on adaptation. Each of the six approaches I propose is itself a collection of more or less closely related approaches I have bundled together in order to follow their practitioners—who often disagree among themselves, even if they share the same general approach—and to make them more pointed and useful. In order to explain in concrete terms how each of these engagements works, I will show how they can be applied to particular adaptations drawn from cinema, television, comic books, videogames, musical performances, and the stage. These examples, like the engagements they display, are meant to be suggestive rather than exhaustive. And each chapter includes a section on *Barbie* to show how all six of these approaches can usefully engage and illuminate a single adaptation.

Finally, and most importantly, I should note that each of these six approaches is designed not to avoid but to accept and ultimately to embrace the marginality of adaptations, for several practical reasons. For one thing, it is entirely realistic to do so in the current academic climate. As the humanities continue to shrink under demands from students and their parents for college majors like engineering and computer science that can be translated into lucrative employment opportunities, every humanities department—from philosophy to literary studies—becomes ever more anxiously territorial, refusing to admit new departmental competitors to the ranks. So adaptation studies is unlikely to emerge as a widely recognized academic discipline any-time soon. This may be a regrettable necessity, but there are also more posi-tive reasons to embrace the marginality of adaptation. The marginalization of adaptation studies gives it the power to question assumptions about lit-erary studies and cinema studies that these more established disciplines tend to avoid. (Think of adaptation scholars as students wising off from the back of the classroom.) Engaging with adaptation can confer the ability to speak truth to the power of these more established disciplines. Finally—and most pertinently to this book—the anti-discipline of adaptation studies is adjacent to a remarkable array of disciplines outside these two fields, including, but not limited to, television studies, moving image studies, digital media studies, translation studies, performance studies, studies in music and art history and creation, border studies, race studies, queer studies, disability studies, and ecocritical studies. Adaptation studies doesn't trump any of these more well-established disciplines, but it has the power to illuminate every one of them in often unexpected ways that make it well worth studying.

Although I have neither the time nor the expertise to provide an exhaustive account of the shifting and often intricate connections between adaptation studies and each of these other fields, this book aims to give you the tools that will empower you to do so on your own. For that reason, it is not meant to serve as a repository of wisdom or to develop a single sustained argument—or even half a dozen self-contained arguments—about how adaptation has been or ought to be engaged. Instead, as this Introduction has already indicated through its own practice, it seeks to use each of these six approaches to generate questions about adaptation and the many other practices and disciplines it engages in turn. Some of these questions are Socratic, rhetorical questions that it raises expressly in order to answer. But most of them—especially those grouped together at the end of every section of every chapter—are open-ended questions meant to encourage you to come up with your own best answers, or with questions of your own. Although this book isn't a "how to make adaptations" version of Syd Field's famous how-to book, *Screenplay*, it has—and aims to cultivate—a lively interest not only in how earlier adaptations have been made, but in how new ones could be made by readers posed to put its approaches into active practice by cre-ating adaptations of their own.

So why study adaptation using any or all of these six approaches? This book's primary goal is to invite you both to consider adaptations more thoughtfully and resourcefully on their own terms and to engage the urgent questions they raise about the powers and limitations of literary canons; the industry behind textual production and distribution; the relations between different kinds of media; the nature of national, political, racialized, gen-dered, and cultural identities; and the ways contemporary digital and social media have profoundly complicated the roles of producers and consumers of texts. Adaptations are worth studying not only because they are engaging on their own, but because the family relationship between adaptation studies and a host of other disciplines has the power to open the doors to new ways of thinking both about adaptation and about many other fields, texts, and assumptions you might otherwise never question.

Questions

- Is *Barbie* an adaptation? Is its categorization by the Academy of Motion Picture Arts and Sciences as "based on material originally presented in another medium" consistent with the Academy's own rules?
- If *Barbie* is an adaptation, then is *The Lego Movie* an adaptation? Are "Making of …" featurettes adaptations? Why, or why not?
- What typically gets adapted: the story, the characters, the fictional world, a text's cultural preoccupations, or something else?
- Can only texts be adapted, or can non-textualized events be adapted as well?
- Does, or should, every adaptation have a single identifiable source it is adapting?
- Should definitions of adaptation be neutral, or should they have positive or negative associations built in?

References

Elliott, Kamilla. *Theorizing Adaptation.* Oxford UP, 2020.
Field, Syd. *Screenplay: The Foundations of Screenwriting.* Revised ed. Delta, 2005.
Hutcheon, Linda, with Siobhan O'Flynn. *A Theory of Adaptation.* Second ed. Routledge, 2012.
Saint Jacques, Jillian. "Preface: Four Fundamental Concepts in Adaptation Studies," *Adaptation Theories.* Edited by Saint Jacques. Jan Van Eyck Academie, 2011, pp. 9–44.
Sanders, Julie. *Adaptation and Appropriation.* Routledge, 2006.
Stam, Robert. "Introduction: The Theory and Practice of Adaptation." *Literature and Film: A Guide to the Theory and Practice of Film Adaptation.* Edited by Robert Stam and Alessandra Raengo. Blackwell, 2005, pp. 1–52.

1 Aesthetic engagements
Adaptation as copy

Adaptation as (generally inferior) copy

The most common engagement with adaptation—one shared by reviewers, fans, English teachers, and most other nonspecialists—focuses on literary works, especially novels, adapted for the movies. Its bedrock assumptions are that the primary goal of studying adaptations is to compare them to the texts they adapt; that the basis for this comparison should be to evaluate them on the grounds of their aesthetic success; and that the result of most evaluations is the verdict that the book is better. This engagement is so common that it has come as a welcome development to have recent adaptation scholars like Lissette Lopez Szwydky and Kamilla Elliott remind us that it is a relatively recent aberration, for "adaptation drives much of the history of fine art" (Lopez Szwydky 1). For most of recorded history, as Elliott has noted, adaptation has been widespread and approved as essential to the creative process. Audiences in ancient Athens could watch tragedies about the House of Atreus—the family of Trojan War hero Agamemnon—by Aeschylus, Sophocles, Euripides, and perhaps other playwrights whose work has not survived. Each of these playwrights was adapting a familiar story whose leading events their audiences would already have known. But because their tragedies depended more on ritual and dramatic irony than on surprise, there is no evidence that audiences ever felt disappointed or cheated that the dramas they were watching were basically copies of earlier myths. No one complained when twentieth-century American playwright Eugene O'Neill drew on the story again for his own trilogy *Mourning Becomes Electra* (1931), or when Helen Fielding used Jane Austen's *Pride and Prejudice* (1813) as the basis for her novel *Bridget Jones's Diary* (1996). Similarly, Roman poet Virgil drew on Homer's epic poems *The Iliad* and *The Odyssey* for his nationalist Latin epic, *The Aeneid* (19 B.C.E.), which in turn inspired later epics from Dante's *Divine Comedy* (1321) to John Milton's *Paradise Lost* (1674), before James Joyce returned to Homer's epic as the ironic foundation for *Ulysses* (1922)—his account of a day in the life of unlikely epic hero Leopold Bloom.

The idea of adaptation as imitation is more pervasive in the non-literary arts. Contemporary painters who train by sitting in museums copying

DOI: 10.4324/9781003438410-2

earlier canvases are following the practice of artists from Rembrandt to Reynolds who drew on biblical and mythological figures, and often on earlier paintings of these figures, for their subjects. In fact, if adaptations produced by the masters of the Italian Renaissance—Giotto, Donatello, Fra Angelico, Michelangelo, Raphael, Leonardo, Botticelli, Bellini, Titian, Caravaggio—were banished as inferior copies, their absence would decimate the collections of museums around the world. Audiences would have found it much harder to follow the stories of ballets like Beethoven's *The Creatures of Prometheus* (1801) and Tchaikovsky's *Sleeping Beauty* (1889) if the outlines of those stories had not already been broadly familiar to them from earlier tales. No one objected to Modest Mussorgsky's decision to base the movements of his piano suite *Pictures at an Exhibition* (1874) on ten paintings by his late friend Viktor Hartman; instead, audiences were delighted by his ingenuity in capturing the spirit of the paintings, just as later generations of audiences were captivated by Maurice Ravel's 1922 orchestration of Mussorgsky's score—one of over two dozen arrangements (the score has also been adapted for organ, trumpet, brass ensemble, piano trio, jazz trio, metal band, synthesizer, and glass harp). Classical composers routinely borrowed forms and themes from other composers and themselves. Mozart, Beethoven, Chopin, Liszt, Max Reger, and Ralph Vaughn Williams all wrote variations on themes drawn from earlier composers. One of Niccolo Paganini's violin etudes served as the basis for both the two books of Johannes Brahms's *Variations on a Theme by Paganini* for piano (1863) and Sergei Rachmaninov's very different *Rhapsody on a Theme of Paganini* for piano and orchestra (1934); and Robert Schumann and Dmitri Shostakovich both pressed brief melodic motifs into service again and again in a series of symphonies, concertos, and works for solo piano. Just as composers have borrowed structures like the sonata and rondo forms from other composers, it is no surprise that poets have borrowed structures like the sonnet and the limerick, and often the subjects and tones these structures imply, instead of inventing their own.

The surprise—at least for many modern audiences—comes in the discovery that none of these forms of quotation, imitation, and copying were looked down on until a relatively short time ago. As recently as the nineteenth century, as Elliott and Linda Hutcheon have noted, adaptations of books and plays, paintings and drawings, music and dance were so widespread that they were accepted without question. In fact, as Martin Meisel has pointed out, "shared structures in the representation arts helped constitute, not just a common style, but a popular style" (Meisel 4). Many features of the story of Frankenstein's monster familiar to modern audiences, from the appearance of Frankenstein's servant Fritz (later renamed Igor) to Frankenstein's exultant cry, "It lives!" (later, "It's alive!"), first appeared not in Mary Wollstonecraft Shelley's 1818 novel, but in Richard Brinsley Peake's 1823 play *Presumption; or, The Fate of Frankenstein*. Shelley's reaction on seeing the play—"But lo & behold! I found myself famous!" (Shelley 378)—proved prophetic, for the theatrical and cinematic adaptations that followed spread her fame far beyond her reading base.

Adaptation, imitation, reinterpretation, and other kinds of copying continue to be popular in contemporary culture. But today, most of these practices are more tightly regulated legally. Producers who want to stage new productions of Samuel Beckett's *Waiting for Godot* (1952) or Heidi Schreck's *What the Constitution Means to Me* (2017) must now pay a fee to the playwright's representatives or descendants. So too must groups planning to cover popular songs like George Gershwin's "Summertime" (1935), Irving Berlin's "White Christmas" (1942), or The Beatles' "Yesterday" (1965)—at least until the copyright expires on the song or play they are performing and it passes into the public domain, as Sherlock Holmes has recently done and Mickey Mouse seems soon to follow. The case of sampling—the incorporation of short segments of pre-recorded music and lyrics into a new recording, a technique essential to hip-hop—is more problematic, since American "fair use" law allows some, but not all, limited uses of copyrighted material without acknowledgment or payment to the copyright holder. Even the song "Happy Birthday to You" (1893?)—sung without acknowledgment or royalty payments at thousands of birthday parties every day—was officially under copyright until 2015, when a court ruling limited Warner/Chappell Music's claim to its copyright to one particular piano arrangement of the song, not its music or lyrics, and the song itself passed into the public domain, making it available for endless performances, celebrations, and adaptations.

Questions

- Why have approaches to adaptation emphasizing fidelity to an original text focused on movies based on novels?
- Are all copies adaptations—and if not, which are adaptations, which are not, and where do you draw the line?
- Are all performances of songs and plays adaptations? Again, how would you determine which are and which are not, and how would you defend this distinction?

Attacking adaptation

Three related developments in the 1800s were largely responsible for the decentering of adaptation as a well-nigh universal aesthetic practice. The first of these was the rise of a new Romantic aesthetic that saw works of art as products of a specific artist's shaping imagination rather than as an imitation of widely accessible models. By positioning artists at the center of the worlds they now claimed to have created rather than copied, this aesthetic, promoted most influentially by William Wordsworth and Samuel Taylor Coleridge, claimed vastly greater moral and economic rights for artists who created successful and popular works.

The second development, theorized most famously by Walter Benjamin, was the discovery and spread of new mechanical technologies that could readily produce the works that had so recently been claimed as Romantic originals, the rightful property of their creators. Though the oldest of these technologies, the printing press, had been invented in the fifteenth century, its commercial potential was not realized until the proliferation of magazines in the 1700s and 1800s; and the other technologies—especially photography, which could capture images that reproduced visual features of their subjects with unprecedented fidelity, and lithography, which carried the power to replicate these photographic images in millions of copies—are nineteenth-century inventions. For Benjamin, "mechanical reproduction emancipates the work of art from its parasitical dependence on ritual" and frees it from "the criterion of authenticity" (Benjamin 224).

The threat these reproductive technologies posed to the artworks that now sought to distinguish themselves from their copies by pronouncing themselves originals was sharpened by a third development that arose in response to what several influential authors had come to perceive as a culture of licentious copying: a series of legal actions to strengthen and enforce copyright laws in Europe and America. These actions—championed by novelists like Charles Dickens and Victor Hugo, who wanted to regulate dramatic adaptations of their novels that neither acknowledged their sources nor paid them any financial compensation—led eventually to the convening of the Berne Convention and the subsequent establishment of international copyright laws that made it illegal to pass literary, visual, and theatrical copies off as original works without acknowledging and compensating the artists who were identified as their original creators. The rise of reproductive technologies that threatened to deprive Romantic and post-Romantic artists of the income they considered their due decentered and denigrated the practice of adaptation, placing what had once been the leading approach to producing artworks in any mode under moral and legal suspicion.

This movement toward denigrating adaptations was dramatically accelerated by the arrival of the cinema, one of the first art forms in history not to be aimed specifically at the cultural elite. Of the many admonitions to early cinema to avoid competing with canonical novels, the most cogent and widely referenced is Virginia Woolf's 1926 injunction that no one should seek to make movies based on literary masterpieces like *Anna Karenina* because no film adaptation could possibly capture the epic sweep of Leo Tolstoy's novel or its psychological subtleties in representing its heroine, whom readers know "almost entirely by the inside of her mind—her charm, her passion, her despair" (Woolf 350): qualities that the cinema, restricted to pictorial (and more recently audiovisual) representations, could not hope to capture. Woolf's view—echoing Gotthold Ephraim Lessing's much earlier dictum in *Laocoön* that "succession of time is the province of the poet just as space is that of the painter" (Lessing 91)—continues to be widely echoed itself in contemporary reviews of both novels and movies, beginning with more recent movies based on *Anna Karenina*. More generally, adaptations in the twen-tieth and twenty-first centuries have been widely dismissed as derivative and inferior copies of canonical works whose integrity and individuality are best respected if they are never imitated.

This hostility to adaptation—fueled by a rearguard cultural elitism that assumes that stories aimed at the general public will always by definition be less complex, less penetrating, and less valuable than stories aimed at niche audiences—has enjoyed the powerful support of the argument crystallized by Siegfried Kracauer's assertion in his 1960 monograph *Theory of Film* that "each medium has a specific nature which invites certain kinds of communications while obstructing others" (Kracauer 3), and developed in detail by Seymour Chatman's influential 1980 essay "What Novels Can Do That Films Can't (and Vice Versa)." The hypothesis that different media excel at representing different kinds of experiences—novels in providing unfettered access to characters' thoughts and emotions, for example, and movies in providing compelling visual images of historical settings and large-scale actions—has played an important role in adaptation studies ever since the publication of George Bluestone's *Novels to Film* in 1957. "Limits of the Novel and of the Film," the long opening chapter of Bluestone's monograph, lays out in meticulous detail the argument that since novels and movies have fundamentally different aesthetics, it is as pointless to compare them as it would be to pronounce the "Johnson's Wax Building better or worse than Tchaikowsky's *Swan Lake*" (Bluestone 6). This position rapidly hardened into a dogma commonly identified as "medium specificity": the belief that every presentational medium has distinctive affinities for some kinds of texts (sonnets for professions of love, watercolors for scenic landscapes, ballets for restaging fairytales, IMAX movies for superhero epics) over others, and that adapting any text into any new medium would inevitably produce differences arising from the different affordances of that medium.

In its own way, Bluestone's attack on fidelity criticism is just as dogmatic as the position it rejects. His proposition that "the novel is a linguistic medium, the film essentially visual" (Bluestone viii) overlooks or minimizes the import-ance of music, sound effects, and dialogue in the movies. And its treatment of novels as a purely verbal medium ignores the interplay of words and images in both illustrated novels and silent movies, in which, as Kamilla Elliott has pointed out, "pictures embellish the initial letters of prose chapters and gar-nish film intertitles" (Elliott 16). His announcement that "twentieth-century novels have abandoned the drama of human thought and action for the drama of linguistic inadequacy" (Bluestone 11)—a reasonable characterization of the high modernist fiction of Woolf and her contemporaries—has inevitably dated as the years passed and adaptations of later twentieth-century novels like Joseph Heller's *Catch-22* (1961), Alice Walker's *The Color Purple* (1982), and George R.R. Martin's *A Game of Thrones* (1996) have resumed a more extroverted focus, raising doubts about his assumptions that "the film has not yet begun to question its ability to render certain types of physical and even psychological reality," and that movies have "difficulty representing streams of consciousness" (Bluestone 14, 47). Bluestone's agreement with film theorist Bela Balász that "pictures have no tenses" and that "time is prior in the novel, and space prior in the film," so that "the novel has three tenses; the film has only one" (Bluestone 57, 61, 48), has been questioned by Sarah Cardwell, who—noting that film adaptations of Vladimir Nabokov's novel *Lolita* rely on far more intricate relations between different times than an indefinite extension of the present tense—concludes that "(1) the film image is not inherently present; it is inherently tenseless; and (2) the filmic medium—films or movies—are capable of representing a range of tenses through the manipulation of images, words, and sounds within a narrative" (Cardwell 88). Bluestone's agreement with Woolf that "the results of conversion from linguistic to visual images are disastrous to both" (Bluestone 23) has been challenged more broadly. Most importantly, his contention that "whereas the moving image comes to us directly through perception, language must be filtered through the screen of conceptual apprehension" (Bluestone 20) has provoked many responses by commentators who find the stories movies tell are just as dependent on audiovisual and generic codes and conventions as the stories novels tell are on linguistic and literary codes and conventions.

Perhaps the most prophetic of Bluestone's general observations is his prediction that the demise of the Motion Picture Producers and Distributors of America, popularly known as the Hays Office—the self-censorship board that policed Hollywood productions from 1934 to 1966, refusing seals of approval to films that did not meet the standards of the 1930 Production Code—would produce "freer cinematic conventions of the future" (Bluestone 218). American movies that are not required to adhere to an industry-backed code that forbade, for example, images showing unpunished crimes, automatic weapons, lace lingerie, two people (even if they were married to each other) sharing a double bed, or "SEX PERVERSION" ("Particular Applications" 287)—widely understood as homosexuality—may still depend on the box office for their success. But they are no longer subject to the censorship that added one more layer of conventions to the imperatives of intelligibility, popularity, and economic success already imposed on them. Bluestone's assertion that "what [the adapter] adapts is a kind of paraphrase of the novel" (Bluestone 62) has been even more influential, especially in the work of Dudley Andrew. Drawing on Lawrence Venuti's contention that what translators translate is not a given text but an "interpretant" that summarizes and conveys a specific interpretation of that text, Andrew suggests that "[r]ather than a mechanical transfer from one semiotic system to another, the filmmaker interprets the source via an audiovisual form that also includes attitudes and concerns brought to the project" (Andrew, "Economies" 32).

Several other commentators, acknowledging that successful adaptations have taken very different approaches to the question of fidelity, have proposed tripartite models based on these different approaches. Geoffrey Wagner distinguishes between "transposition" ("a novel is given directly on screen"), "commentary" (the novel is "either purposely or inadvertently altered in some respect"), and analogy ("a fairly considerable departure for the sake of making *another* work of art") (Wagner 222, 223, 227). Michael Klein proposes similar categories: "close" (an adaptation that translates "the text into the language of film"); "intermediate" (an adaptation that "retains the structure of the narrative while significantly altering" that source text); and "loose" (an adaptation "that regards the source merely as raw material ... for an original work" (Klein 9–10). John M. Desmond and Peter Hawkes similarly distinguish between adaptations that feature "*close, loose, or inter-mediate* interpretation" (Desmond and Hawkes 3); and Linda Costanzo Cahir between "literal translation," "traditional translation," and "radical translation" (Cahir 16–17). Andrew's three categories—which complicate this close/pretty close/not at all close model—are "borrowing" ("the artist employs, more or less extensively, the material, idea, or form of an earlier, generally successful text"); "intersecting" ("the uniqueness of the original text is preserved to such an extent that it is intentionally left unassimilated in adaptation"); and "transforming" ("the reproduction in cinema of something essential about an original work") (Andrew, "Adaptation" 98, 99, 100).

Questions

- Bluestone concludes *Novels into Film* by remarking that since "[t]he film and the novel remain separate institutions, each one achieving its best results by exploring unique and specific properties," it might be better if "film-makers ... abandon adaptation entirely and write directly for the screen" (218). What are the advantages of basing films on novels and basing them on original screenplays?
- What are the differences between fidelity criticism and medium-specific criticism? Is it possible to endorse, combine, or practice both fidelity criticism and medium-specific criticism?
- Of the commentators who outline three different approaches films take to their sources, Desmond, Hawkes, and Cahir indicate no particular preference between them, but Andrew is clearly attached to intersecting and impatient with transforming. Which approach do you favor in the adaptations you know and why?

Attacking fidelity

Although Bluestone's medium-specific approach to adaptations arose specifically as a reaction against approaches that mandated fidelity to the adapted text, both approaches were often criticized for the same reasons. Writing in 2003, I argued:

Fidelity to its source text—whether it is conceived as success in re-creating specific textual details or the effect of the whole—is a hopelessly fallacious measure of a given adaptation's value because it is unattainable, undesirable, and theoretically possible only in a trivial sense. Like translations to a new language, adaptations will always reveal their sources' superiority because whatever their faults, the source texts will always be better at being themselves.

(Leitch, "Twelve Fallacies" 152)

I further contended that "Chatman's arguments ... apply not to essential properties of novels and films, but to specific reading habits that are grounded in the history of fashion, taste, and analysis rather than in any specific technical properties of novels and films" (Leitch, "Twelve Fallacies" 161). Robert Stam combined these two criticisms with elegant concision by emphasizing the fidelity imperative they shared:

Another variation on "fidelity" discourse suggests that an adaptation should be faithful not so much to the source text but rather to the essential traits of the medium of expression. This 'medium-specificity' approach assumes that every medium is inherently 'good at' certain things and 'bad at' others.

(Stam 19)

Even scholars who have announced the incommensurability of novels and movies routinely go on to compare specific novels and their film adaptations anyway, as Chatman does briefly with Jean Renoir's 1936 adaptation of Guy de Maupassant's story "A Day in the Country" and Bluestone and Brian McFarlane each do in extended chapters analyzing specific films adapted from novels that their theories maintain could not possibly be adapted to the cinema. The contradiction between the apparent demands of medium specificity as a theory and the comparative analysis of novels and their film adaptations as a practice reveals three other imperatives buried within approaches to adaptation that emphasize either fidelity or medium specificity.

One of these is obvious: the belief that the leading mode of adaptation in our time is feature films based on novels. Despite the popularity of theatrical adaptations from *Rip Van Winkle* (1897) to *The Whale* (2022), aesthetic or archival accounts of adaptation have most often focused on films based on novels. The older medium has typically been held in higher esteem because it is more established; because it requires a literate audience; because it is weightier—surprisingly little has been written about the many feature films adapted from short stories—and because it is older. This approach to adaptation considers adaptations as copies of works that have been previously validated and accepted into the literary canon. Focusing on novel-to-film adaptations allows Bluestone, as he acknowledges himself, to emphasize the movies' response to the rise of modernist novels by Joyce, Woolf, Henry James, Joseph Conrad, and Marcel Proust, which strive ever more directly to use external incidents to dramatize their true subject: the operation of individual characters' consciousness. And it elevates the modernist novel, which seems in Bluestone's hands to have arisen specifically in revolt against the exteriority of the movies, as a typical representative of all novels.

This imperative is undergirded by a second, more general imperative: that the central concern of adaptation studies is to compare specific adaptations with the texts they adapt, comparing exactly one adaptation to one adapted text; and that the basis of this case study—a model that Robert R. Ray found so reductive that he was convinced it would drastically limit the scope of an adaptation studies that "did not see that the cinema's very different deter-minations (commercial exposure, collaborative production, and public con-sumption) made irrelevant the methods of analysis developed for 'serious literature'" (Ray 46)—is aesthetically evaluative.

This comparative evaluation is based in turn on a third imperative: the business of adaptation scholars is not only to evaluate the success or failure of the adaptation, but to evaluate its success or failure in replicating the experience provided by the novel it is adapting. This third imperative tilts the field decisively in terms of the novel, which not only provides a culturally privileged norm against which film adaptations are to be judged but gets to dictate the terms of this judgment. This move effectively rules movies that are widely held to be better than their novels—like *Psycho* (1960), *The Graduate* (1967), *The Godfather* (1972), *Jaws* (1975), and *Fight Club* (1999)—out of court as marginal cases or contradictions in terms. Unlike Virginia Woolf, who feels no compunction about condemning adaptations of Tolstoy as unauthorized poaching by practitioners of a second-rate medium, Bluestone and Chatman craft a neutral, medium-specific theory of adaptation that they violate at will because their own professional orientation, which far precedes their interest in adaptation, is aesthetic, and the comparisons between novels and films into which they feel they have been forced therefore involve com-parative evaluation.

The establishment of adaptation studies as an academic field of study over the second half of the twentieth century arose largely in reaction against the characterization of adaptations as mere copies of canonical literary originals. Forty years after Bluestone's impatient dismissal of fidelity as a criterion for judging adaptations, McFarlane complained in 1996 that adaptation studies had been repeatedly "inhibited and blurred" by adaptation scholars' "near-fixation with the issue of fidelity" (McFarlane 194). Sarah Cardwell argued that instead of viewing television adaptations as versions of texts whose pri-mary authors continued to be Jane Austen and George Eliot, "[i]t would be more accurate to view adaptation as the gradual development of a 'meta-text'" that "may draw on any earlier adaptations, as well as upon the pri-mary source text" (Cardwell 25). In her contribution to the 2005 Literature/Film Association conference proceedings published as *In/Fidelity*, Rochelle Hurst contended that "[t]he discourse of adaptation theory, informed by the binary opposition that underlies Bluestone's approach, posits literature and film as innately different, diametrically opposed, and hierarchically positioned" (Hurst 179). Instead, she proposed adaptation as "somewhat separable from both the novel in which it has its origins and the film in which it finds its form. Occupying the overlap, the adaptation complicates the novel/film binary." By "refuting the hierarchy that situates the novel as innately superior to the film," adaptation "render[s] problematic the desire for fidelity" (Hurst 187). My own much briefer contribution to the proceedings, which recommended "treating fidelity as a specific but by no means privileged possibility" (Leitch, "Fidelity Discourse" 208), was titled "Fidelity Discourse: Its Cause and Cure."

This widespread dismissal of fidelity as a touchstone for grading adaptations up or down was thoroughly logical for the field of adaptation studies because it was highly unlikely that scholars looking to make a name for themselves would venture into an infant discipline devoted to the study of second-rate copies. At the same time, however, it was highly ironic because it marked a decisive break from approaches to adaptation based on fidelity and on medium specificity and a more general break from the ways adaptation was viewed by academic specialists and by the general public. For over 20 years, in fact, adaptation scholars routinely criticized their colleagues in the nascent field for their allegiance to fidelity as a criterion for judging adaptations even though most of these colleagues as far back as Bluestone had never dismissed adaptations as mere copies and never agreed that fidelity to their sources should be the primary criterion in evaluating adaptations, leaving this position for literary scholars and film reviewers. As J.D. Connor put it:

> What I am calling the fidelity reflex … is not the persistence of the discourse, but the persistent call for it to end. For adaptation theory to have any chance of success, it must do two things. First, it must account for the persistence of fidelity discourse despite decades of resourceful argument against it. Second, it must account for its own blind spot: What has the campaign against fidelity failed to get at? And given this consistent failure to achieve its goals, why do critics persist in calling for an end to fidelity?
>
> (Connor)

Questions

- Why have some stories, and some versions of these stories, become canonical while others have not?
- Whose interests are served by specific canons and canons in general?
- What alternative models might adaptation offer to the model of the literary canon and its copies?

When does fidelity matter?

Even though more adaptation scholars have attacked than defended the proposition that adaptations should be judged for their fidelity to the texts they adapt, making fidelity into something like the F-word in adaptation studies, this proposition continues to have its adherents. Christine Geraghty has made a wonderfully succinct case for fidelity: "Faithfulness matters if it matters to the viewer" (*Now a Major Motion Picture* 3). It is clear that faithfulness is particularly important to television viewers watching BBC adaptations of Shakespeare, Austen, or Dickens, and to moviegoers drawn to theaters by the promise that the movie they have come to see is "based on the novel by …" Hence the proliferation of lists like that the staff of online resource Literary Hub assembled of "10 Screen Adaptations Much, Much Worse Than the Books They're Based On."

Numerous commentators have taken approaches to fidelity that avoid either wholeheartedly accepting or rejecting it. In his 1948 essay "Adaptation, or the Cinema as Digest," André Bazin imagined that "we are moving toward a reign of the adaptation in which the notion of the unity of the work of art, if not the very notion of the author himself, will be destroyed" by the confluence of a given novel and its theatrical and cinematic adaptations into "a single work reflected through all three art forms, an artistic pyramid with three sides, all equal in the eyes of the critic" (Bazin, "Adaptation" 26). Returning to the subject four years later, he championed the cinema as a distinctive art form while attacking essentialist notions of "cinema with a capital C" in his 1952 essay "In Defense of Mixed Cinema" (Bazin, "In Defense" 70). He rejected the widespread belief that adaptations cheapened the novels they adapted, since an adaptation "cannot harm the original in the eyes of those who know it," and since "to adapt is no longer to betray but to respect" (Bazin, "In Defense" 65, 69). Noting the significant influence of cinematic techniques on American novelists like John Dos Passos, Ernest Hemingway, and Erskine Caldwell, Bazin argued that there is no such thing as pure cinema, for the same reason that there is no such thing as pure literature or pure drama: all these ways of presenting stories are mixed media that depend on learning from each other for their continued development and success. At the same time, Bazin believed that "an original scenario is preferable to an adaptation, all else being equal," and that "the film-maker has everything to gain from fidelity"—"not the illusory fidelity of a replica," but a fidelity based on "an intimate understanding of its own true aesthetic structure which is a prerequisite and necessary condition of respect for the works it is about to make its own" (Bazin, "In Defense" 70–71, 65, 70).

Following Bazin, Kamilla Elliott argued against what she called "the word and image divide" that presumably made it impossible for visual texts like movies to adapt verbal texts like novels, whose representational strategies were assumed to be both analogous to those of movies and so categorically different from them that they made faithful adaptations impossible, so that "even though analogical rhetoric pervades the novel and film debate, categorical approaches have dominated its theorization" (Elliott 4, 11). Focusing her analysis on a series of illustrated Victorian novels, Elliott recommended replacing what critics largely framed as a competition between novels and films with a model of them as "reciprocal looking-glass analogies," each reflecting the properties of the other while marking its distance from the other in a "reciprocity [that] creates a mutual and inherent rather than a hierarchical and averse dynamic" (Elliott 210, 212). For Elliott, as for Bazin, cinema is literary for the same reasons literature is cinematic.

Other scholars have defended fidelity as an evaluative criterion by attacking the assumption that it is inevitably opposed to novelty. George Raitt argues that " 'sameness' and 'difference' are not binary opposites, that 'difference' may be observed even where there is 'sameness' or 'equivalence' " (Raitt 47). And Casie Hermansson, noting that "the main objection to fidelity is its evaluative focus," observed that "any comparative adaptation criticism that draws heavily on the source literature, no matter the dominant method-ology, has become tarred with the same brush as fidelity and has come to be treated as inseparable from it" (Hermansson 148). Surveying recent attempts by adaptation scholars to acknowledge the importance of fidelity without endorsing it as a categorically privileged criterion for judging adaptations, she concludes:

> [I]t is time to include fidelity—aporias and all—in the intertextual toolbox of adaptation criticism. It is one tool among many, and sometimes not the right tool for the job. But at other times, and perhaps in combination with other tools, it is the only one that will do.
>
> (Hermansson 156)

Hence, using "both/and … instead of either/or" models that combine fidelity with other values "will surely result in the more productive criticism and theory that adaptation critics persistently call for" (Hermansson 157).

The most extensive contemporary defense of fidelity is the essays Colin MacCabe, Kathleen Murray, and Rick Warner collected in *True to the Sprit: Film Adaptation and the Question of Fidelity* (2011). MacCabe's introductory essay, aptly titled "Bazinian Adaptation," suggests that by sharing a "commitment to the value of both books and films analyzed," the volume's contributors could focus on "that particular form of productivity that preserves identity at the same moments that it multiplies it" (MacCabe 9, 7). Fredric Jameson, in his Afterword to the volume, dismisses attacks on fidelity as strategies for avoiding "the illusion that there could ever be any-thing like an organic or referential unity in what the printed text shares with its moving image" (Jameson 215). Starting from the proposition that "the novel and its film adaptation must not be of equal quality" (217), Jameson analyzes Andrei Tarkovsky's 1972 film adaptation of Stanislaw Lem's 1961 novel *Solaris* under the corollary that "it can happen that the two texts are of equal merit, but then in that case the film must be utterly different from, utterly unfaithful to, its original" (Jameson 217, 218). He concludes with the deeply anti-Bazinian recommendation that "individual works, either as external adaptations or as internal echo-chambers of the various media, be

grasped as allegories of their never-ending and unresolvable struggles for primacy" (Jameson 232). Among the other contributions, Kathleen Murray's
essay stands out for proposing the "adaptive system" behind Howard
Hawks's 1944 film *To Have and Have Not*, which "needs to be thought of
as a Warners picture, a Hawks film, a Hemingway adaptation, a Faulkner
screenplay, a response to *Casablanca*, and a Bogart/Bacall vehicle simultaneously" (Murray 91, 111).

The most provocative of all the essays in *True to the Spirit* is Dudley
Andrew's "The Economies of Adaptation" because it extends the
author's long no-but-yes tango with fidelity. As early as 1980, Andrew
had remarked about transforming, the third approach to adaptation he
considered: "Unquestionably the most frequent and most tiresome discussion
of adaptation (and of film and literature relations as well) concerns fidelity and
transformation" (Andrew, "Adaptation" 101). Having denounced discussions
of fidelity, he recommended that "[i]t is time for adaptation studies to take a
sociological turn" toward a future in which scholars can "use [adaptation] as
we use all cultural practices, to understand the world from which it comes and
the one toward which it points" (Andrew, "Adaptation" 104, 106). In "The
Economies of Adaptation," by contrast, he notes that adaptation is

> the humming motor of uncontrollable textual proliferation—the *hori-
> zontal* spread of a title, an author, an idea from medium to medium, lan-
> guage to language—but it can also function as an antidote or alternative.
> For if the *vertical* line that anchors it to the bedrock of its source remains
> intact, a contemporary film can draw away from the system, submerging
> its audience in a different sensibility and set of values. That chain bears the
> troubled name "fidelity."
>
> (Andrew, "Economies" 32)

Deploring adaptation scholars' movement away from "the *vertical* line
that anchors a film to its literary substrate" and their decision "to detach
the anchor and let the film float free" (27–28), Andrew proposes situating
adaptations within both a "vertical economy ... ruled by past and future,
measured by the ancestors and the gods from whom literary, religious, and
moral values derive," and a "horizontal economy [that] creates value in
spreading this patrimony out as widely as possible" (Andrew, "Economies"
34–35). Because "[f]ilm adaptations are icons of canonical literary creations,"
Andrew follows Bazin in suggesting: "We should use adaptations, just as we
use images ... to get at the truths to which they point. Cinema brings us
closer to a fidelity to truth" (Andrew, "Economies" 35, 37). Ironically, his
climactic defense of fidelity—"Genuine fidelity abandons vain and simple-
minded matching for creative transformation" (Andrew, "Economies" 38)—
sounds remarkably like Hurst's attack on fidelity.

Medium-specific comparative aesthetic evaluation, by contrast, continues
to play a leading role in the work of adaptation scholars who renounce it as

a theory while engaging in it in practice. Rare indeed are adaptation scholars of whatever theoretical persuasion who do not indulge in expressions of preference for some texts over others; and even rarer are scholars like Elliott, whose admirable monograph *Theorizing Adaptation* contains not a single case study. But contemporary scholars committed to comparative evaluation as a methodology rather than merely a series of ad hoc preferences have more tools at their disposal today than they did when Bluestone wrote. Aesthetically based adaptation studies can take its cue from contemporary translation studies, a parallel discipline whose path has often echoed and sometimes anticipated developments in adaptation studies. Instead of comparing translations of poems and plays and novels to the texts they translate, which invariably set standards for the translations' success as demanding as they may be accidental, recent translation theorists from George Steiner to Lawrence Venuti have defined translation as a practice to be judged in terms of its success in using source texts as the basis for translations that address the political, ideological, and cultural needs of their target audiences rather than its success in replicating the beauties of those source texts. And adaptation studies can draw inspiration and key terms from performance studies, which considers archival texts from *The Iliad* to *Anna Karenina* to lie dormant and inaccessible to contemporary audiences until new performances—or, we might say, new adaptations—breathe new life into them. When literary history meets performance studies, adaptation is no longer the enemy of the canon. Just as the status of the original depends for Jacques Derrida on the copy, canons, as Lopez Szwydky points out, depend on the adaptations that ensure their "continued cultural relevance, accessibility, and survival" (Lopez Szwydky 25).

Questions

- If so few adaptation scholars promote fidelity as a touchstone, why does it keep resurfacing?
- Which stakeholders endorse it and why?
- What foundational assumptions or desires does fidelity criticism depend on?
- What foundational assumptions does medium-specific criticism depend on?
- Which stakeholders in the production, distribution, and consumption of adaptations—authors, screenwriters, directors, studio heads, publicists, reviewers, audiences, or academic critics—are most likely to endorse fidelity criticism or medium-specific criticism and why?
- Which of the two approaches is better categorized as aesthetic and what makes it so?
- Do aesthetic approaches to adaptation typically lead to generalizations about literature and film? If so, what form do these generalizations take?

Fidelity to what?

Special problems with the aesthetic model of adaptation emerge in cross-over adaptations like *Frankenstein Meets the Wolf Man* (1943), *Billy the Kid Versus Dracula* (1966), and *The League of Extraordinary Gentlemen* (2003), which seek to graft two or more existing franchises together. The strain to be faithful to the rules and conventions of multiple sources has given crossover adaptations as a group a bad reputation. The most successful are those that capitalize on this tension by milking their stress points for farce. The mixture of jump scares and ridiculous reactions by a well-known comedy team made *Abbott and Costello Meet Frankenstein* (1948), which also included appearances by Dracula and the Wolf Man, so successful that Universal—the studio that had survived the Great Depression by creating profitable franchises featuring all these monsters before using *Buck Privates* (1941) to launch a series of 20 comedies starring radio comedians Bud Abbott and Lou Costello—followed it with *Bud Abbott and Lou Costello Meet the Killer, Boris Karloff* (1949), *Bud Abbott and Lou Costello Meet the Invisible Man* (1951), *Abbott and Costello Meet Dr. Jekyll and Mr. Hyde* (1953), and *Abbott and Costello Meet the Mummy* (1955), all of which capitalized on the same humorous discrepancy between the Universal monsters and the clueless pair who encountered them. *Murder by Death* (1976) invites half a dozen fictional detectives—clearly burlesquing Hercule Poirot, Jane Marple, Sam Spade, Nick and Nora Charles, and Charlie Chan—to dinner, where they follow their own very different paths in an attempt to figure out who has killed their host. *Cowboys & Aliens* (2011) humorously mashes up tropes from the two genres indicated by its title.

Even film adaptations that identify only one source in their credits can raise problems of their own about what would count as fidelity to that source. The most obvious of these problems is the difficulty in drawing a line between things that are adaptations and things that are not. Are James Bond movies that are not based on any of the Bond novels Ian Fleming wrote still adaptations? The Academy of Motion Picture Arts and Sciences says that they are, because, like *Toy Story 3* (2010) and *Borat 2* (2020), they are still adapting a pre-existing character. But the Academy ruled that the screenplay for *My Big Fat Greek Wedding* (2002), which was based on a one-woman stage show by its star, Nia Vardalos, was eligible in the Best Original Screenplay category. Many fans were outraged over the ruling by the Writers Branch executive committee of the Academy that the screenplay Greta Gerwig and Noah Baumbach wrote for the 2023 film *Barbie*—which included the credit, "Based on 'Barbie' by Mattel"—was eligible for nomination only as Best Adapted Screenplay because they felt that identifying the film as an adaptation diminished its satirical achievement, and because the Golden Globe and Critics Choice awards had both allowed it to be nominated as Best Original Screenplay.

Even if everyone agreed that *Barbie* was an adaptation, questions would remain. The film is amusingly determined to replicate many details of its source material, from Barbie's involuntarily arched feet, designed to fit into high-heeled shoes, to its cascade of accurately named costumes and properties to its roster of supporting characters—Skipper, Midge, Allan, and of course Ken—from among Barbie's friends and relatives. And its star, Margot Robbie, is costumed and made up to look uncannily like the doll Mattel introduced in 1959. But its cast of characters also includes Dr. Barbie, Lawyer Barbie, Judge Barbie, Writer Barbie, Physicist Barbie, and President Barbie—all of whom copy different Barbies Mattel has created and marketed. The most memorable of these alternative Barbies is Weird Barbie, played by the scene-stealing Kate McKinnon—a character who has no direct precursor in Mattel's vast array of Barbies. Most audiences have identified Robbie's Barbie, who acknowledges that she is Stereotypical Barbie, with the real Barbie; but although the film makes her its most prominent and proactive character, it never identifies her as more real than any of the other Barbies. In addition to maintaining an exaggerated faithfulness to Barbie's Dreamhouse, Barbie's convertible, and the pastel color scheme of Barbieland, the film playfully invokes the established personas of Ryan Gosling—whose portrayal of Ken as first comically inept and then eager to seize patriarchal power over Barbie's Dreamhouse, which he renames Ken's Mojo Dojo Casa House, and Barbieland, which he renames Kendom—and Margot Robbie, whose tearful assertion that she is no longer beautiful is greeted by Helen Mirren's voiceover: "Note to the filmmakers: Margot Robbie is the wrong person to cast if you want to make this point." Mirren's observation can readily be generalized: you can't get more aesthetically perfect than *Barbie*, and that's exactly why the film complicates both its heroine and her world by giving her an intimation of mortality that sets the plot in motion and leads to her decision to change from a perfect doll to an imperfect human being. Exploring the implications of a copy's fidelity to previous models, in fact, is the central business of the film.

A very different range of questions about what exactly is being adapted arise in Gerwig's preceding film, her 2019 adaptation of *Little Women*. Louisa May Alcott's 1868 novel about Meg, Jo, Amy, and Beth, the four sisters of the March family, has been adapted half a dozen times into feature films and even more often into television programs or miniseries, including two Japanese *anime* series, *Wakakusa no Yon Shimai* (1981) and *Ai no Wakakusa Monogatari* (1987). The most influential of these earlier adaptations, David O. Selznick's production of George Cukor's 1933 film for RKO, established the literary adaptation, which for years had been considered box-office poison, as a genre with the ability to attract audiences across the socioeconomic spectrum. Mervyn Le Roy's star-studded 1949 adaptation for MGM and Gillian Armstrong's 1994 adaptation for Columbia had both proved successful with reviewers and audiences alike.

Gerwig's film differs from earlier *Little Women* in attempting to square Alcott's traditional coming-of-age story about young women whose prescribed mission in life was to marry and raise families of their own with contemporary feminist values. The result is a frankly revisionist reading of both Alcott's novel and Alcott herself. Reviewing Gerwig's film for *Slate*, Dana Stevens describes it as:

> a piece of metafiction—or, to be more precise, a *poioumenon*, the rhetorical term for a work of art that tells the story of its own making. The leather-bound edition of *Little Women* that serves as the movie's opening title, its red leather cover stamped in gold with the name "L.M. Alcott," reappears in identical form at the end—all except for the name, which has become "J.M. March." And … there's a hint in Jo's last scene with the publisher that the ending of her own story as we've just seen it may not match up 100 percent with the ending of the manuscript she delivers. In a movie that's all about female agency and the importance of owning one's own story—in both the emotional and financial senses—that shift from object to subject, from character to author, is key.
>
> (Stevens)

Figure 1.1a and 1.1b The opening and closing sequences of Greta Gerwig's 2019 adaptation of *Little Women* conflate the novel's author and its heroine by framing the film with images of *Little Women* that indicate two different authors

Stevens's assessment of the film has been broadly shared. In introducing her interview with Gerwig for *Film Comment*, Devika Girish suggests that:

> Gerwig doesn't quite reinvent the novel but rather discerns, with X-ray-like intuition, the kernel that has made *Little Women* so formative for generations of ambitious women: it's the story of a woman who wants to write, and write she does. And Gerwig also understands that this woman

isn't just Jo March—the tempestuous tomboy-protagonist of the novel—but also its author, Louisa May Alcott.

(Girish)

This conflation of author and heroine has a long history. Alcott made no secret of the fact that Meg, Amy, and Beth March were all based on her own sisters; and that she used herself as the model for Jo, who resisted the advances of smitten neighbor Laurie Lawrence in pursuit of her independence and her vocation as a writer. In fact, both she and her publisher worked to foster "the perception that author and heroine were interchangeable. Alcott's work was marketed to encourage the illusion not only that Jo was Alcott but that Alcott was Jo" (Sicherman 252–53). In Gerwig's adaptation, this conflation of the author and her heroine drives the story, as Jo's quest for professional recognition, respect, and success emerges as the leading motivation in her life. As a result, this is the only film adaptation of Alcott's novel that does not make it clear that Jo (Saoirse Ronan) has accepted the marriage proposal of Professor Friedrich Bhaer (Louis Garrel), leaving the audience to decide for themselves whether she will marry him. Although the film erases most of the specific details of Alcott's life, its focus on her professional career and its framing by an opening scene showing her new novel being accepted for publication and a closing scene showing Jo watching raptly as the first copies of *Little Women* roll off the press raises the question of whether the movie is most invested in being faithful to Alcott's novel, to Alcott's life, or to the principles of third-wave feminism.

Gerwig told Girish:

> [W]hen I started writing, I started looking at the two parts of the book as two separate books ... I wanted to give the March women back what they had as girls. That felt to me like part of the task of this film, because I can't tell you how many women are like, "I only read the first part." If the thing we're telling girls is that once you become an adult, it's all over, that's not good enough, because then there's nothing left to desire, there's nothing to look towards. If there's no bravery and ambition and scope once you're an adult, if it all existed as a girl and then you put away your childish things, it just feels not right. So I wanted to ground it in adulthood.
>
> (Girish)

This self-assessment raises a series of pointed questions. Is Gerwig channeling Alcott the writer or Alcott's novel? What would it mean to be faithful to the facts of an author's life, to the author's sensibility, or to the author's historical circumstances (e.g., the novel's setting in Concord, Massachusetts or its repeated invocations of the Civil War, in which Mr. March is serving), rather than her book? Is it legitimate to sacrifice historical or biographical accuracy to entertainment? Where should we draw the line between fiction and autobiography, or biography in general? Does the up-to-date feminism of Gerwig's film restore the letter and the spirit of Alcott's novel, as André Bazin bids? Is what we take to be the spirit of Alcott's novel inevitably informed and shaped by our own cultural contexts and assumptions? Given that all feature films based on the novel except for Claire Niederpruem's 2018 adaptation are period pieces set during the American Civil War, would it be possible to adapt *Little Women* without updating it, or are all adaptations necessarily updates? Does Gerwig's film, like most other adaptations of *Little Women*, present itself as a copy of Alcott's novel? Is it a *poioumenon*, a work of art that tells the story of its own making, as Stevens suggests? Or is it an anti-adaptation, one that aspires to be superior to Alcott's novel by enlisting a revised Alcott in updated cultural debates—an anti-adaptation that is particularly invested in avoiding specific questionable tropes like little women submitting themselves to men as they grow into an adulthood that is more boring and subservient than their childhood? What kind of work did audiences want and expect *Little Women* and its adaptations to do in 2019, and how are those expectations likely to change in the future?

Questions

- What is the relation between the credits "Based on the novel by Louisa May Alcott" and "Based on 'Barbie' by Mattel?"
- What is the most illuminating, or the most defensible, way to approach *Little Women*'s relation to Alcott's novel?
- Does Gerwig's film seek to be true to the spirit of the novel? Does it assume that you have read the novel? Does it assume that you know anything in particular about the novel?
- What features of Alcott's novel is Gerwig's film most invested in preserving, and what is the nature of that preservation?
- Does the film seek to make Alcott's story speak to us in particular—and if so, what does it think Alcott has to say to audiences in the twenty-first century?
- Does the film seek to improve on the novel by updating it, by re-historicizing or otherwise recontextualizing it, or by judiciously adding appealing features or deleting dated or otherwise less appealing features?
- More generally, what does it mean to say that a film is based on a novel?
- Do we need other ways of thinking about adaptation rather than as copy, or can this approach itself be adapted to address the questions raised by *Barbie* and *Little Women*?

Fidelity redux

The most sustained and ambitious attempt to revive fidelity as a criterion for evaluating adaptations is Ursula Vooght's monograph *The Great Gatsby Meets Alain Badiou: Rethinking Fidelity in Film Adaptation* (2023), which draws on the work of philosopher Alain Badiou to devise an approach that can distinguish more and less successful adaptations. Observing the number of adaptation scholars who have expressed impatience with continued appeals to fidelity, she lists some of the leading ways the topic has been presented:

> excluding or relocating ideas of value, excluding so-called individual opinion to focus on form, or form to focus on reception or sociological context; attempts to avoid a fidelity of transference, that result in a focus only on differences; privileging source or adaptation over one another; removing a consideration of the source text to alleviate the idea of the adapted text being constantly at a disadvantage; and refocusing fidelity on to the pragmatic use of fidelity by filmmakers and studio, or the desire for it by the public.
>
> (Vooght 26–27)

Noting the problems implicit in this variety of ways of thinking about fidelity, Vooght contends that "these issues should be reframed holistically" under the banner of Badiou (Vooght 27). For Badiou, "fidelity and truth are linked together," even though he maintains that "a truth cannot be articulated"; instead, "[o]ne knows the existence of a truth by its effects":

> To access a truth in Badouian terms clearly requires some kind of openness to the void, the uncountable, the part that cannot be assimilated in the situation. It is an approach of fidelity that maintains this openness. For Badiou, when a subject embraces a truth-event with fidelity, it allows a truth to be both made and discovered.
>
> (Vooght 29, 37)

In support of his contention that "[f]idelity is … essential to the realisation of truth's possibilities," Badiou distinguishes among several different kinds of fidelity. "Dogmatic fidelities 'pretend' every multiple is connected to the event and hence are institutionalising; spontaneist fidelities suggest that only those who made the event can take part in it"; and "generic fidelity"— Badiou's preferred mode—"allows for more of a universal response" (Vooght 40). This type of fidelity, which does not rely on any prior knowledge, can "gather together and distinguish what in the situation depends on an event" (Vooght 41). Since Badiou's " 'truth' is the same for all," the path to truth for every individual involves "an active, unprejudiced process of sincere and faithful engagement" (Vooght 41).

Vooght judges film adaptations of *The Great Gatsby* in terms of their fidelity not to the particulars of F. Scott Fitzgerald's novel but to "the global truth-event of modernity" it dramatizes: "a global Badouian event, reorienting every aspect of life and culture" (Vooght 47, 57). Emphasizing the novel's "contradiction of style versus content" and "the contradiction of the celebration and repudiation of material excess," along with its deep ambivalence toward the American Dream of "personal freedom, education, the rise of the middle class and success through personal effort," she describes the novel's "fidelity to modernity in being both and neither, creative and destructive, hopeful and despairing" (Vooght 63, 64, 66).

Vooght's analyses of the four film adaptations of *The Great Gatsby* are framed by her accounts of their commercial imperatives, the impact of their star personas, their marketing campaigns, their contemporaneous reviews, and the surprisingly different agendas of their directors. Herbert Brenon, the contract director in charge of the 1926 film, "apparently insisted on a happy ending, with the Buchanans' marriage restored to harmony," which was entirely consistent with Fitzgerald's status as "a popular author" whose work could be altered in fundamental ways without provoking an outcry (Vooght 97). Elliott Nugent, who directed the 1949 film, "had [such] a very high opinion of the novel he was working with" that he was convinced that "a film version could be little more than a poor imitation" (Vooght 97). Jack Clayton's self-satisfied assessment of the 1974 film he directed—"We've made the book"—"clearly indicates his goal—not to create a film but to render a book" (Vooght 98). Baz Luhrmann's attitude toward his 2013 film is more complicated: "Luhrmann tends to use Fitzgerald and his status to justify certain decisions, whilst at the same time pushing his own individual changes when convenient," justifying these changes by "claim[ing] a link between his own and Fitzgerald's unorthodoxy" (Vooght 101).

When she turns to a textual analysis of the four adaptations, Vooght unmasks the superficiality of their attempts at a "correspondence" to the particulars of Fitzgerald's novel, its increasingly canonical status, and its period setting, which they increasingly fetishize:

> [T]hat correspondence, where it is obvious, usually extends only to surface depictions or has been commandeered to perform other roles within the screenplay ... [C]hanges that serve to close down Fitzgerald's openness will work against the possibility of a Badouian fidelity.
>
> (Vooght 168)

The films' literalization of themes like Gatsby's exclusion from the Buchanans' social class and the underworld connections on which his success depended, and iconic images like the eyes of Dr. T.J. Eckelberg, the green light at the end of Daisy's pier, and the excessively opulent parties Gatsby hosts, have positioned Fitzgerald's novel more and more as "a source of fixed meanings [that] suppressed his text's more politically contentious aspects" (Vooght 199).

Vooght concludes not by pronouncing any of the four adaptations superior or inferior to the others but by indicating that although none of them is, or could be, entirely faithful to *The Great Gatsby*, its author, its period, and its canonical status, each of them achieves more limited fidelity of a different kind. The 1926 film, which has not survived, evidently succeeded "as a crowd pleaser" with "little desire to make a connection with Fitzgerald's prose style" (Vooght 229). The 1949 film, though limited by a "clunky script and studio setting," stands out for its underappreciated "depiction of Gatsby's subtle exclusion from the moneyed upper classes" (Vooght 229). The 1974 film, marked by "overly binary contrasts" between rich and poor and a "cold and narcissistic" depiction of the trappings of wealth, is most successful in dramatizing "larger themes, such as the tension between modernity and the fading values of an older America" (Vooght 230). And Luhrmann's "shallow and reifying" return to "ideas of Fitzgerald's canonical and commercial value" repeatedly undermines his attempts "to create a connection with the ambiguous and 'open' aspects of Fitzgerald's prose in a cinematic way"— attempts that, as Badiou might say, are most successful when they remain most open (Vooght 230).

Instead of focusing, as all these adaptations do, on the replication of specific details from Fitzgerald's novel, Vooght proposes a recipe for a successful adaptation that embodies "an exploratory, integrated and holistic view of fidelity which allows for the consideration of the source text as an evental site" (Vooght 232):

> The attitude to the source text must be connection ... Then, the makers must intend to be 'faithful to this fidelity,' [keeping in mind that] literalising through the reproduction of details in the text works against the unknowable meanings of the text ... There must be room for contradiction, for inconclusiveness, and for emotional trajectories that go beyond the stated facts on the screen ... [A]daptations must tap into their own contemporary zeitgeist, as well as those traces that reactivate past truth-events, continually rearticulating and reproducing their truths.
>
> (Vooght 232)

Questions

- If we shift from asking, "Do we want to use fidelity in assessing adaptations?" to "How do we want to use fidelity in assessing adaptations?", what are the best ways to use fidelity in analyzing adaptations?
- What place does fidelity, however you define and use it, have among the other characteristics of adaptations you think are most important?
- What do you want to use fidelity, or discussions of fidelity, to do?

The ethics of fidelity

Buried in all discussions of fidelity are ethical assumptions and imperatives that become more explicit whenever commentators berate an adaptation for not being faithful to its source. As Robert Stam observes, these accusations, even when they remain implicit, can be remarkably wide-ranging:

> The conventional language of adaptation criticism has often been profoundly moralistic, rich in terms that imply that that the cinema has somehow done a *disservice* to literature. Terms like "infidelity," "betrayal," "deform-ation," "violation," "bastardization," "vulgarization," and "desecration" proliferate in adaptation discourse, each word carrying its specific charge of opprobrium. "Infidelity" carries overtones of Victorian prudishness; "betrayal" evokes ethical perfidy; "bastardization" connotes illegitimacy; "deformation" implies aesthetic disgust and monstrosity; "violation" calls to mind sexual violence; "vulgarization" conjures up class degradation; and "desecration" intimates sacrilege and blasphemy."
>
> (Stam 3)

Commentators have used derogatory and dismissive tags like these so freely that it is surprising to see how few of them have seriously considered the eth-ical implications of adaptations that seek to be faithful to the texts they are adapting. If infidelity is unethical, then fidelity must presumably be ethical. But even critics who profess outrage at unfaithful film adaptations "ignore the problems that arise from dealing with backers, studios, stars, technicians, publicists, and stage mothers to focus their attention on exactly one party, the author of the original property" (Leitch, "Ethics" 62). In fact, since authors whose copyrighted works are subject to duly licensed adaptation are acknowledged and compensated whether the adaptations at hand are faithful or not, the sole beneficiary of a faithful adapter's ethical solicitude is the adapted work itself, which is presumably beyond caring.

In "The Ethics of Infidelity," I proposed some specific ethical reasons why *Alice's Adventures in Wonderland* might have chosen to be unfaithful to the photographs Charles Lutwidge Dodgson took of Alice Liddell, the model for his fictional heroine—to avoid "a serious violation of her privacy"; and why Gus Van Sant's exceptionally close remake of Alfred Hitchcock's *Psycho* might at certain strategic points have departed from its model—to reveal "a powerful, if largely overlooked, case for fidelity as psychosis" (Leitch, "Ethics" 70, 75). But most adaptation scholars have continued to invoke the ethical overtones of fidelity discourse without coming to terms with its implications.

The most notable exception to this reluctance to engage the ethics of fidelity and infidelity is Shelley Cobb. Following Lori Chamberlain—who argues, in Cobb's words, that "faithfulness, as a criterion for translation, is used metaphorically to evoke Western cultural expectations for the gendered relationship of heterosexual marriage and romance"—Cobb contends:

> [T]he language of fidelity constructs a gendered possession of authority and paternity for the source text within adaptation: the film as faithful

wife to the novel as paternal husband. In this way, fidelity legitimizes both the relationship between the two texts and the act of (re)production.

(Cobb 30)

Cobb presents three exhibits that reveal this invidious gendering. The first is from Brian McFarlane's *Novel to Film*. Despite McFarlane's admonition that "words like 'tampering' and 'interference,' and even 'violation,' give the whole process [of adaptation] an air of deeply sinister molestation" (McFarlane 12), Cobb notes, he "displaces the object of sanctity from the original text to the *viewer's memory* of it" in a passage in which the word *violence* continues to "uphold the gendered language of fidelity and its moralising" (Cobb 31). The second is my essay "Adaptation, the Genre," which uses adaptations of the novels of Alexandre Dumas *père* and *fils* to argue that "the *genre* of adaptation has been dominated, if not defined, by feminine romantic love adaptations rather than masculine romantic adventure adaptations," and that the "solution to the problem of adaptation as a genre is to foreground the *masculine* romantic adventure adaptation" as less likely to be preoccupied with fidelity to its source or castigated for lacking that fidelity (Cobb 33). The third is Stam's Introduction to *Literature and Film*, which rejects fidelity discourse for "a new set of tropes for speaking of adaptation" and recommends as one possibility "the 'Pygmalion model, where the adaptation brings the novel to 'life' " (Stam 24). Cobb dismisses this model as a "return of the repressed" value of gendered fidelity: "the image of the male artist who sees only his own version of woman as worthy of love is hardly a revolution against fidelity" (Cobb 35).

Although she does not "argue for the value of a *feminine* approach to adaptations" (Cobb 33), Cobb recommends that everyone who encounters adaptations be aware of potentially gendered ways of thinking and talking about them. Her advice could well be generalized: every act of creating, consuming, and analyzing adaptations is fraught with ethical overtones, and every party to these transactions should keep these overtones in mind.

Questions

- Do adaptations have a specifically ethical responsibility to be faithful to the texts they adapt? If so, why? If not, what ethical responsibilities do they have to authors or other parties?
- How do these responsibilities compare to other ethical responsibilities they have to other shareholders in the adaptive process?
- Many fans of *Watchmen* harshly criticized Zack Snyder's film adaptation of Dave Gibbons's graphic novel when it was first released in 2009 because they saw it as a slavish attempt to imitate the novel. If fidelity is a virtue, is it possible for an adaptation to be too faithful to the text it is adapting?
- Are aesthetic approaches to adaptation necessarily ethical approaches?

- Are ethical approaches to adaptation necessarily aesthetic approaches?
- What do aesthetic engagements allow or reveal about adaptations that other engagements don't?

References

Andrew, Dudley. "Adaptation." *Concepts in Film Theory*. Oxford UP, 1984, pp. 96–106.

Andrew, Dudley. "The Economies of Adaptation." *True to the Spirit: Film Adaptation and the Question of Fidelity*. Edited by Colin MacCabe, Kathleen Murray, and Rick Warner. Oxford UP, 2011, pp. 27–39.

Bazin, André. "In Defense of Mixed Cinema." Bazin, *What Is Cinema?* Vol. 1. Translated and edited by Hugh Gray. U of California P, 1967, pp. 53–75.

Bazin, André. "Adaptation, or the Cinema as Digest." Translated by Alain Piette and Bert Cardullo. *Bazin at Work* (1997). Rpt. in *Film Adaptation*. Edited by James Naremore. Rutgers UP, 2000, pp. 19–27.

Benjamin, Walter. "The Work of Art in the Age of Mechanical Reproduction." *Illuminations*. Edited by Hannah Arendt, translated by Harry Zohn. Schocken, 1969, pp. 217–51.

Bluestone, George. *Novels into Film*. Johns Hopkins UP, 1967.

Cahir, Linda Costanzo. *Literature into Film: Theory and Practical Approaches*. McFarland, 2006.

Cardwell, Sarah. *Adaptation Revisited: Television and the Classic Novel*. Manchester UP, 2002.

Cardwell, Sarah. "About Time: Theorizing Adaptation, Temporality, and Tense." *Literature/Film Quarterly*, vol. 31, no. 1 (Jan. 2003), pp. 82–92.

Chatman, Seymour. "What Novels Can Do That Films Can't (and Vice Versa)." *Critical Inquiry*, vol. 7, no. 1 (1980), pp. 121–40.

Cobb, Shelley. "Adaptation, Fidelity, and Gendered Discourses." *Adaptation*, vol. 4, no. 1 (2010), pp. 28–37.

Connor, J.D. "The Persistence of Fidelity: Adaptation Theory Today." *M/C Journal*, vol. 10, no. 2 (2007), doi: https://doi.org/10.5204/mcj.2652.

Desmond, John M. and Peter Hawkes. *Adaptation: Studying Film and Literature*. McGraw-Hill, 2005.

Elliott, Kamilla. *Rethinking the Novel/Film Debate*. Cambridge UP, 2003.

Geraghty, Christine. *Now a Major Motion Picture: Film Adaptations of Literature and Drama*. Rowman and Littlefield, 2007.

Girish, Devika. "Life's Work." *Film Comment*, Nov.–Dec. 2019, https://www.film comment.com/article/lifes-work/.

Hermansson, Casie. "Flogging Fidelity: In Defense of the (Un)Dead Horse." *Adaptation* vol. 8, no. 2 (2015), pp. 147–60.

Hurst, Rochelle. "Adaptation as an Undecidable: Fidelity and Binarity from Bluestone to Derrida." *In/Fidelity: Essays on Film Adaptation*. Edited by David L. Kranz and Nancy Mellerski. Cambridge Scholars P, 2008, pp. 172–96.

Jameson, Fredric. "Afterword: Adaptation as a Philosophical Problem." *True to the Spirit: Film Adaptation and the Question of Fidelity*. Edited by Colin MacCabe, Kathleen Murray, and Rick Warner. Oxford UP, 2011, pp. 215–33.

Klein, Michael. "Introduction: Film and Literature." *The English Novel and the Movies*. Edited by Michael Klein and Gillian Parker. Ungar, 1981, pp. 1–13.

Kracauer, Siegfried. *Theory of Film: The Redemption of Physical Reality*. Oxford UP, 1960.

Leitch, Thomas. "Twelve Fallacies in Contemporary Adaptation Theory." *Criticism*, vol. 45, no. 2 (Spring 2003), pp. 149–71.

Leitch, Thomas. "Adaptation, the Genre." *Adaptation*, vol. 1, no. 2 (Fall 2008), pp. 106–20.

Leitch, Thomas. "Fidelity Discourse: Its Cause and Cure." *In/Fidelity: Essays on Film Adaptation*. Edited by David L. Kranz and Nancy Mellerski. Cambridge Scholars, 2008, pp. 205–8.

Leitch, Thomas. "The Ethics of Infidelity." *Adaptation Studies: New Approaches*. Edited by Dennis Cutchins and Christa Albrecht–Crane. Fairleigh Dickinson UP, 2010, pp. 61–77.

Lessing, Gotthold Ephraim. *Laocoön: An Essay on the Limits of Painting and Poetry*. Translated by Edward Allen McCormick. Johns Hopkins UP, 1984.

Literary Hub. "10 Screen Adaptations Much, Much Worse Than the Books They're Based On." https://lithub.com/10-screen-adaptations-much-much-worse-than-the-books-theyre-based-on/?utm_source=join1440&utm_medium=email&utm_pl acement=newsletter.

Lopez Szwydky, Lissette. *Transmedia Adaptation in the Nineteenth Century*. Ohio State UP, 2020.

MacCabe, Colin. "Introduction: Bazinian Adaptation: *The Butcher Boy* as Example." *True to the Spirit: Film Adaptation and the Question of Fidelity*. Edited by Colin MacCabe, Kathleen Murray, and Rick Warner. Oxford UP, 2011, pp. 3–25.

McFarlane, Brian. *Novel to Film: An Introduction to the Theory of Adaptation*. Clarendon, 1996.

Meisel, Martin. *Realizations: Narrative, Pictorial, and Theatrical Arts in Nineteenth-Century England*. Princeton UP, 1983.

Murray, Kathleen. "*To Have and Have Not*: An Adaptive System." *True to the Spirit: Film Adaptation and the Question of Fidelity*. Edited by Colin MacCabe, Kathleen Murray, and Rick Warner. Oxford UP, 2011, pp. 91–113.

"Particular Applications of the Code and the Reasons Therefore [Addenda to the 1930 Code]." Appendix II to Martin, Olga J. *Hollywood's Movie Commandments*. Arno, 1970, pp. 285–88.

Raitt, George. "Still Lusting After Fidelity?" *Literature/Film Quarterly*, vol. 38, no. 1 (2010), pp. 47–58.

Ray, Robert B. "The Field of 'Literature and Film.'" *Film Adaptation*. Edited by James Naremore. Rutgers UP, 2000, pp. 38–53.

Shelley, Mary Wollstonecraft. *The Letters of Mary Wollstonecraft Shelley: Volume I: "A Part of the Elect."* Edited by Betty T. Burnett. Johns Hopkins UP, 1980.

Sicherman, Barbara. "Reading *Little Women*: The Many Lives of a Text." *U.S. History as Women's History: New Feminist Essays*. Edited by Linda K. Kerber, Alice Kessler-Harris, and Kathryn Kish Sklar. U of North Carolina P, 1995, pp. 245–66.

Stam, Robert. "Introduction: The Theory and Practice of Adaptation." *Literature and Film: A Guide to the Theory and Practice of Adaptation*. Edited by Stam and Alessandra Raengo. Blackwell, 2005, pp. 1–52.

Stevens, Dana. "Greta Gerwig Has Made Cinema's Greatest *Little Women*." *Slate*, 4 Dec. 2019, https://slate.com/culture/2019/12/little-women-review-2019-movie-adaptation-greta-gerwig.html.

Vooght, Ursula. *The Great Gatsby Meets Alain Badiou: Rethinking Fidelity in Film Adaptation*. Aosis, 2023, https://books.aosis.co.za/index.php/ob/catalog/book/421.

Wagner, Geoffrey. *The Novel and the Cinema*. Fairleigh Dickinson UP, 1975.

Woolf, Virginia. "The Cinema." 1926. Rpt. in *The Essays of Virginia Woolf, Volume 4: 1925–1928*. Edited by Andrew McNeillie. Hogarth, 1994, pp. 348–54.

2 Intertextual engagements
Adaptation as process

Product or process?

In *A Theory of Adaptation*, Linda Hutcheon—following John Bryant's proposition that, because "writing is a process," it is a mistake "to define a material text—and by that I mean the physical writing on the page—as a fixed thing" (Bryant 3, 2)—defines adaptation as a term that can refer to both a process and a series of products created by that process:

> First, seen as a *formal entity or product*, an adaptation is an announced and extensive transposition of a particular work or works …
>
> Second, as a *process of creation*, the act of adaptation always involves both (re-)interpretation and then (re-)creation; this has been called both appropriation and salvaging …
>
> Third, seen from the perspective of its *process of reception*, adaptation is a form of intertextuality: we experience adaptations (*as adaptations*) as palimpsests through our memory of other works that resonate through repetition with variation.
>
> (Hutcheon 7–8)

In a later section of her chapter "Final Questions," entitled "What Is *Not* an Adaptation?" (170), Hutcheon acknowledges several problems with her definition of adaptation as product, especially in the terms *announced* and *extensive*. If adaptations have to announce themselves as adaptations, then is the 1979 movie *Apocalypse Now* an adaptation of Joseph Conrad's 1899 novella "The Heart of Darkness," which writer and director Francis Ford Coppola frequently mentioned as his inspiration without ever identifying it in the film's credits; and is the 1995 movie *Clueless* an adaptation of Jane Austen's 1815 novel *Emma*, which its credits never cite but which writer and director Amy Heckerling constantly referred to as a source during her publicity tour? And how extensive do their borrowings have to be to make

DOI: 10.4324/9781003438410-3

them adaptations? Distinguishing "adaptation proper" from other works on "the continuum of fluid relationships between prior works and later—and lateral—revisitations of them," Hutcheon rules that "short intertextual allusions to other works or bits of sampled music would not be included. But parodies would" (Hutcheon 171, 170).

Regardless of problems in Hutcheon's definition that adaptation scholars continue to debate, the distinctions between adaptation as a productive process, adaptation as a receptive process, and adaptation as a series of products generated by these two processes have had a decisive impact on adaptation studies. If aesthetic approaches to adaptation emphasize the status of individual adaptations as products, intertextual approaches emphasize the nature of adaptation as a process. Writing about popular film genres like the Western and the musical, Rick Altman described these genres, which casual audiences might assume to be fixed and enduring, as "the temporary by-product of an ongoing *process*" of "genrefication" (Altman 54, 62). "Genrefication," the term Altman coins to describe this process, might make his explanation sound hard to swallow. But it would be much easier to describe individual adaptations as more or less incidental byproducts of the ceaseless activity of adapting.

This process, which has consistently been identified with the twenty-first century, has much deeper roots in texts like Petronius' *Satyricon* (first century A.D.), Miguel de Cervantes' *Don Quixote* (1605/1615), Laurence Sterne's *Tristram Shandy* (1759–66), Denis Diderot's *Jacques le fataliste et son maître* (1796), and Lewis Carroll's *Alice's Adventures in Wonderland* (1865), which both imitated and parodied a wide range of texts, from accounts of dining to chivalric romances to autobiographies. Instead of backing away from the challenges that have bedeviled so many crossover adaptations, the literary tradition of Menippean satire, whose targets are typically social attitudes and mores rather than specific authors or works, grasps these challenges eagerly, forging material from multiple sources into something (not entirely) new. This tradition reaches a twentieth-century climax in the later novels of James Joyce. Instead of adopting a reparative approach to Homer's *Odyssey*, as Virgil's *Aeneid* (19 B.C.E.) does in bringing its hero's morals into closer accord with the morals of imperial Rome, Joyce's modern Irish epic *Ulysses* (1922) poses endless connections between its nominal source and hundreds of other texts it adapts, cites, or alludes to. Joyce explores this territory even more deeply in *Finnegans Wake* (1939), deliberately subordinating both the novel's throughline and the nominal sourcetext announced by its title to an intricate network of references that continues to occupy scholars 100 years on.

Questions

- What are the relations between (thinking about) adaptation as process and (thinking about) adaptations as products?

- Where would you draw the line between things that are adaptations and things that are not?
- What family resemblances can you find between *Alice in Wonderland*, *Ulysses*, and contemporary Menippean satires like *Barbie*?

From copies to intertexts

Robert Stam, the leading scholar associated with the emergence of adaptation as a process of production and reception, takes exactly this approach to his subject. Contending that too much of the discussion of adaptation "has focused on the rather subjective nature of the **quality** of adaptations," he seeks to direct attention to "the more interesting issues of (1) the theoretical *status* of adaptation, and (2) the analytical *interest* of adaptations" (Stam, "Introduction" 4). For Stam, all texts, whether or not they are explicitly marked as adaptations, are always in dialogue with other texts whose values and markers they have internalized to a greater or lesser extent. Since texts are "caught up in the ongoing whirl of intertextual reference and transformation, of texts generating other texts in an endless process of recycling, transformation, and transmutation, with no clear point of origin" (Stam, "Introduction" 31), adaptation as a process is incessant and inevitable.

In some ways, Stam's intertextual model of adaptation marks a return to the ancient models the nineteenth and twentieth centuries had left behind. Adaptation, in Stam's view, is not the exception but the rule—the force behind all literary, audiovisual, and narrative production. Since he finds adaptation "less a resuscitation of an originary word than a turn in an ongoing dialogical process" (Stam, *Literature* 4), he consistently subordinates adaptations as variously successful works of art to adaptation as an ongoing process. Hence there is no such thing as an authoritative text. More precisely, textual authority is not eternally endowed by aesthetic achievements that elevate a few chosen works to a timeless canon but is constantly up for grabs as different texts—and different versions of texts—struggle to speak for and against different cultural norms and ideals. Stam recalls how Jacques Derrida "dismantled the hierarchy of 'original' and 'copy'" by arguing that "the auratic prestige of the original does not run counter to the copy; rather, the prestige of the original is *created* by the copies, without which the idea of the original has no meaning" (Stam, "Introduction" 8). Following Derrida, he concludes that "the 'original' always turns out to be partially 'copied' from something earlier" (Stam, "Introduction" 8). Stam's quest "to deconstruct the unstated doxa which subtly construct the subaltern *status* of adaptation (and the filmic image) vis-à-vis novels (and the literary word)" (Stam, "Introduction" 4) has allowed other commentators to rewrite the genealogy of adaptations. Thomas Van Parys notes that "an adapted text can ... be related to its source text, rather than subordinated to it" (Van Parys 433). And Lissette Lopez Szwydky suggests "[a]pproaching adaptation as an entry point to literature" (Lopez Szwydky 25).

Stam's citation of Derrida and his use of terms like "doxa" and "subaltern" echo the poststructuralism that swept through the academy in the 1960s and 1970s, upending aesthetic hierarchies and canonical certitudes. Just as he notes that the ceaseless process of adaptation calls into the question the very possibility of originality, Stam owes much of his own analysis to earlier theorists. The most important of these are Mikhail Bakhtin, Julia Kristeva, and Gérard Genette. Kamilla Elliott has aptly summarized the impact of their theories of intertextuality on adaptation studies:

> Julia Kristeva coined the term in 1966. Radicalizing Mikhail Bakhtin's theory of dialogics by joining it to Derridean poststructuralism, Althusserian political ideology, generative grammar, and Lacanian psychoanalysis, she challenged then dominant views that located meaning in deliberate speech acts, conscious author intent, and agenda-driven cultural discourses with a theory in which intertextuality is a feature of all texts in which meaning is therefore variable, contested, and unfixed, continually renegotiated among authors, texts, readers, and cultural contexts, which are themselves unstable.
>
> (Elliott, "Tie-Intertextuality," 192)

Instead of assuming that individual texts and canonical archives are characterized by an aesthetic and thematic unity directed by authorial intention and agency, Stam draws on Bakhtin's idea that texts from Rabelais's *Gargantua and Pantagruel* (1532–64) to Dostoevsky's "Notes from Underground" (1864) are carnivals that provide showcases for dialogues among many different incompletely internalized and resolved voices that are often pointedly at odds with each other. Just as circus fans do not go to carnivals to enjoy well-defined, unified experiences that will be the same for every audience because they have been prescribed by the features of the carnival, audiences of Bakhtin, Kristeva, and Stam do not read or watch or listen to texts with the expectation of taking away pleasures predetermined by the selection and placement of every word, sound, and image. Bakhtin, who prized unresolved dialogues between competing voices above all other fictional elements, considered the novel to be the most obviously dialogic of all genres because it was the one most clearly driven by conflicts within incompletely internalized voices borrowed from or inflected by a potentially limitless range of earlier texts. Dennis Cutchins has noted that for Bakhtin, "an adaptation is primarily not a kind of text, but *a way of looking at texts*" (Cutchins 80). Bakhtin sets "canonical texts," whose bodies are "entirely finished, completed," against "grotesque texts," each of them "a body in the act of becoming" that is "never completed; it is continually built, created, and builds and creates another body." Noting that the excesses and exaggerations of grotesque texts "constantly invite the reader or viewer to perceive interconnections," Cutchins quotes Bakhtin, who argues that "we perceive [grotesque] texts as adaptations more readily," and that they "invite adaptation more often" than canonical texts (Cutchins 82; see Bakhtin 320, 317).

For Stam, who finds the cinema just as dialogic and grotesque as the novel in its profusion of unreconciled voices, adaptation is the joyous, jagged tip of an iceberg that includes every text ever produced. His account of Bakhtinian dialogism is supplemented by Kristeva, whose "intertextuality theory" he claims is "rooted in and literally translating Bakhtin's 'dialogism'" (Stam, "Introduction" 8). Since Kristeva considers every text "*an intersection of textual surfaces* rather than a *point* of fixed meaning," every term in narrative is "at least *double*" (Kristeva 36, 37).

An even more important predecessor to Stam is Genette, who replaces Kristeva's term "intertextuality" with what Stam calls "the more inclusive term 'transtextuality' to refer to 'all that puts one text in relation, whether manifest or secret, with other texts" (Stam, "Introduction" 27). Genette distinguishes five different types of transtextual relationships that define "literature in the second degree." "Intertextuality," or "the effective co-presence of two texts," involves the quotation, allusion, or plagiarism of one text by another (Genette 1). "Paratextuality" concerns the relation between "the text proper" and "titles, prefaces, postfaces, epigraphs, dedications, illustrations, and even book jackets and signed autographs, in short all the accessory messages and commentaries which come to surround the text and which at times become virtually indistinguishable from it" (Genette 4, 3). "Metatextuality," which is characterized by an overtly "critical relation between one text and another" (Genette 4), includes not only academic studies of canonical texts but rewritings like Jean Rhys's *Wide Sargasso Sea* (1966) and J.M. Coetzee's *Foe* (1986), whose attitude toward the texts they are revisiting—in this case, *Jane Eyre* (1847) and *Robinson Crusoe* (1719) respectively—is fundamentally revisionist and critical. "Architextuality" indicates "the generic taxonomies suggested or refused by the titles or subtitles of a text," however imprecise or misleading these labels may be (Genette 4). Of all Genette's categories, Stam considers "hypertextuality"—referring to "the relation between one text, which Genette calls 'hypertext,' to an anterior text or 'hypotext,' which the former transforms, modifies, elaborates, or extends"—to be "the type most clearly relevant to adaptation" (Stam, "Introduction" 31; see Genette 5). As if in agreement with this conclusion, Genette concludes his own volume by proposing that "every successive state of a written text functions like a hypertext in relation to the state that precedes it and a hypotext in relation to the one that follows" (Genette 395).

Stam's analysis, which has had a profound impact on more recent work in adaptation studies, raises two other important questions. The first concerns the ethics of adaptation. What ethical issues do discussions of adaptation as process rather than product necessarily raise? When Cutchins considers the question of "*why* we ... experience this doubled perception" of adaptation in some texts but not in others, he asserts that "[t]he answer to this question ... is for Bakhtin neither structural nor theoretical but ethical." Because "works of art … create their own artistic validity, their own weight, meaning, value, or power, only through the kinds of intertextuality I have been describing," it follows that "[m]uch of the power of an adaptation … derives from its relationships with source texts and other texts on its boundaries" (Cutchins 84). And these relationships inevitably have at least two moral or ethical dimensions. The first depends on their creators' intentions, which may range from reverence (citations of the Hebrew Bible in the Gospels) to revisionist correction (*Wide Sargasso Sea*, which retells the story of *Jane Eyre* from Bertha Mason's proto-feminist perspective rather than Jane's) to criminal trespass (countless cases of plagiarism). The second depends on the attitudes different audiences adopt toward them (uncritical acceptance? Engaged dialogue? Summary rejection?) and the uses to which different audiences put them.

Stam, who had established a reputation as a scholar of postcolonial litera- ture before he turned to adaptation, is particularly sensitive to "postcolonial [film] adaptations of colonialist novels like *Robinson Crusoe*, for example *Man Friday* (1976)," which "liberate the oppressed colonial characters of the original" (Stam, "Introduction" 42), and film adaptations like *The Grapes of Wrath* (1940), *Madame Bovary* (1949), and *Lolita* (1962), which have been shaped by censorship. Both his background and his methodology make him less sympathetic to adaptations that push the stories they borrow "to the 'right,' by naturalizing and justifying social hierarchies based on class, race, sexuality, gender, region, and national belonging," than to those that move "to the 'left' by interrogating or leveling hierarchies in an egalitarian manner" (Stam, "Introduction" 42). Along similar lines, Cristina Bacchilega suggests that "consider[ing] the gender politics of fairy-tale adaptations in relation to other dynamics of power and experiences of disjunction" would encourage "the emergence of a renewed poetics and politics of wonder that, although hardly cohesive, are situated responses to the hegemony of a colon- izing, Orientalizing, and commercialized poetics of magic" (Bacchilega ix).

This preference for left-leaning over right-leaning adaptation suggests a second question: what kinds of evaluative judgments are possible and appro- priate when adaptation is considered primarily as an ongoing process that spins off individual adaptations along the way? Some observers might decide that shifting the definition of adaptations from copies of single canonical texts to byproducts of the ceaseless process of adaptation renders compara- tive evaluation irrelevant, since no texts enjoy the privilege of being original touchstones against which their copies should be measured. Cutchins notes that for Bakhtin, canonical texts that "don't open themselves to interpene- tration or even to interpretation" end up "no longer hav[ing] literary value"; whereas imperfect texts like *Sense and Sensibility* "seem … almost to demand rewriting" (Cutchins 82, 83). Stam himself argues:

> By adopting an intertextual as opposed to a judgmental approach rooted in assumptions about a putative superiority of literature, we have not

abandoned all notions of judgment and evaluation. But our discussion will be less moralistic, less implicated in unacknowledged hierarchies. We can still speak of successful or unsuccessful adaptations, but this time oriented not by inchoate notions of "fidelity" but rather by attention to "transfers of creative energy," or to specific dialogical responses, to "readings" and "critiques" and "interpretations" and "rewritings" of source novels, in analyses which always take into account the gaps between very different media and materials of expression.

(Stam, "Introduction" 46)

The most important word in these two accounts is one that does not appear in either of them: *power*. Value judgments that subordinate particular adaptations to adaptation as a process are likely to be judgments about how those adaptations handle the power dynamics they find in the texts they adapt—how they seek to replicate, question, alter, or reverse the power dynamics and differentials that made the texts they adapt worth adapting in the first place.

As these examples indicate, not everyone who focuses on adaptation as an intertextual process takes the same approach to evaluating individual adaptations. But everyone who does pronounce some adaptations more faithful than others implicitly accepts a hierarchy that defines the adapted text as a center rather than as "a sponge [that] is literally all surface" (Cutchins 79). The following section examines two approaches that are particularly dramatic in the different ways they consider the question of evaluation.

Questions

- On what basis is it most reasonable and defensible to evaluate different adaptations—or should we avoid evaluating them at all?
- Given the transactional nature of authority, what makes a given version—for example, a play by Shakespeare—authoritative?
- Are there authoritative versions of any fairytales?
- What is at stake, and what changes, when we define an adaptation (or indeed any text) as an intertext rather than a text?

Better texts through adaptation

Stam's intertextual account of adaptation is marked by surprising continuities with the aesthetic theories he attacks when he singles out for special attention adaptations that confront the tyranny of the European canon and its avowedly universal aesthetic by talking back to Shakespeare and his ilk. Echoing "Towards a Third Cinema"—the 1969 manifesto by Fernando Solañas and Octavio Getino that rejected the First Cinema of Hollywood as crassly commercial and the Second Cinema of European art films as hermetically elitist—he sees the pointedly revisionist adaptations of Third Cinema as products of a radical politics whose deepest meanings arise not from their relation to the texts they choose to adapt but to the political contexts from which they arise and the political actions they seek to provoke. In connection with their political agenda, adaptations from Joseph Gai Ramaka's 2002 Senegalese film *Karmen Gei,* which "both queers and Africanizes the story of Carmen," to the Oficina Theatre Company's 2009 production of *Hamlet,* in which Jose Celso Martinez Correa and his collaborators transformed Shakespeare's play into "an anthropophagic musical" (Stam, "Revisionist" 243, 241), serve as lenses that focus critical attention on canonical texts in transgressive new ways—especially when they illuminate acts of imperialistic suppression those canonical texts had sought to conceal under the cloak of universality.

Despite his occasional forays into theater, Stam implicitly accepts aesthetic theorists' assumption that novel-to-film adaptation is the privileged, or at least the unmarked, mode of adaptation. And he often makes evaluative comments about adaptations. Some of these are marginal, like his preference for certain adaptations of *Robinson Crusoe, Madame Bovary,* and *Lolita* over others. Others are systemic, like his endorsement of the anti-imperialistic left-wing political agenda he uses to grade adaptations up or down—an endorsement that led Lawrence Venuti to conclude disapprovingly, "In adaptation studies informed by the discourse of intertextuality, the film is not compared directly to the literary text, but rather to a version of it mediated by an ideological critique" that implicitly demands "that the film should somehow inscribe that and only that ideology" (Venuti 28).

For all these limitations, which may well be inevitable effects of Stam's politically driven account of adaptation, the intertextual approach he championed has been prodigiously influential on adaptation studies. It plays a central role in Linda Hutcheon's 2006 monograph *A Theory of Adaptation,* whose attempt to survey a wide variety of approaches to adaptation and package them within a single theory gave decisive weight to intertextual over aesthetic accounts. It inspires Kate Newell to conclude that "a networked model of adaptation" can reveal "that cultural understandings of literary works originate not exclusively or even necessarily in source texts but in patterns of repetition and reiteration" (Newell 197). And it continues to influence scholars who seek to incorporate the adaptations of Third Cinema into a more extensive body of anti-imperialistic adaptations. The leading figure in this movement is Douglas Lanier, who discusses portraits of Shakespeare, Shakespearean fanfiction, Shakespeare tourism and festivals, and fictionalized biographies from *Shakespeare in Love* (1998) to "Shakespeare's Ghost Writer" —a 1947 episode in *Superman Comics* in which Clark Kent and Lois Lane are accidentally transported back to Shakespeare's day and Superman, Kent's powerful alter ego, lends the playwright, who is seriously pressed for time, crucial assistance in writing *Macbeth* (Lanier, *Shakespeare and Modern* 136). In a 2018 conference paper, Lanier coined the term "reparative Shakespeare" to describe the ways in which revisionist performances and adaptations of Shakespeare's plays seek to extract hitherto hidden meanings and implications in the most canonical of all Anglophone authors that can "create a positive effect in a performer" (Lanier, "Shakespeare and the Reparative Turn").

Elaborating on Lanier's argument, Alexa Alice Joubin notes that a "reparative approach to the arts, coupled with political reasoning that makes an adaptation relevant and compelling, fosters stronger affective connections to a play, because the neural mechanisms underlying emotion and motivation are intertwined" (Joubin, *Shakespeare* 73). Joubin—who surveys East Asian Shakespeares from Akira Kurosawa's films *Throne of Blood* (1957), based on *Macbeth* (ca. 1606); *The Bad Sleep Well* (1960), based on *Hamlet* (ca. 1600); and *Ran* (1985), based on *King Lear* (ca. 1606), to the Shakespeare Festivals in Hong Kong, Beijing, Shanghai, and Taipei—distinguishes two "strands of recuperative adaptations" that "emerge out of the tradition of using literature as a coping strategy in times of crisis" (Joubin, *Shakespeare* 72, 73):

> The first comprises more conservative approaches to Shakespeare based on an assumption that the dramatic situations exemplify moral universality. Earnest performances of artistic reparative efficacy propose that Shakespeare can improve one's character and social circumstances ... The second consists of adaptations, particularly those in a parodic vein, that problematize heteronormativity and psychological universals in liberal humanist visions of Shakespeare ... The moralist impulse is informed by the therapeutic self-help ethos, while the parodic approach questions the canon's capacity for emotional transformation.
>
> (Joubin, *Shakespeare* 72–73)

Nor is heteronormativity the only universalizing impulse reparative adaptations can unmask, interrogate, and deconstruct. Joubin's 2020 essay "Screening Social Justice: Performing Reparative Shakespeare against Vocal Disability" adds "performances that appear to diagnose and recuperate disability" (Joubin, "Screening" 192). Tom Hooper's 2010 film *The King's Speech* epitomizes the first approach to reparative adaptation, which "depicts how Shakespeare's moral universals can empower and redeem disabled individuals" (Joubin, "Screening" 194) like the stuttering King George VI (Colin Firth). "By problematizing psychological universals allegedly found in Shakespeare," on the other hand, Cheeah Chee Kong's 2000 *Chicken Rice War* "urges its audiences to ask: why does one have to 'improve' accents and speech patterns deemed non-normative by the dominant culture?" (Joubin, "Screening" 199). By actively seeking to rectify or reverse the cultural damage inflicted by the hegemony of earlier texts on the cultures they colonize, including their own host cultures, the parodic second strand represented by *Chicken Rice War* may be seen as repairing not only the audience but Shakespeare himself, who, as Lanier says, "is often as much the object as the agent of legitimation" (Lanier, "Minstrelsy" 2).

In examining the relation between the "highbrow art" of Shakespeare's plays and the "popular American cultures" represented by "African American music," Lanier argues:

> [M]id-century jazz adaptations of Shakespeare serve as an ambivalent middle-term between Shakespearean minstrelsy of the nineteenth century ... and contemporary hip-hop, where musicians have reclaimed Shakespeare as a minor yet symbolically significant point of reference for African American music.
>
> (Lanier, "Minstrelsy" 2, 3)

Of the many jazz adaptations of Shakespeare that Lanier examines, two stand out as especially significant. The more straightforward of these is Basil Dearden's 1961 film *All Night Long*, whose screenplay—written by the blacklisted Paul Jarrico under the pseudonym Peter Achilles (Shakespeare is not credited)—transports the story of *Othello* to a London warehouse whose owner, Rod Hamilton (Richard Attenborough), uses it as a private jazz club where performers like Charles Mingus, Dave Brubeck, Tubby Hayes, John Dankworth, and Johnny Scott chat, take turns in solo and ensemble numbers, and then leave. Their music provides a powerful auditory background to the film's take on *Othello*, in which drummer Johnny Cousins (Patrick McGoohan) persuades Black bandleader Aurelius Rex (Paul Harris) that Delia Lane (Marti Stevens), his wife of one year, is cheating on him with Cass Michaels (Keith Mitchell), the band's manager and sax player. In Lanier's reading, the film soft-pedals racial prejudice—white and Black characters mix comfortably throughout the single evening in which the action unfolds in "a miniature racial and jazz utopia," and Cousins' final tirade against love turns his "earlier race-oriented comments into symptoms of his own personal psychology, twisted by ambition and self-loathing, rather than indicators of a more pervasive racial politics"—to focus on "the vexed business of jazz," which underlies Rod's pivotal importance as financier, Johnny's vengeful plotting against Rex and Delia, and Rex's anger at Delia for joining Cass in "a bopped-up version of the standard 'I Never Knew'" that shows "she has taken up performing again and in a musical style pointedly not his own" (Lanier, "Minstrelsy" 18, 20, 18, 19).

In addition to jazzing up Shakespeare, the film modifies *Othello* in several other ways. Like *10 Things I Hate about You* (1999), *Hamlet* (2000), and *O* (completed 1999, released 2001), it updates Shakespeare, setting itself apart from period film adaptations like those starring Orson Welles (1951), Laurence Olivier (1965), and Laurence Fishburne (1995). It changes the story's setting from Venice and Cyprus to South London. It is more narrowly determined psychologically, providing Johnny with an easily identifiable motive—his fury that Delia, who has retired from singing, has not only rejected his romantic overtures but refused to form a partnership with him that will secure Rod's financial backing—for acting against Delia and Rex.

And it adds a happy ending in which Delia recovers from Rex's attempt to choke her to death. Each of these changes raises further questions about the whole project of reparative adaptation.

The most openly debated of these involves casting. Should Othello, the Moor of Venice, be played by a Black man? Fishburne—like Moses Gunn, who played the role on Broadway—is Black; Welles and Olivier, both of whom played the role in heavy makeup, are not. Recent reactions against "blackface" performances, in which white performers don makeup to play Black characters, have led to three developments among theatrical producers: a call for racially accurate casting insisting that Black roles like Othello be reserved for Black performers; a call for color-blind casting that rules each role should be given to the performer best qualified and best prepared to play it; and a call for more diverse casting that ensures the entire cast of any given production reflects the ethnic and racial diversity of its audience or their larger culture rather than that of the play at hand. The first and second of these imperatives are obviously at odds with each other, since Black, Asian, and Minority Ethnic (BAME) roles can either be reserved for BAME performers or not. But so are the second and third of them, as Christine Geraghty has pointed out: "On the one hand, audiences are expected not to take ethnicity and skin colour as semiotically significant while, on the other, they are meant to recognize that the cast as a whole represents a society marked by multicultural diversity" (Geraghty 171).

Figure 2.1 Adjoa Andoh as Lady Danbury and Golda Roshuevel as Queen Charlotte effortlessly cross the color line of the British aristocracy in the first episode of *Bridgerton*'s second season

Out of all the adaptations that have sought to follow contradictory ethical guidelines in racial casting, the one that has attracted the most attention is the Netflix television series *Bridgerton* (2020–), based on a cycle of eight Regency romance novels Julia Quinn published between 2000 and

2006. Unlike the novels—whose characters, in the absence of any racial labels or markers, audiences have assumed were all white—the TV series presents an anachronistic view of early nineteenth-century London, frequently described as alternate history, populated by both white and BAME characters. In fact, one of the most powerful characters in the series, Queen Charlotte, is played by the mixed-race Golda Rosheuval, and her confidante Lady Danbury by Adjoa Andoh, who is Black. Audiences' reactions were predictably mixed to the announcement by series creator Chris Van Dusen, the showrunner for the first two seasons, that the series is not "color-blind" because "that would imply that color and race were never considered, when color and race are part of the show" (Komonibo and Newman-Bremang). Reviewing the first season for the *New York Times*, Salamishah Tillet rejoiced in the fact that "Bridgerton provides a blueprint for British period shows in which Black characters can thrive within the melodramatic story lines, extravagant costumes and bucolic beauty ... without having to be servants or enslaved" (Tillet). But Alyssa Rosenberg, writing in the *Washington Post*, demurred:

> There is no sign that any of the White families on the show feel the slightest anxiety about integration; it's only the Black characters who discuss the new order in any real way. Nor is there any exploration of how the king's innovation [taking a mixed-race queen] has resonated outside of the nobility. Neither his race nor the supposed tenuousness of his title make the Duke of Hastings any less of a catch to the ambitious mothers who target him. Telling us that the show is presenting a daring exploration of race and class is not the same as actually making it so.
>
> (Rosenberg)

Fans have been sharply divided in their reactions to some of the changes the series has wrought on Quinn's novels. But the many viewers who have made *Bridgerton* so popular attest to at least some audiences' abilities to accept the logical inconsistencies of BAME casting, to revel in its promise of things to come, or to ignore it entirely in their consumption of erotic, plushly mounted period romance.

Questions

- Are period adaptations more faithful to Shakespeare because they are set in what we imagine his time and place to have looked like, or are updated adaptations more faithful because they engage contemporary social problems that either endorse or question Shakespeare's universality?
- Given its longstanding position as a tragedy, could you defend repositioning *Othello*, whose "themes of racial violence" recent producers like Trevor Nunn have directly addressed, as one of Shakespeare's "problem plays," like *All's Well That Ends Well* and *Measure for Measure*?

- Given our historical and cultural distance from Shakespeare's take on race, is it advisable or even possible to film *Othello* without updating it?
- Do adaptations that update *Othello*, like *All Night Long* and *O*, seek to improve it?
- Does *All Night Long*'s decision to bring Delia back from her apparent death amount to a redemptive arc for Rex, a heretical betrayal of Shakespeare, or an assumption that movie audiences have a limited tolerance for tragedy?
- Since Giuseppe Verdi's opera *Otello* (1887)—despite working equally dramatic changes on Shakespeare, beginning by cutting the play's entire Act I—has found an honored place in the cultural canon, why has *All Night Long* remained largely unknown?
- Does the television adaptation of *Bridgerton* have the greatest responsibility to be faithful to Julia Quinn's novels, to the mores of the period in which they are set, or to contemporary fans' own sensibilities, ideas, and wishes?

Sound, race, and adaptation

The canonical status of *Otello*, and more generally of opera—which Linda and Michael Hutcheon have called "the Ur-adaptive art" (Hutcheon and Hutcheon 305) because it combines musical, textual, and theatrical media in a single performance—provides a provocative context for an even more challenging Shakespearean adaptation Lanier considers: Duke Ellington's 1957 album *Such Sweet Thunder*, a recording of 11 numbers composed by Ellington and Billy Strayhorn. Because the titles of most of the numbers, from "Sonnet in Search of a Moor" to "Madness in Great Ones," contain obvious allusions to different Shakespeare plays, Lanier concludes that "Ellington conceives of the suite as a series of musical portraits of Shakespearean characters," framed by portraits of Othello ("Such Sweet Thunder") and Cleopatra ("Half the Fun"), which, along with "Sonnet in Search of a Moor," "actively celebrate black erotic power—as the pun on 'a moor'/'amour' suggests—and defy stereotypes of black sexuality by stressing these characters' sophistication and sly charm" (Lanier, "Minstrelsy" 13). Despite Ellington's obvious intent to evoke Shakespeare through these paratextual markers, it is harder to make a case for the purely instrumental numbers in *Such Sweet Thunder* as adaptations of Shakespeare than it would be to make a case for *Otello* or other musical Shakespearean adaptations like Hector Berlioz's choral symphony *Romeo et Juliette* (1839), Otto Nicolai's opera *The Merry Wives of Windsor* (1849), or George Russell's 1968 *Othello Ballet Suite*, which Lanier describes "not as a master ideological narrative about race, but as an abstract psychological study of human nature in crisis" (Lanier, "Minstrelsy" 17). It would be entirely possible for audiences who were unfamiliar with the titles of the numbers to miss their Shakespearean connections, and even more likely that they would not realize that "Circle of Fourths"—the twelfth number that Ellington added to the suite later—was "a musical tribute to Shakespeare himself" (Lanier, "Minstrelsy" 13). Indeed, Stuart Hampton-Reeves notes that "[t]wo of the tunes on *Such Sweet Thunder* had already been performed under different names before Ellington came up with the project" and retitled them "The Star-Crossed Lovers" and "Half the Fun" (Hampton-Reeves 278, 281). Presumably it was only their retitling that turned them into Shakespearean adaptations, even though Hampton-Reeves's Google search for the words "such sweet thunder" convinced him that the words "used to be Shakespeare's but now they belong to the Duke" (Hampton-Reeves 279).

Is it possible to adapt theatrical texts like Shakespeare's plays to instrumental music? Generations of program music—Beethoven's *Coriolan Overture* (1807), Hector Berlioz's *Symphonie Fantastique* (1830), Franz Liszt's *Faust Symphony* (1857), Peter Ilych Tchaikovsky's *Romeo and Juliet Overture-Fantasia* (1880), Richard Strauss's *Don Quixote* (1898)—indicate that many composers and audiences have been convinced that it is. Although Hampton-Reeves admits that the Shakespearean reference in the title "The Telecasters"—which, according to the album's liner notes, refers to Iago and the three witches in *Macbeth* because "they all have something to say"—"goes over my head" (Hampton-Reeves 282), he has no hesitation in calling the numbers "adaptations." Of the four sonnets, he notes that each one, adapting a poem of 14 lines, is "exactly twenty-eight bars long in two-bar sections, with a melody of ten notes every two bars … [O]ne can sing any of Shakespeare's sonnets with these pieces" (Hampton-Reeves 283).

If Ellington's instrumental music can adapt Shakespeare, can it also adapt him from a Black perspective? Julie Sanders, noting that Black performers like Paul Robeson "had given new cultural agency to the role," concludes that "*Such Sweet Thunder*, like Liszt's *Hamlet*, is a rich aesthetic response to the stage performances of its day" (Sanders 18). In *The Sonic Color Line*, Jennifer Lynn Stoever pushes this question further: "What is the historical relationship between sonic and visual racial regimes?" (Stoever 6–7). Stoever argues that race is not just seen but heard, or pointedly not heard: "The sonic color line describes the process of racializing sound … The listening ear drives the sonic color line; it is a figure for how dominant listening practices accrue—and change—over time" (Stoever 7). Following W.E.B. Du Bois—whose *Dusk of Dawn* warns that "[a]ny literary, artistic, or political project challenging race … will be gravely complicated by the fact that whites not only have been conditioned to see *and* hear the world differently but also have labeled and propagated this sensory configuration as universal, objective truth"—she contends that "both race and gender—along with sexuality and class—impact how one sounds and listens" (Stoever 10, 21; see Du Bois 130–31). Hence the sonic color line

> enables listeners to construct and discern racial identities based on voices, sounds, and particular soundscapes—the clang and rumble of urban life versus suburban "peace and quiet," for instance—and, in turn, to mobilize

racially coded batteries of sounds as discrimination by assigning them differential cultural, social, and political value.

(Stoever 11)

This raises the very real possibility that these adaptations can get us to hear and see race differently, beginning with the fact that most jazz performances—unlike the tightly scripted scores of *Such Sweet Thunder*—are built on 12-bar improvisations on existing themes, making jazz itself, like opera, a radically adaptive mode.

Questions

- Is it possible to produce recognizable adaptations of Shakespeare using purely instrumental music?
- How can musical compositions most successfully adapt literary texts?
- How can, or how should, you listen to musical adaptations? Should you listen first or read the liner notes or commentaries first?
- Is it possible to adapt theatrical plays to non-verbal music?

Descriptive adaptation studies

The thorny evaluative questions raised by the scholars of postcolonial and reparative adaptation who follow in the path of Stam, Lanier, and Joubin are treated in an entirely different way by proponents of Descriptive Adaptation Studies (DAS), whose most notable practitioner is Patrick Cattrysse. Cattrysse's analysis of adaptation is rooted in the Polysystem Studies (PS) analysis of translation developed by Itamar Even-Zohar and Gideon Toury in the 1970s, which redirected attention from the question of how faithful different translations were to their sources to what roles they played in their target cultures. When it was first applied to adaptation, this forward-thinking approach

> allowed scholars to study adaptations in a more consistent way. In an effort to eschew value judgments, it aimed at a descriptive-explanatory approach. In an attempt to step beyond the endless accumulation of *ad hoc* selected case studies, the PS approach called for the development of broader corpus-based research. It also entailed a break with the customary fidelity-based discourse and the single source text model. It suggested looking at adaptations as adaptations, the production and reception of which are determined by multiple conditioners to be found in both source and target contexts.

(Cattrysse 11)

Despite the echoes of Cutchins ("an effort to eschew value judgments"), Hutcheon ("looking at adaptations as adaptations"), and Bluestone ("a break with the customary fidelity-based discourse"), Cattrysse's approach departs from these other theorists in fundamental ways. Unlike Stam, it finds Bakhtin a less valuable forerunner of adaptation studies than the Russian formalists and Prague structuralists who were his contemporaries (Cattrysse 150–53). It regards particular adaptations not as individual achievements or failures but as nodes in a larger intertextual system. Practitioners of DAS, as its title announces, do not evaluate specific adaptations in terms of their faithfulness to the letter or the spirit of the texts they adapt; in fact, they do not evaluate them at all but attempt instead to describe them as neutrally and scientifically as possible, treating earlier evaluations as either methodological errors or cultural evidence to be mined and studied rather than embraced or refuted.

Cattrysse summarizes the PS approach as

- a descriptive rather than a prescriptive approach. This entails a 'functional' [rather than an aesthetic] definition of the object of study.
- a target (con)text-oriented rather than a fidelity-based and therefore predominantly source (con)text oriented approach.
- a trans-individual, systemic, and corpus-based approach rather than an endless accumulation of *ad hoc* case studies and a glorification of the genius Auteur.

(Cattrysse 51)

Although it joins the poststructuralist attack on aesthetics, fidelity, and authorship, the PS approach is more structuralist than poststructuralist. It breaks with Hutcheon in defining adaptations as texts that are perceived as adaptations, assuming instead that "pseudo-originals or hidden/secret adaptations greatly outnumber overt adaptations" (Cattrysse 123), and incorporating these unacknowledged adaptations into the adaptive system. And it rejects deductive and evaluative approaches to adaptation in favor of those that promise "scientific validity" (Cattrysse 136).

Placing its faith in systems that agglomerate vast quantities of details, DAS finds the truth of adaptation in those systems. Cattrysse's analysis of two film adaptations of Raymond Chandler's 1940 novel *Farewell, My Lovely*— *The Falcon Takes Over* (1942) and *Murder, My Sweet* (1944)—persuasively argues that the former "recycles the narrative source materials to continue the successful 1930s tradition of the gentleman-detective comedy in the *Falcon* series"; whereas the latter, released only two years later, " 'uses' these and other source-modeling materials to confirm an innovating trend begun a few years later in the hardboiled detective genre" that would soon "be labeled the *film noir* style" (Cattrysse 151). On the whole, however, Cattrysse is less interested in the textual details of individual noir adaptations than in the general patterns that emerge from the corpus of these adaptations. In order to determine the most important authors for adaptations of film noir, he compiles a list of 604 films listed in 11 filmographies published between 1940 and 1990 and gives each author one point for each novel or story adapted into a film noir mentioned in each filmography. The resulting list of "top-scoring adapted authors" is headed by Cornell Woolrich, followed by Raymond Chandler, Steve Fisher, William R. Burnett, and Jonathan Latimer (Cattrysse 258). The comparatively low ranking of James M. Cain (#7 on the list) and Dashiell Hammett (who fails to make the top ten) is presumably due to the relatively small number of novels and stories they had written that were adapted to the screen, however influential these adaptations—from *The Maltese Falcon* to *Double Indemnity*—might have been.

Such a scientific, statistics-driven approach to adaptation might seem likely to inhibit debate. But in fact, Cattrysse considers DAS less a "theory" ("a set of answers") than a "research program" ("a set of questions") (Cattrysse 44). The questions he raises are well worth pondering. What, for example, is the relation between "description and explanation," or between "description and prediction" (Cattrysse 336)? Should researchers in adaptation be able to predict the appearance and characteristics of future adaptations? More pragmatically, "how do personal and collective career values match or conflict with the epistemic values of the discipline and thereby cause the discipline to progress or regress; and what can research communities do about this?" (Cattrysse 339). Finally, given that "the respective objects of study of a meta-theoretical study of adaptations and a study of adaptations are very different indeed," how can adaptation scholars best address "the gap between theory and practice" in the study of adaptation (Cattrysse 341)? Both Cattrysse's scientific approach to adaptation and the highly speculative questions it raises lay the groundwork for still another intertextual approach.

Questions

- What are the most fruitful ways to integrate the theory of adaptation, whether or not it is drawn from DAS, with the analysis of particular adaptations?
- What are the implications of organizing scholarly fields either by the kinds of spatial models represented by diagrams and maps or by temporal models like histories and commentaries for the treatment of such subjects as fidelity, selection, and scholarly inheritance?
- Which of these models, spatial or temporal, is best suited to which sorts of explanations for which phenomena presented to which audiences?
- Should adaptation studies be considered either "a science-based discipline" (Cattrysse 333) that seeks results that can be universally validated and replicated, or a field of play that thrives on exactly the kinds of ad hoc, intuitive, endlessly debatable, revisitable, adaptable questions, insights, and leaps of faith?

Adaptation vs. intermediality

The most ambitious and comprehensive of all intertextual approaches to adaptation is rooted in the concept of intermediality, first introduced as

Intermedialität by Aage A. Hansen-Löve in 1983 and further developed in Irina O. Rajewsky's 2002 monograph *Intermedialität*. Rajewsky differentiates between intramediality—phenomena that occur in only one medium; intermediality—phenomena that can cross media boundaries to move between two or more media; and transmediality—non-media-specific phenomena that can be delivered in different media using the means specific to the respective medium, without the assumption that a contact-providing source medium is important or possible (Rajewsky 13). Werner Wolf takes up Rajewsky's three terms but defines them somewhat differently. For Wolf, transmediality "concerns phenomena that appear in more than one medium without being (viewed as) specific to, or having an origin in, any of them" (Wolf 461). Wolf's theoretical model redefines "transmediality" as one of three subcategories of intermediality, alongside intermedial transposition (e.g., film adaptations of novels), intermedial reference (allusions to films in novels), and plurimediality (graphic novels). In Wolf's account, which has been highly influential on other transmedial scholars, intermediality emphasizes the relations between different media over the relations between specific works.

In their discussions of intermediality, both Rajewsky and Wolf therefore return to the age-old question Gotthold Ephraim Lessing had placed at the center of *Laocoön*: the relations between different presentational media like music, painting, and poetry. This question had already returned for further discussion among early commentators on film and literature and again in the work of interart theorist W.J.T. Mitchell, who asserts that "[a]ll media are mixed media" (Mitchell 211), and in contemporary research on ekphrasis—the process by which artworks are represented in other artworks in different media, as in John Keats's "Ode on a Grecian Urn" and Wallace Stevens's "Anecdote of the Jar." More recently, it has been given new urgency by the emergence of digital media, whose ability to produce, transmit, and transform texts across multiple platforms often appears to challenge traditional artistic practices and assumptions about autonomy and originality.

Marie-Laure Ryan, noting that the term "media" can mean very different things to different observers, has proposed three more general ways in which the term has been used:

- Materials and technologies (clay, stone, the human body; technologies such as writing, print, and digital encoding)
- Semiotic media: verbal, visual, auditory, olfactory, gustatory, tactile, or … iconic (classical painting), indexical (music, abstract painting), symbolic (verbal arts)
- Cultural media (literature, film, TV, radio, etc.) as both practices and institutions.

(Ryan 14–16)

Marina Grishakova, who provides this summary of Ryan's definitions, adds a fourth way of thinking about media—"as aesthetic expressive systems that involve sets of specific features, conventions, and forms"—and suggests that these four understandings of media can alternatively be considered "as *four levels of mediation or medium-ness* present in any intermedial works" (Grishakova 18).

This last suggestion has clearly been influenced by a schema proposed by Lars Elleström focusing not on the distinctive properties of different media or on different understandings of media, but on what Elleström calls "the four modalities of media" (Elleström, "Modalities" 17). The "*material modality*" is "the latent corporeal interface of the medium" (the changing images on the flat screens of televisions and movie theaters; the unchanging flat surfaces of book pages; the "extended, generally solid materiality" of sculptures). "The *sensorial modality* is the physical and mental acts of perceiving the present interface of the medium through the sense faculties" (hearing in music; seeing in reading; hearing and seeing in theater). "The *spatiotemporal modality* of media covers the structuring of the sensorial perception of sense-data of the material interface into experiences and conceptions of space and time" governed by "four dimensions: width, height, depth, and time." Photographs have only two dimensions, sculptures three, and dance performances all four. The "*semiotic modality*"—the most complex of the four— "involves the creation of meaning in the spatiotemporally conceived medium by way of different sorts of thinking and sign interpretation" (Elleström, "Modalities" 17,18, 21, 22).

For all their different ways of theorizing media, transmediality, and intermediality, all these approaches share a common assumption: that the practices and products of adaptation occupy a relatively limited place in the vastly larger array of intermedia products and practices. In general, there has been limited dialogue between adaptation scholars and intermedial scholars. But Elleström has advanced a highly useful critique of adaptation studies, in the form of ten propositions that focus on "the borders of adaptation studies" (Elleström, "Adaptation" 513) as it is currently practiced, that is worth considering at length.

Elleström begins by observing that "*Adaptation is a transfer of media characteristics among media products, not qualified media*" (Elleström, "Modalities" 514). In other words, adaptation studies focuses on specific intermedial adaptations, not on the general characteristics that distinguish different media from each other. This would have been less true 70 to 100 years ago, when literature-to-film studies were dominated by discussions of the general properties and representational affinities of literature and film, like those of Vachel Lindsay, Hugo Münsterberg, Virginia Woolf, Allardyce Nicoll, Sergei Eisenstein, Alexandre Astruc, and especially André Bazin. Although George Bluestone's *Novels to Film* marked a turn from this model, followed by the specific novel-to-film studies in Morris Beja, Joy Gould Boyum, James Griffith, Brian McFarlane, and any number of articles in *Literature/Film Quarterly*, several notable studies after Bluestone—Seymour Chatman's 1980 essay "What Novels Can Do That Films Can't (and Vice

Versa)", Keith Cohen's 1979 *Film and Fiction,* and Bruce Morrissette's 1985 *Novel and Film*—continued to maintain a double focus on both individual media products and media in general; and Timothy Corrigan and Kamilla Elliott—who, along with Patrick Cattrysse, has continued to advocate for studies of adaptation that do not focus on specific case studies—have called for Bazin's medial theories to replace Bluestone's case studies as a model for contemporary adaptation studies.

According to Elleström, "*[a]daptation is a transfer of media characteristics among self-reliant media, not assisting media*" (Elleström, "Modalities" 515). In other words, adaptation studies as it is currently practiced focuses on finished media products, not the incidental byproducts like musical scores, opera librettos, artists' notebooks, and film screenplays generated in the course of producing adaptations. It is clearly true, as Elleström claims, that "the study of self-reliant media as source media still clearly dominates the field" (Elleström, "Modalities" 515). But recent work in adaptation studies— from Simone Murray's research on the adaptation industry to the growing body of work in screenplay studies pioneered by Jack Boozer—defines fewer and fewer media products as self-reliant. More generally, Henry Jenkins's widely influential work on convergence culture has taught a generation of scholars to see texts from *Frankenstein* (1818) to *The Matrix* (1999) as nodes in an ever-expanding universe of meaning and experience rather than as independent works that happen to share the same characters and settings. The inevitable rise of artificial intelligence technologies like ChatGPT is bound to accelerate and complicate this universe by blurring the boundaries between self-reliant and assisting media products—all of which it increasingly casts as works-in-progress.

Elleström notes that "*[a]daptation is a transfer of media characteristics among artistic media, not non-artistic media,*" and that "*[a]daptation is a transfer of media characteristics among premeditated media, not casual media*" (Elleström, "Modalities" 515, 516). Adaptation studies has so far focused on media traditionally defined as artistic productions—novels, plays, poems, paintings, drawings, sculptures, movies, operas, tone poems, ballets—to the virtual exclusion of non-artistic media like "news reports and advertisements" and unpremeditated utterances like "ordinary speech, gestures, and email messages" (Elleström, "Modalities" 516). Like the previous critique, these critiques are still accurate but grow more dated every year. The essays on adaptations of history in the collections edited by Lawrence Raw and Defne Ersin Tutan and by Pascal Nicklas and Dan Hassler-Forest are less concerned with individual histories as artistic products than with their implications for history itself as an adaptive practice. And as the profusion of digital platforms like Facebook, Twitter, Instagram, Vimeo, Spotify, and TikTok continues, adaptation studies—and indeed textual, intertextual, and transmedial studies in general—will be increasingly challenged to adjust their orientation from premeditated to casual media. Individual adaptation scholars will have to decide whether their own orientation will be hierarchical, favoring some texts over others on the grounds of their aesthetics, politics, or premeditation, or egalitarian, emphasizing analysis over evaluation. And different scholars are likely to decide this question differently. The rise of an attention economy aimed at short-term rather than long-term attention is likely to pose a broader challenge that may ultimately devalue premeditated long-form media from operas to novels simply because no one is interested in them anymore.

Elleström's charges that "*[a]daptation is a transfer of media characteristics from literature or theater to film, not among other qualified media,*" and that "*[a]daptation is a transfer of narrative traits, not other media characteristics*" (Elleström, "Modalities" 516, 517), are both debatable and provocative. Although adaptation studies has expanded its remit to consider novels based on films, cartoons based on novels, operas based on novels and plays, films based on oral narrative, songs based on novels, and films based on songs, it is probably true that "the implicit literature- or theater-to-film formula continues to have a firm grip on adaptation studies" (Elleström, "Modalities" 517)—largely because adaptation theory continues to focus primarily on the ways narratives and narrative elements like plots, characters, and storyworlds are adapted. Paintings and sculptures like Michelangelo's *David* (1504) and the different scenes he painted on the ceiling of the Sistine Chapel (1512) often adapt narrative elements. But adaptations often incorporate transmedial elements that are not narrative, from the long history of representational portraiture to Picasso's *Guernica* (1937). Berlioz's *Symphonie Fantastique* and several of Richard Strauss's tone poems use musical sounds to recreate narrative elements; if you listen closely to the Introduction to Act 1 of Strauss's opera *Der Rosenkavalier* (1911), you can hear Octavian and the Marschallin making love even before the curtain goes up. But there is nothing narrative about the birdcalls we hear toward the end of the second movement of Beethoven's Pastoral Symphony (1808), or the wordless vocal lines that frame the final movement of Vaughn Williams's Pastoral Symphony (1922). Since, as Elleström notes, several theorists have dissented from the assumption that adaptation focuses on narrative elements without theorizing their dissent, it is fair to ask how adaptation studies would change if it explicitly broadened its purview to embrace the ways non-narrative features are adapted to new media.

Another pair of Elleström's propositions—"*[a]daptation is a transfer of media characteristics from one medium to the other, not from several media*" and "*[a]daptation is a transfer of media characteristics among complete media, not parts of media*" (Elleström, "Modalities" 518, 519)—targets adaptation studies' focus on adaptations involving exactly one source text to one adaptation. He notes that any number of adaptation scholars, from Cattrysse to Linda Hutcheon, have disputed the first of these assumptions. His corrective formulation—"most media products, and also qualified media, may well be knitted together in a huge and ever-unfinished web of media transformations," in which "the target in one specific case of media transformation may be viewed as the source of yet another target" (Elleström, "Modalities" 519)—echoes interventions in adaptation studies by Gérard Genette and Robert Stam, who already define adaptation as a continuous rather than a binary process. The target of the second critique is presumably Hutcheon's definition of adaptation as "an announced and extensive transposition of a particular work or works"—a formulation whose last two words directly anticipate and deflect the first of these two critiques—and her distinction between "adaptation proper" and such intertextual modes as allusion, quotation, parody, pastiche, and other "spin-offs" (Hutcheon 171). Elleström notes that although his argument that "both sources and targets should be considered in their entirety, not piecemeal ... is tacitly understood as the norm, I think that few would defend it at any length"—especially since analyses of particular adaptations inevitably "consider only parts of the source medium, the target medium, or both" (Elleström, "Modalities" 519). Indeed, a little-noted paradox of adaptation studies—as of textual studies generally—is that close readings of carefully chosen passages from long novels like *Bleak House* (1852–53) and *The Brothers Karamazov* (1880) and their adaptations are typically presented as synecdoches that provide analyses of those entire works.

The final pair of Elleström's critiques—"*[a]daptation is a direct, not an indirect, transfer of media characteristics among media*" and "*[a]daptation is a transfer of media characteristics in one direction only, not two*" (Elleström, "Modalities" 519, 520)—maintain that adaptation studies focuses exclusively on source and target media, not on intermediate media, whether these are assisting media like screenplays and librettos or self-reliant media like nineteenth-century plays about Frankenstein. I anticipated the first of these arguments myself when I suggested that movies that claim to be based on true stories—from Penny Marshall's 1990 medical drama *Awakenings*, the first film to use this credit, to Edward Zwick's 2008 World War II drama *Defiance*, which announces even more forthrightly, "This is a true story," over a visual mashup of wartime clips accompanied by an obviously post-synchronized soundtrack—do so

> not to establish truth or fidelity to the truth as a predicate of the discourse but to use the category of a true story as a privileged master text that justifies the film's claims to certain kinds of authority—ideally by placing them beyond question.
>
> (Leitch, *Film Adaptation* 286)

I have extended this argument to deal with the many stories about Robin Hood and his Merry Men, all of them clearly adaptations of something—although it is practically impossible to pin most of them down to a single source text because "there is no single definitive account of Robin Hood and almost certainly never was" (Leitch, "Adaptations" 286). Elleström concedes that the latter critique—that adaptations establish themselves as modifications of source texts that continue to exist unchanged throughout the process—is self-evidently true "from a practical point of view," but not necessarily "from a hermeneutical perspective" (Elleström, "Modalities" 520). In fact, it may not be true even from a practical point of view, since once an artist has filled a canvas with paint, every additional stroke in an oil painting produces a new painting literally on top of the surface of the old, contradicting Elleström's assertion that "no source media products are materially modified when they are adapted" (Elleström, "Modalities" 520). More to the point, the hermeneutical perspective he singles out as an exception has become ever more powerful since 2003, when Kamilla Elliott, in a passage he cites, defined the last of her seven models of adaptation—the looking-glass model—as explicitly establishing a "mutual and reciprocal inverse transformation that nevertheless restores neither [the film nor the novel] to its original place" (Elleström, "Modalities" 520; see Elliott, *Theorizing* 229). A growing number of studies have confirmed the commonsensical idea that it is impossible to see an original text in the same way once you have seen its adaptation, and that it is impossible to see it as an original text if you have seen the adaptation first. The ever-increasing tendency of adaptations to modify their originals beyond recognition, and beyond the point at which they are identified as originals, is likely to become a non-story in the new age of textual proliferation, whose reaction to the retrospective hermeneutical and even material destruction of original texts is likely to be, "Who cares?"

Questions

- How would you define the relation between adaptations and other kinds of intertexts?
- How would you define the relation between adaptation and other intermedial or transmedial practices?
- How would adaptation studies change if its focus changed from media products to qualified media, or if its focus expanded to include both media products and qualified media?
- How would adaptation studies and intermedial studies change if they treated all media—artistic and non-artistic, self-reliant and assisting, premeditated and casual—as equal?
- Can you draw and defend a sharp distinction between narrative and non-narrative elements in a given text and indicate the relations between them?

The logic of dialogical adaptations

Whatever their future impact on the practices and products of adaptation, recent developments in digital media have given new life to the tradition of carnivalistic adaptations Bakhtin traces back to Rabelais. This tradition had already survived in Stam's revisionist adaptations, Lanier's reparative adaptations, and a series of freewheeling satirical comedies that often took their cue from Monty Python, the British comedy troupe whose BBC television series *Monty Python's Flying Circus* (1969–74) juiced its sketch comedy with cross-dressing skits, satires of the absurdity of British mores, surreal animation, sexual innuendo, and highbrow allusions to figures from Mary Queen of Scots to Jean-Paul Sartre. Monty Python's television success led to a long series of theatrical tours, five feature films—from the compilation *And Now for Something Completely Different* (1971) to *Monty Python's The Meaning of Life* (1983)—and over two dozen books and recordings that reprised their favorite routines. The frenetic mashups of high and low culture Monty Python popularized inspired many followers. The Flying Karamazov Brothers—a theatrical troupe of four buskers, none of them actually related to each other—have incorporated pop music and juggling into their anarchic performances of repertory staples like Shakespeare's *Comedy of Errors* since 1973. And the three members of the Reduced Shakespeare Company, who made their debut in 1981, have presented thousands of performances of *The Complete Plays of Mr. William Shakespeare (Abridged)*, *The Complete History of America (Abridged)*, and *The Bible: The Complete Word of God (Abridged)*.

Blossoming alongside these farcical adaptations, an even more widely seen series of transmedia mashups has brought together heroes, adventures, and franchises that originally existed in different fictional worlds set mostly during the same time period. Inspired by the 1960 film *The League of Gentlemen*, writer Alan Moore and artist Kevin O'Neill created the comic book *The League of Extraordinary Gentlemen* in 1999. The series, originally intended as Victorian England's answer to DC Comics' Justice League of America, swiftly gravitated toward the genre of steampunk, a subgenre of science fiction centered on anachronistically futuristic technologies as they might have been imagined by citizens of nineteenth-century worlds largely driven by steam power. The sensibility of *The League of Extraordinary Gentlemen* delighted in the logical contradictions between Victorian and postmodern habits and ideas. Its cast of characters—drawn almost entirely from Victorian works of popular fiction—was headed by Mina Murray, the heroine of Bram Stoker's vampire novel *Dracula* (1897); Allan Quatermain, the explorer hero of H. Rider Haggard's *King Solomon's Mines* (1885); Captain Nemo, from Jules Verne's *Twenty Thousand Leagues Under the Sea* (1870); Hawley Harvey Griffin, the eponymous Invisible Man from H.G. Wells's 1897 novella; A.J. Raffles, the gentleman thief E.W. Hornung created in 1898; and Dr. Jekyll and Mr. Hyde, from Robert Louis Stevenson's 1886 shilling shocker. These were incongruously joined by Carnacki, the occult investigator created by horror specialist William Hope Hodgson in 1910; Orlando, the sexually fluid protagonist of Virginia Woolf's 1928 historical fantasy; and Emma Knight, the crime-fighting partner of John Steed in 1960s television series *The Avengers*.

Moore and O'Neill's series, which eventually ran to 21 issues and a standalone graphic novel, was a remarkably capacious adaptation. In addition to adapting its iconic leading figures, it added many minor characters drawn from lesser-known works, prompting diehard fans to work overtime to identify them all. In addition, its storyworld adapted elements from Victorian popular fiction, Victorian and postmodern technology, and earlier steampunk fiction. Stephen Norrington's 2003 film adaptation of the series added still more layers of adaptation by including Dorian Gray, the immortal subject of a painting that aged instead of him in Oscar Wilde's 1891 novel, presenting him now as Mina Murray's former lover; Ishmael, the first mate in Herman Melville's 1851 novel *Moby-Dick*; and Tom Sawyer, now grown up from the boy in Mark Twain's 1876 novel to become a U.S. Secret Service agent recruited by Quatermain to join the League in the battle against Professor Moriarty, the nemesis of Sherlock Holmes, who shares important features with Marcel Allain and Pierre Souvestre's fictional villain Fantômas and M, the chief of the Secret Intelligence Service in Ian Fleming's twentieth-century novels about James Bond. And of course the film also poses as an adaptation of the comic books that adapt all these other features. The result is a carnival that mashes up two media, a dozen fictional franchises, several distinct historical eras, and its target audience's assumptions about the nature of history itself.

The League of Extraordinary Gentlemen was followed by a dizzying number of other dialogical adaptations and mashups. Even as the ridicule that greeted Roland Joffé's 1995 film adaptation of *The Scarlet Letter*, which updated Nathaniel Hawthorne's 1850 novel, added sexually explicit scenes to it, and capped it with a happy ending, discouraged adapters who might have been tempted to attempt other revisionist adaptations of canonical nineteenth-century literary works, audiences flocked to *Midnight in Paris* (1996), whose hero travels through time from contemporary Paris to the Paris of the 1920s—populated by future celebrities like Gertrude Stein, Ernest Hemingway, F. Scott Fitzgerald, Pablo Picasso, and Salvador Dalí— and ultimately to *Belle Epoque* Paris, where he meets Paul Gauguin, Edgar Degas, and Henri de Toulouse-Lautrec. The film, which became the greatest box-office success for its writer and director, Woody Allen, is a Menippean satire that uses honored figures from the past to satirize the beliefs of present-day characters and audiences. Some of the most notable of recent revisionist adaptations include the 2013–17 television series *Bates Motel*—an extended prequel to Alfred Hitchcock's feature *Psycho* (1960), which had already spawned two sequels, one prequel, and Gus Van Sant's notoriously close remake; *Penny Dreadful*, another neo-Victorian mashup which ran from 2014 to 2016; *The Handmaid's Tale* (2017–22), a dystopian fantasy based on Margaret Atwood's 1985 novel, which had already been adapted as a feature film directed by Volker Schlöndorff in 1990; and *Fargo*, whose five seasons to date (2014–24) returned to the chilly North Dakota landscape of Joel and Ethan Coen's 1994 black comedy to follow new criminal plots over each series, laced with references to other Coen movies like *Raising Arizona*, *Barton Fink*, *The Man Who Wasn't There*, *The Big Lebowski*, *No Country for Old Men*, and *A Serious Man*.

Finally, *Barbie*, in addition to being an adaptation of a canonical toy, reveals new dimensions when viewed through an intertextual lens. Its narrative clearly takes the form of a revisionist adaptation whose heroine—at first rejoicing in her unchanging status as the perfect doll, then bewildered and troubled by the unbidden thoughts of death that force her to confront her own mortality—embarks on a quest that seeks and ultimately discovers her fulfillment as an adaptive figure: a doll so deeply informed by human wishes and desires that she becomes human. This narrative trajectory might seem forbiddingly grim, as indeed it does to Barbie early on, if it were not leavened from the beginning with several features that invite the audience to pull away from an immersion in its plot and characters and view it more critically as a text in dialogue with other texts. One of these features is its transgressive mashup of allusions to Stanley Kubrick's 1968 sci-fi epic *2001: A Space Odyssey*, the 1995 BBC television miniseries *Pride and Prejudice*, Francis Ford Coppola's 1972 gangster epic *The Godfather*, and a wide range of other cultural touchstones that mark the film as another Menippean satire, illuminating specific moments, scenes, and patterns in its story without ever determining its outcome. Another is the heroine's abrupt switches from naiveté to sophistication, as when she tells Weird Barbie: "I know I'm Stereotypical Barbie and therefore don't form conjectures concerning the causality of adjacent unfolding events, but some things have been happening that might be related." A third is its own persistent sense of self-consciousness, figured most prominently by Helen Mirren's intermittent voiceover commentary, like her acute observation in the film's opening minutes that "Barbie changed everything. Then she changed it all again."

Barbie's appointment with her obstetrician in the film's closing scene marks the end of the heroine's own development even as it confirms the film's status as a reparative adaptation in the second of Joubin's two senses: an adaptation that therapeutically addresses and seeks to correct and heal the flaws—superficiality, conformity, insensitivity, sterility, and an absolute inability to change—of its iconic source text. In the process, the film both demystifies what Walter Benjamin might have called the aura of its most obvious sourcetext and challenges the whole notion of a text as something singular, deliberately created, and unified, replacing it with a Barthesian field of force first figured by Weird Barbie and ultimately internalized by the heroine, whom most viewers will persist in considering the real Barbie no matter what changes she goes through. Just because an adaptation seeks to improve on the texts that inspired it, the film seems to suggest, there's no need to get all serious about the project.

Questions

• How does defining adaptation intertextually change its ethical import?
• How closely does the search for knowledge in the humanities resemble the search for knowledge in the sciences?

- Given the critiques of the canon and its rationale, do you find aesthetics to be shareable, principled, or authoritative—or is it simply reducible to a series of individual opinions that cannot be generalized?
- What do intertextual engagements allow or reveal about adaptations that other engagements don't?

References

Altman, Rick. *Film/Genre*. British Film Institute, 2000.

Bacchilega, Cristina. *Fairy Tales Transformed? Twenty-First-Century Adaptations and the Politics of Wonder*. Wayne State UP, 2013.

Bakhtin, Mikhail. *Rabelais and His World*. Translated by Hélène Iswolsky. Indiana UP, 1985.

Bryant, John. *The Fluid Text: A Theory of Revision and Editing for Book and Screen*. U Michigan P, 2002.

Cattrysse, Patrick. *Descriptive Adaptation Studies: Epistemological and Methodological Issues*. Garant, 2014.

Cutchins, Dennis. "Bakhtin, Intertextuality, and Adaptation." *The Oxford Handbook of Adaptation Studies*. Edited by Thomas Leitch. Oxford UP, 2017, pp. 71–86.

Du Bois, W.E. Burghardt. *Dusk of Dawn: An Essay Toward an Autobiography of a Race Concept*. Harcourt, Brace, 1940.

Elleström, Lars. "The Modalities of Media: A Model for Understanding Intermedial Relations." *Media Borders, Multimodality and Intermediality*. Edited by Lars Elleström. Palgrave Macmillan, 2010, pp. 11–48.

Elleström, Lars. "Adaptation and Intermediality." *The Oxford Handbook of Adaptation Studies*. Edited by Thomas Leitch. Oxford UP, 2017, pp. 509–26.

Elliott, Kamilla. "Tie-Intertextuality, or, Intertextuality as Incorporation in the Tie-in Merchandise to Disney's *Alice in Wonderland* (2010)." *Adaptation*, vol. 7, no. 2 (2014), pp. 191–211.

Elliott, Kamilla. *Theorizing Adaptation*. Oxford UP, 2020.

Geraghty, Christine. "Casting for the Public Good: BAME Casting in British Film and Television in the 2010s." *Adaptation*, vol. 14, no. 2 (Aug. 2021), pp. 168–86.

Grishakova, Marina. "Intermediality: Introducing Terminology and Approaches in the Field." *The Palgrave Handbook of Intermediality*. Edited by Jørgen Bruhn, Asun López-Varela Azcárate, and Miriam de Paiva Viveira. Palgrave Macmillan, 2024, pp. 13–29.

Hampton-Reeves, Stuart. "'A Noise of Thunder': Shakespeare and Jazz." *The Oxford Handbook of Shakespeare and Music*. Edited by Christopher R. Wilson and Mervyn Cooke. Oxford UP, 2022, pp. 274–94.

Hansen-Löve, Aage A. "Intermedialität und Intertextualität: Probleme der Korrelation in Wort- und Bildkunst: Am Beispiel der russischen Moderne." *Dialog der Texte*. Vienna, 1983, pp. 291–360.

Hutcheon, Linda and Michael Hutcheon. "Adaptation and Opera." *The Oxford Handbook of Adaptation Studies*. Edited by Thomas Leitch. Oxford UP, 2017, pp. 305–23.

Hutcheon, Linda, with Siobhan O'Flynn. *A Theory of Adaptation*. Second ed. Routledge, 2012.

Joubin, Alexa Alice. *Shakespeare and East Asia*. Oxford UP, 2021.

Joubin, Alexa Alice. "Screening Social Justice: Performing Reparative Shakespeare against Vocal Disability." *Adaptation*, vol. 14, no. 2 (Aug. 2021), pp. 187–205.

Komonibo, Ineye and Kathleen Newman-Bremang. "A Double Hot Take on *Bridgerton*, Race and Romance." *Refinery*, no. 29 (Jan. 4, 2021), https://www.refinery29.com/en-gb/2020/12/10244616/bridgerton-review-blackness-represe ntation.

Kristeva, Julia. "Word, Dialogue and Novel." Translated by Alice Jardine, Thomas Gora, and Leon S. Roudiez. *The Kristeva Reader*. Edited by Toril Moi. Columbia UP, 1986, pp. 34–61.

Lanier, Douglas. *Shakespeare and Modern Popular Culture*. Oxford UP, 2002.

Lanier, Douglas. "Minstrelsy, Jazz, Rap: Shakespeare, African American Music, and Cultural Legitimation." *Borrowers and Lenders: An Electronic Journal of Shakespearean Appropriation*. vol. 1, no. 1 (2005), https://borrowers-ojs-azsu.tdl. org/borrowers/article/view/17.

Lanier, Douglas. "Shakespeare and the Reparative Turn." Paper presented at the 2018 conference of La Société Français Shakespeare, Paris, January 18–20, 2018.

Leitch, Thomas. *Film Adaptation and Its Discontents: From Gone with the Wind to The Passion of the Christ*. Johns Hopkins UP, 2007.

Leitch, Thomas. "Adaptations without Sources: The Adventures of Robin Hood." *Literature/Film Quarterly*, vol. 36, no. 1 (2008), pp. 21–30.

Lopez Szwydky, Lissette. *Transmedia Adaptation in the Nineteenth Century*. Ohio State UP, 2020.

Mitchell, W.J.T. *What Do Pictures Want? The Lives and Loves of Images*. U of Chicago P, 2005.

Newell, Kate. *Expanding Adaptation Networks: From Illustration to Novelization*. Palgrave Macmillan, 2017.

Rajewsky, Irina O. *Intermedialität*. A. Francke UTB, 2002.

Rosenberg, Alyssa. " 'Bridgerton' meant to integrate period romances. So why is it so hard on Black women?" *Washington Post*, Dec. 28, 2020, https://www.washing tonpost.com/opinions/2020/12/28/bridgerton-meant-integrate-period-romances-so-why-is-it-so-hard-black-women/.

Ryan, Marie-Laure. "Media and Narrative." *Routledge Encyclopedia of Narrative Theory*. Edited by David Herman, Manfred Jahn, and Marie-Laure Ryan. Routledge, 2005, pp. 14–16.

Sanders, Julie. *Shakespeare and Music: Afterlives and Borrowings*. Polity, 2007.

Stam, Robert. *Literature Through Film: Realism, Magic, and the Art of Adaptation*. Blackwell, 2004.

Stam, Robert. "Introduction: The Theory and Practice of Adaptation." *Literature and Film: A Guide to the Theory and Practice of Adaptation*. Edited by Robert Stam and Alessandra Raengo. Blackwell, 2005, pp. 1–52.

Stam, Robert. "Revisionist Adaptation: Transtextuality, Cross-Cultural Dialogism, and Performative Infidelities." *The Oxford Handbook of Adaptation Studies*. Edited by Thomas Leitch. Oxford UP, 2017, pp. 239–50.

Stoever, Jennifer Lynn. *The Sonic Color Line: Race and the Cultural Politics of Listening*. New York UP, 2016.

Tillet, Salamishah. "*Bridgerton* Takes on Race. But Its Core is Escapism." *New York Times*, Jan. 5, 2021, https://www.nytimes.com/2021/01/05/arts/television/bridger ton-race-netflix.html.

Van Parys, Thomas. "Against Fidelity: Contemporary Adaptation Studies and the Example of Novelisation." *Adaptation Theories*. Edited by Jillian Saint Jacques. Jan Van Eyck Academie, 2011, pp. 407–43.

Venuti, Lawrence. "Adaptation, Translation, Critique." *Journal of Visual Culture*, vol. 6, no. 1 (2007), pp. 25–43, https://citeseerx.ist.psu.edu/document?repid= rep1&type=pdf&doi=91133d9b5f299464c6ac9f8d1b6c5f2b8c7a4c81.

Wolf, Werner. "Literature and Music: Theory." *Handbook of Intermediality: Literature– Image – Sound – Music*. Edited by Gabriele Rippl. De Gruyter, 2015, pp. 459–74.

3 Industrial engagements

Adaptation as product

The adaptation industry

The current state of adaptation—a free-for-all that makes it possible for fans to post sequels, prequels, parodies, and mashups of their favorite stories online and share them with strangers they will never meet—makes it easy to forget that throughout the twentieth century, adaptation did not involve simply the kinds of copies made by fans and other amateurs but copies specifically designed to make money both directly, by promoting new sales, and indirectly, by promoting the value of the properties they drew on. This commercial incentive behind so many adaptations features briefly in the work of commentators from Virginia Woolf, who deplores it as inevitably cheapening and betraying the texts under adaptation, to George Bluestone, who regards it as a necessary evil in the business of adaptation. It features even more briefly in the contributions of intertextual scholars like Robert Stam, Patrick Cattrysse, Irina O. Rajewsky, and Lars Elleström, who subordinate the study of specific adaptations to the more general study of adaptation as a process and practice. It is not until the work of Simone Murray that the commercial motives behind adaptation come to the fore.

Surveying the field of adaptation studies in 2012, Murray regards it as at once burgeoning, exciting, and deeply compromised by its continuing investments in the disciplines of literary studies and cinema studies. This investment is neatly encapsulated in the original name of the Association of Adaptation Studies, which from 2006 to 2007 was called the Association of Literature on Screen Studies. Murray criticizes the field's persistent emphasis on the comparative textual analysis of case studies and its corresponding refusal to respond to Dudley Andrew's call, first issued in 1981, that "it is time for adaptation studies to take a sociological turn" (Andrew 104). In *The Adaptation Industry: The Cultural Economy of Contemporary Literary Adaptation,* Murray announces that "the governing impetus behind the present volume is to reconfigure the discipline of adaptation studies by rethinking adaptation sociologically" (Murray 103)—a perspective she organizes around the business of encouraging, producing, performing, publicizing, and consuming adaptations.

DOI: 10.4324/9781003438410-4

Despite this label, Murray's focus is not so much sociological as economic. She sees adaptation neither as a series of inferior copies nor as a series of byproducts spun off by an endless process of dialogic intertextually but as "a *material* phenomenon produced by a system of interlinked interests and actors" (Murray 16), motivated by the imperatives of what she calls the "adaptation industry." So her project, informed by the cultural theory of Pierre Bourdieu, is defined neither as "comparative aesthetic evaluation" nor as "ideologically alert deconstruction" (Murray 4). Instead, as her title indicates, it focuses on the sociology of the adaptation industry itself, whose governing imperative in generating and assessing adaptations as products is not to challenge or uphold aesthetic standards but to extract the greatest possible profits from these products. In combining "political economy of media," the "history of the book," and "cultural theory," Murray seeks to reframe "questions of literary value" as arising "from their sitting at the juncture of two philosophically hostile conceptual systems: the aesthetic and the commercial" (Murray 17–19, 16).

Murray's model of the adaptation industry avoids both textual analysis and "media studies' traditional tripartite division into production/text/audience categories" (Murray 23) in favor of an approach that pointedly excludes both texts and audiences from the "six key stakeholder groups" she identifies as the foundation of the adaptation industry—"authors; agents; publishers, writers' [sic] and film festival directors; literary prize–judging committees; screenwriters; and producers and distributors" (Murray 20)—whose negotiations between aesthetic and commercial interests repeatedly end up tilted heavily in favor of the commercial. This is hardly surprising given the long history of cinema's on-again, off-again relationship with literary prestige. Until the commercial success of *Little Women* in 1933, Hollywood studios treated literary classics as box-office poison. And during the heyday of the studios, from the 1920s through the 1960s, executives and publicists routinely distinguished prestige productions like *The Wizard of Oz* (1939), designed to burnish the studio's image, from commercial productions like *Gone with the Wind* (1939), designed to make money. *Gone with the Wind*, marketed as both a sweeping historical epic and an adaptation of Margaret Mitchell's Pulitzer Prize-winning 1936 novel, became the highest-grossing film in the studio's history. But although MGM publicized *The Wizard of Oz* as both an adaptation of a 40-year-old children's classic by L. Frank Baum and the studio's first film to be shot (mostly) in Technicolor, it did not expect the enormously expensive production to earn back the costs of producing and publicizing it, and the movie "did not really make money until it was leased to television" (Harmetz 288), beginning in the 1950s.

Despite the different and sometimes contradictory aims of the stakeholders Murray identifies in the adaptation industry, they all share the goal of promoting adaptation as a widely recognized, critically accepted, and commercially successful enterprise. Instead of viewing literature as a field that is repeatedly violated by inferior adaptations, Murray sees publishing as an industry that is actively complicit in adaptation, encouraging the publication of exactly those novels that are most likely to make more money through successful adaptation. This encouragement can be so proactive and seminal that it extends to awarding prospective authors contracts for unwritten books that hold the greatest promise for "content franchises based upon their work" (Murray 26)—franchises that can extend from the initial book to an avalanche of publicity, a constellation of theatrical or cinematic adaptations, or a series of sequels produced by the original author or a factory of other, perhaps unacknowledged authors.

Of all Murray's stakeholders, those who are most clearly committed to recognizing and rewarding artistic success are the committees that judge literary prizes like the Man Booker Prize, the prestigious British award for fiction she singles out for close examination. Although "facilitating adaptation was not the Booker's original *raison d'être*," Murray notes that such

> self-described literary awards have for several decades had a significant impact in the marketplace: prompting new cover designs and re-jacketing of a winning author's backlist; reorienting bookshop layout by guaranteeing preferential display of winning titles; and also influencing readers' reception of a work through mentions of a title's prize-winning status in book reviews and the broader literary sphere.
>
> (Murray 105)

The Booker Prize in particular has generated a remarkable number of film adaptations. Over the first 40 years of its history, an impressive 21% of the novels that won or were shortlisted for the Booker were adapted to the cinema.

After years of wrestling with the "'culture versus trash' binary logic" implicit in the Booker Prize's rejection of middle-class commercial success in favor of elitist literary value, Ion Trewin, the Booker's Literary Director, embraced the intimacy between the Booker's literary cachet and the commercial possibilities it opened for prize-winning novels made into movies— "harnessing," in Murray's terms, "the Booker's cross-media commercial impact *as evidence of* its cultural clout" by positioning the prize as

> a sifting device bringing contemporary fiction of the highest calibre to the attention of a broad English-language reading public; should film producers then take up this content to adapt for acclaimed films that only serves to bring the title, novelist and prize to a still wider audience, validating in turn the Booker's role as sagacious judge of cultural value in the first instance.
>
> (Murray 117)

This positioning of the Booker as both aesthetically validating and commercially predictive may seem to mark a triumphant accord for commerce and art, but it does not solve the problems of how to adapt particular Booker-winning novels to film. So, despite her suspicion of "textual analysis," Murray looks more closely at the laborious process by which Ian McEwan's novel *Atonement*, which was shortlisted for the 2001 Booker Prize, and Thomas Kenneally's *Schindler's Ark*, which won the 1982 Prize, were adapted to the screen years after their consecration. Because she notes that "the peculiarly literary qualities that the Booker shortlist typically celebrates—strongly interiorised point-of view [sic], linguistic self-consciousness, playful metafictionality—tend to make these amongst the most difficult texts to translate to audio-visual media," she focuses on the "onscreen strategies to flag Booker consecration and directorial reverence for print culture, while aiming to create a filmic text both commercially successful as well as critically esteemed by the cinematic community" (Murray 4, 118). The result, in the case of Steven Spielberg's 1993 adaptation *Schindler's List*, is "the most extreme example of the contradictory attraction-repulsion dynamic filmmakers have long manifested with regard to Booker texts" (Murray 128).

Using his research into the company Best Seller to Box Office (BS2BO), whose subscription website provides "[a]ccess to an online library of over 65,857 curated books from all over the world specifically evaluated for screen adaptation" (Best Seller to Box Office), Jean-Louis Jeannelle argues in support of Murray's position that since "in BS2BO spec sheets, the original work is imagined exclusively as a function of producer needs and expectations," its engagement with adaptation is diametrically opposed to that of academics: "Adaptation professionals think of the process as always working towards the film," whereas adaptation scholars

> insist upon thinking of adaptation in terms of the book, or at the very least, as a fruitful dialectic between the two extreme ends of the process, without taking into account the constraints imposed upon the agents implied in each of the adaptation's phases.
>
> (Jeanelle 103)

Observers reluctant to take sides in the debate between forward thinking and backward thinking may take comfort in the fact that even though Murray's resistance to close reading extends to apologies she offers on each of the rare occasions when she descends into the analysis of specific adaptations like *Atonement* and *Schindler's List*, these analyses show that her industrial approach, like the intertextual approach pioneered by Stam, is eminently compatible with textual analysis, using it as a corrective supplement rather than a new model that supersedes the canonical model.

Questions

- Murray contends that "fidelity is an absolute value; once a source text has been 'strayed' from, the critical measuring stick of 'fidelity' loses its evaluative rigour" (Murray 8). What place do questions about fidelity have in industrial approaches to adaptation?

- How does Murray's notion of collaboration compare to those of Robert Stam, Douglas Lanier, and Alexa Alice Joubin?
- Disputing Robert B. Ray's assumption that authors "have (for better or worse) been largely able to write whatever pleased them, without regard for audience or expense" (Murray 13; see Ray 42), and Robert Stam's assertion that "questions of material infrastructure enter only at the point of distribution" (Stam 56), Murray argues that adaptation "is now factored in and avidly pursued from the earliest phases of book production" (Murray 13). At what point do you think commercial concerns first enter the process of producing any particular adaptation, or any non-adapted text?
- For Murray, "contemporary media content" is "adaptation operating under a different name" (Murray 17). In what ways have digital video productions and platforms changed the economic status of adaptation?

The business of comic book adaptations

The particular relevance of Murray's industrial approach to contemporary adaptation practices is indicated by her deliberate decision to focus on the period "*circa* 1980 to the present [2012]" (Murray 20): a period marked by the rise of "spreadable media" (Jenkins et al. 3) whose material can be readily transferred from one media platform to the next. As Siobhan O'Flynn notes in her Epilogue to the revised edition of *A Theory of Adaptation*, some of this content is presented as incomplete and interdependent, so that every manifestation of *The Matrix*, for example, depends on other manifestations for its full understanding; others simply "expand tentpole franchises" that are already coherent and complete on their own. Observing that "media conglomerates no longer own the channels of production and distribution in the way that they did in the last century," O'Flynn follows Lawrence Lessig in noting that industry protocols often conflict with "the ethos of a Web 2.0 fan community" in a battle between Lessig's "commercial and sharing economies" (O'Flynn 192, 186, 189).

Nowhere are these complications and conflicts more dramatically demonstrated than in adaptations of superhero comics. Building on Murray's economic approach, and particularly on her emphasis on the ways that approach has driven recent developments in the adaptation industry, Liam Burke's aptly subtitled monograph *The Comic Book Film Adaptation: Exploring Modern Hollywood's Leading Genre* (2015) develops a business model in which corporations like Marvel Studios depend for their survival and indefinite expansion on a potentially endless series of new adaptations, sequels, prequels, reboots, and combinations of familiar superhero entries in the Marvel Universe. Making no attempt to adapt individual issues or stories or narrative arcs in the sources they draw on, Marvel Studios treats all these sources—including earlier films the studio produced itself—as raw material to be mined for the purpose of generating new blockbusters that will dominate Hollywood's summer box office.

These blockbusters are so frequently described as industrial franchises that it might be tempting to assume that Hollywood is the original home of commercial franchises. But comic book movies are based on comic books, or "sequential art," as Will Eisner, creator of comic-book hero the Spirit has called it, or graphic novels—a genre often said to descend from Eisner's 1978 book *A Contract with God*, which aspires, as Burke puts it, "to produce a work that has greater depth and permanency" (Burke 8). These comic books are equally industrial franchises that are typically commissioned by publishers and written, illustrated, colored, and lettered by shifting, collaborative teams of creators aiming to reach the widest possible audience—for example, with the teasing promise that in this issue, a member of the Justice League of America will die or Superman will marry Lois Lane.

Comic books in turn are based on a still older commercial undertaking: the comic strips that Burke traces back to British magazines like *Punch* (1841) and the *Illustrated London News* (1842), and the Sunday supplements to American newspapers like Joseph Pulitzer's *New York World* and William Randolph Hearst's *New York Journal*. In fact, "the first defining forms of popular seriality were developed in media characterized by relatively fast rhythms of production and reception, such as newspapers and radio" (Kelleter and Loock 128). Noting that "two factors—the use of continuing characters and their appearance in mass circulated newspapers—set American comics apart from the earlier European form and made them mass market products," Ian Gordon argues that "comic art contributed significantly to the formation of a culture of consumption" (Gordon 7, 9). The adventures of early comic strip heroes like the Yellow Kid and Buster Brown were designed to boost newspapers' circulation by providing readers comic relief from the news through figures readers could follow, like the news, from day to day and year to year. By providing a reassuring sense of continuity despite their discontinuous appearance, comic strips encouraged their audiences to read the newspapers in which they appeared as stages for a series of entertaining, continuous narratives whose every installment they needed to keep up with. Some comic strips, from *Gasoline Alley* (1918–) to *For Better or for Worse* (1979–2008), have shown their characters growing older with the passing years; others, like *Calvin and Hobbes* (1985–95) and *Dilbert* (1989–), have kept them the same age; still others, like *Blondie* (1930–), have allowed them to grow older up to a certain point and then frozen them in time. These changes mirror the inevitable changes in the production staffs behind long-running comic strips. The retirement of Bill Watterson and the death of Charles M. Schulz respectively brought *Calvin and Hobbes* and *Peanuts* (1950–2000) to an end, but *Dick Tracy* (1931–) and *Blondie* have outlived their creators by many years, transforming themselves ever more decisively from individual acts of creation to industrial franchises marketed to as many newspapers as possible. Although many newspapers have declined to run comic strips, the papers that do typically devote an entire page or two to a collection of strips, offering the funny pages—whether or not their individual entries are funny—as one of their selling points.

When comic strips first became collected in books in *Famous Funnies: A Carnival of Comics* in 1933 and were then produced specifically for comic books in the aptly titled *New Comics* in 1935, several changes appeared in their production and consumption. Comic books were more likely than comic strips to be produced in color. Their freedom from the obligation to provide either a punchline or a cliffhanger in every installment encouraged a shift to less episodic and less "comic" comics. And audiences now consumed them not as supplements to the newspapers in which they were embedded but as independent narratives that were worth spending money on. The birth of superhero comics followed soon afterward with the first appearance of *Superman* in 1938. Unlike the telenovelas that remain popular throughout Latin America today, comic books produced in the United States increasingly tilted away from soap-opera romance toward the adventures of superheroes. With rare exceptions like the 1930s and 1940s live-action franchises based on *Blondie* and *Dick Tracy*, and more recent films like *Garfield* (2024) and the *Peanuts* movies and television programs (1965–2023), superheroes have been far more likely to generate commercially successful movies than their comical counterparts.

Of the many questions these adaptations raise, the most obvious concerns what exactly they are adapting. Although many superhero movie franchises return repeatedly to present different, often contradictory versions of their heroes' origin stories, most—with a few notable exceptions like *Watchmen* (2009)—refuse to adapt any single story from the hundreds or thousands to choose from in those heroes' print history. In that case, what exactly are they adapting: the superheroes themselves, their storyworlds or universes, or their visuals, which can range from costumes different superhero movies either preserve or change dramatically to their color scheme, like the muted and often monochromatic visuals Batman movies borrow from *The Dark Knight Returns* (1986) and other graphic novels featuring the Caped Crusader? Burke complicates this question further by noting the ways "superhero movies have been subsumed into a larger genre that is most often termed 'the comic book movie'" (Burke 8): a genre that includes movies like *Dick Tracy* (1990) and *Sin City* (2005), which do not feature superheroes; and television series like *Creepshow* (2019–) and movies like *The Matrix* (1999), which "have adopted characteristics of the comic book form and its film adaptations" even though they are not adaptations of any particular comic book franchise themselves (Burke 8, 9).

For these reasons, it makes sense that "[c]omic book fans, like the readers of most cult texts, prioritize the source. However, they are not as dogmatic about the original's primacy as some literary purists. Although readers prize 'fidelity,' the term most often used is 'continuity,'" which refers to "character consistency, interrelated books, and cumulative events" (Burke 19). As every fan knows, the notions of consistency and continuity are frequently challenged by successive entries in most franchises, which change details of the heroes' costumes, information about their backstories and origins, and retrospective updates that tax the ingenuity of fans looking to construct a consistent timeline for the cumulative movie adventures of their favorite heroes. So Burke, following Clare Parody, sees superhero adaptations as prioritizing "transmedia *franchises*" over logically consistent "storytelling" (Burke 21; see Parody on franchise adaptation as "brand management," 215), thus fulfilling André Bazin's prophecy that critics of adaptation in 2050 would find "not a novel out of which a play and a film had been 'made,' but a single work reflected through three art forms, an artistic pyramid with three sides, all equal in the eyes of the critic" (Bazin 26).

Questions

- Burke observes that "at the start of the 21st century Hollywood faced certain cultural, technological, and industrial challenges that comics were uniquely equipped to surmount" (Burke 2). Since not every movie made since 2000 has been a comic book adaptation, what other kinds of material have been helpful in surmounting the industrial difficulties he describes?
- How consistent are the "[s]tudies of comic adaptation audiences" (Burke 10) Burke refers to by other commentators and uses himself in support of his analysis with Murray's industrial approach to adaptation?
- Burke quotes former DC president Paul Levitz as saying that "there are 4,000 Batman stories: which one, or ones, am I going to do? Which are going to be my ideal version?" (Burke 13). How do comic book adaptations answer this question?
- Burke argues that "discounting fidelity discourse is at odds with the field's wider calls for audience-centric research" (Burke 18). In what ways does fidelity remain an important consideration in industrial approaches to adaptation, and who gets to decide what has to be faithful to what?

Evaluating superhero franchises

Whether or not fans of superhero franchises prize continuity over fidelity, a signal advantage of industrial approaches to adaptation is that they offer an obvious metric for evaluation: the best adaptations are those that make the most money. Since the hallmark of commercially successful franchises is the largest number of the most devoted fans—audiences who can be counted on to pay to see every new entry in a franchise, some of them perhaps more than once—it is the moviegoing public, not critics, who determine which franchises are the most successful. And Burke's useful Appendix (Burke 269–71) shows that the verdict among fans in English-speaking countries is clear: entries in the Marvel Universe were judged superior to entries in the DC Universe through 2014, with the notable exception of movies about Batman, whose adventures were consistently more successful than those of other DC heroes.

But this simple observation is clouded by several complications. For one thing, decisions about which superhero franchises to develop, combine, and abandon are made by studio executives, not fans; and although the executives do their best to follow the money, they sometimes misread fans' wishes or make changes meant to strengthen their franchises that hurt them instead. Spencer Harrison, Anne Carlsen, and Miha Škerlavaj contend that "Marvel's success rests on four principles: (1) selecting for experienced inexperience, (2) leveraging a stable core, (3) continually challenging the formula, and (4) cultivating customers' curiosity" (Harrison et al.). These principles, which echo the tension Murray finds between aesthetic and economic imperatives, are constantly in conflict with each other, driven at once by a desire to expand the Marvel Universe into intriguing new realms and a determination to preserve an economically successful formula. "The secret," add Harrison, Carlsen, and Škerlavaj, "seems to be finding the right balance between creating innovative films and retaining enough continuity to make them all recognizably part of a coherent family" (Harrison et al.). This balance can be hard to find, since many films meant to launch franchises fail at the box office, and even successful franchises usually meet with declining critical approval and box-office success. Even though many observers of the Marvel Universe's reliance on superheroes, action sequences, and special effects may have wondered, "Were people just watching the same movie over and over again?", Harrison, Carlsen, and Škerlavaj conclude that Marvel "fans go to the next film looking for something different" (Harrison et al.).

By contrast, they note, longtime fans' widespread rejection of *Star Wars: The Last Jedi*, which actively sought to depart from the dramatic arc and visual style of earlier *Star Wars* movies, indicates that "franchises that have stuck closer to a winning formula run into trouble when they attempt to renew themselves" (Harrison et al.). The Marvel Universe, which is clearly driven by the creative vision of producer Kevin Feige, avoids recycling familiar origin stories and often gives more screen time to previously lesser-known superheroes like Iron Man, Nick Fury, and Falcon, whom the movies feel free to transform from their comic book avatars. Zack Snyder, the director who is the leading creative force behind the DC Universe, faces much greater challenges, because DC heroes like Superman, Batman, Wonder Woman, and the Flash have long, well-documented histories from which the movies depart at their peril—histories that have so little to do with each other that they are hard to knit together into a stable franchise universe. So Marvel's decision to sell Spider-Man and other popular heroes to other production companies turned out to be an advantage, since it left Marvel more freedom to reassemble the remaining parts and add the lost heroes into the universe as the studio recovered the rights. As Mike Ryan has said: "DC legitimately has the best toy collection—they have access to every DC character, as opposed to Marvel, who doesn't. The problem is, they just don't know how to display or position that collection" (Ryan). Charlie Ridgely adds:

> Warner Bros. and DC have taken a more standalone approach to their films as of late, embracing the styles and stories of individual filmmakers before trying to fit everything into the greater connected universe. The Marvel Cinematic Universe, on the other hand, is all about its connective tissue. There are different styles to be found in the different projects, but the goal for every title is to serve the greater narrative.
>
> (Ridgely)

Fans have noted other differences between the two universes. DC movies are often dark dramas and Marvel movies, which meld performers and characters more closely, are often comedies; but DC movies are often campy, whereas Marvel movies deliver the goods without further irony. They can do so because Marvel comics are already notably self-referential and self-reflective, often speaking directly to their audience through facetious marginal captions. So Marvel movies can comfortably accommodate a meta-dimension without departing from the tone of the comics, whereas DC movies have to make sometimes awkward choices between playing with their material and playing it straight.

The most striking exception to Marvel's economic domination of DC movies is Batman, the only DC franchise that seriously rivals the success of the Marvel Universe. Batman movies have been more successful than those featuring any other DC hero for several reasons. Batman has been played by a wide variety of performers—Lewis Wilson, Robert Lowery, Adam West, Michael Keaton, Val Kilmer, George Clooney, Christian Bale, Ben Affleck, Dante Pereira-Olson, and Robert Pattison—most of whom have enriched the role without ever becoming exclusively identified with it. Precisely because Batman, unlike superheroes from Superman to Spider-Man, has no superpowers, his physical limitations and his mortality make him a more interesting character subject to a wider range of possible developments. And in many versions of his story, he is mysterious in ways that invite audiences to fill in the blanks to their own taste.

In addition, the world of most Batman movies is more highly stylized visually than that of competing DC or Marvel superheroes. Tim Burton's 1989 film *Batman* established something like a definitive *mise en scène* for future installments of the franchise, its color palette sharply limited by a pervasive and foreboding sense of darkness. Although sequels from *Batman Returns* (1992) to *Batman & Robin* (1997) successively lightened this palette and the mood it projected, it returned with a vengeance in Christopher Nolan's trilogy: *Batman Begins* (2005), *The Dark Knight* (2008), and *The Dark Knight Rises* (2012). The most recent screen adaptation, Matt Reeves's *The Batman* (2022), creates a *mise en scène* and a mood that are even darker as it explores a formative period in the lives of both Bruce Wayne/Batman (Robert

Pattinson) and Selina Kyle/Catwoman (Zoë Kravitz), and it is no surprise that the film ends with an announcement—"I can already see things will get worse before they get better"—that both confirms its dark tone and indicates more sequels to come. DC's decision to launch a younger version of Batman that would coexist with his older counterpart in the DC Universe, although it risks confusing or alienating fans, opens still further possibilities for complicating the character.

Figure 3.1 Batman (Robert Pattinson) and Catwoman (Zoë Kravitz) share a characteristically dark moment of distanced intimacy in *The Batman* (2022)

It is not only Batman's individual character that makes his films compelling. He has confronted an impressive array of franchise villains—the Joker, the Penguin, Catwoman, the Riddler, Two-Face, Mr. Freeze, Poison Ivy, Bane, Scarecrow, Ra's al Ghul, and Tania al Ghul—each of them with dramatic origin stories of their own. Although none of these villains is as evil or as monstrously effective as Loki is in the Marvel Universe, they are all visually and psychologically striking grotesques who help balance the interest of their films—many fans thought that Jack Nicholson's Joker completely upstaged Michael Keaton's Batman in the 1989 film—even as they serve as worthy antagonists to the hero. Batman's more complex relationship to these villains is suggested in the comic book *Ego and Other Tails*, whose Bruce Wayne is bedeviled by his dark double Batman, who taunts him: "[C]ould it be that the great Batman needs his archnemesis in order to feel complete?" (Cooke 52). The codependency between Batman and his adversaries is only the most obvious sign of the many disabilities that make him the most fallible and the most human of the great superheroes. Different incarnations of Batman have presented him as asocial, bipolar, or schizophrenic.

Instead of casting him as a disabled or other-abled superhero like Superior or the Hulk, the stories in which Batman appears repeatedly link his psychology to the sociology of his world. Gotham City, where millionaire Bruce Wayne makes his home, is every bit as dark as he is. Especially in the films directed by Tim Burton, Christopher Nolan, and Matt Reeves, it is a far more troubled setting than Clark Kent's fictional home of Metropolis or Peter Parker's home in the real-life New York borough of Queens. Like Batman, Gotham City could be described as disabled—not by a traumatic past or social withdrawal, but by political corruption or infighting. So Batman, who is "out to clean up a city that likes being dirty" (Miller and Mazzucchelli 82), has a codependent relationship not only with his criminal antagonists but with his hometown. Since Frank Miller describes Batman as "a hero who wishes he didn't have to exist" (Miller and Mazzuchelli, "Afterword: The Weird Creature of Darkness"), a hero whose vocation is to heal the wounds of a city from which he can't separate himself, it marks a significant breakthrough when, in the comic-book story *Ego*, he realizes that "I can't appreciably change the city—I've begun to wonder if the only thing I can change is myself" (Cooke 12).

For all these reasons, Batman's career raises more ethical questions than those of most other superheroes. These questions begin with the hero's motivations and behavior, which are often questioned by Police Commissioner Gordon and other politically powerful figures in Gotham City. How much more virtuous is Batman than the city guardians who often challenge him and the villains he confronts? These questions can be expanded not only across but outside Batman's universe. How do Batman's ethics change when he is portrayed across different media and played by different performers? What ethical issues arise when fans demand strict fidelity to a character who is always white, or Christian, or a playboy? What are the ethics of DC's management of their most popular franchise hero? Should popular media seek to teach their audiences moral lessons, or grapple with the ethical complications arising from their potentially competing imperatives, or simply present entertainment that provides fans with the enjoyment arising from wish fulfillment and nostalgia and the corporations with profit? Most pointedly in Batman's case: should audiences approach franchise superheroes as heroic role models or as psychologically and morally cautionary figures?

In the ten years since Burke wrote, life has unquestionably become harder for superhero adaptations. A variety of factors can reasonably be cited. The dramatic changes to life during the COVID-19 pandemic caused a precipitous drop in attendance at movie theaters, and fans had long thought superhero films too big for television watching. Marvel's strategy of subordinating every hero and every hero's story to a larger storyworld and a longer narrative arc required audiences to keep informed about a lengthening series of earlier installments, and some viewers eschewed the challenge. Given the decline of once-popular genres like the Western and the musical, there is no reason to assume that superhero films will retain their popularity indefinitely, even with the generation of audiences who have grown up loving them. It is entirely possible that, as Batman would say, things will get worse before they get better.

In the meantime, one final complication arising from the apparently simple question of how to assess the success of superhero adaptations is implicit in the number of different ways to measure that success. Analysts weighing the success of any particular franchise entry would presumably consider its box-office returns and its ratings on sites like Metacritic and Rotten Tomatoes. But these two metrics often point in different directions. So do economic indicators like domestic and foreign grosses and box-office grosses versus the costs of producing and publicizing a given franchise entry. The situation becomes even more complicated if we attempt to measure the success of a whole franchise. How should we balance the number of movies the franchise has generated, the number of times it has been rebooted by different hands, and the income generated by comic books or other merchandise it has promoted? For that matter, what exactly counts as a Black Widow film—films that Black Widow has appeared in, or only films that she has headlined? Given the ways many superheroes have changed in the course of their long comic-book runs and the fact that, as Amanda Conner puts it, "the wonderful world of comics has morphed into a brave new world where all sorts of different styles are becoming the norm" (Conner 6), the only constant in superhero franchises might seem to be change. At the same time, however, Superman and Deadpool, who are always recognizable as such, might seem to provide anchors affording stable identities to their ever-changing franchises—unless, of course, they get married in one of the Imaginary Stories that pop up in some of their comic-book franchises or switch from being villains to heroes in the course of the franchise. The rest of this chapter moves outside the superhero multiverse to explore some of these complications in greater detail.

Questions

- Is there any single definitive adaptation of any particular superhero? Given the fact that many audiences accept Sophocles' *Oedipus the King*, the 1939 *The Wizard of Oz*, and any number of Disney cartoon features as definitive adaptations, why do superheroes resist such definitive adaptation?
- Why do so many Batman movies keep returning to or rewriting his origin story?
- Do all superheroes require or imply a dysfunctional cultural context?
- When you follow a superhero franchise, are you more interested in the story it tells or in its connections to earlier entries in the franchise? Do you watch for Easter eggs and other embedded meta-perspectives? Do you

seek original meta-perspectives of your own? Or do you prefer to immerse yourself in the franchise universe and watch for the story?
• Should superhero franchises aim to create multiple universes or one coherent universe from a fan's perspective—or from a corporate perspective?

Complicating the economic imperative

Industrial approaches to adaptation emphasize the status of adaptations as reworkings of legally acquired properties. Although these terms have long been familiar to Hollywood lawyers, there are several ways to engage with them that reveal further complexities implicit in these industrial approaches.

One of these ways involves a renewed focus on the material features of adaptations that Kyle Meikle thinks are largely neglected by Murray's industrial approach despite the goal announced in "Materializing Adaptation Theory," the title of the essay that became her Introduction to *The Adaptation Industry*. In "Rematerializing Adaptation Theory," Meikle argues that Murray's materialist approach is metaphorical rather than literal, limited to the human agents and institutions within the adaptation industry. "[R]ethinking adaptation in terms of raw materiality," he points out, "would allow for nonhuman actors to take their rightful place alongside the adaptation industry's more literal and literary agents," recasting "Murray's adaptation industry as a Latourian collective of humans and nonhumans" (Meikle 174). Such a rethinking along the lines suggested by Bruno Latour would enlarge the field of adaptation's raw materials from a given story or characters or source material to the physical media of adaptations—materials like paper, canvas, and celluloid filmstock—"mak[ing] way for an *intermaterial* model of adaptation to complement the *intertextual* and *intermedial* models already at play in the field of adaptation study" (Meikle 175).

Further complexities in industrial approaches to adaptation are revealed if we turn from adapted literary, theatrical, cinematic, and televisual texts to tie-in merchandise, swag, and other typically material appropriations. These exceptionally wide-ranging "tie-in" adaptations, as Kamilla Elliott calls them, were once dismissed as marginal but are increasingly recognized by Murray and others as foundational to the adaptation industry. When one of the students in my adaptation seminar invited the others to bring in their favorite adaptations for a show-and-tell session, the closest thing to a traditional textual adaptation anyone brought was a copy of the script for *The Batman*. The range of the other items was astonishing. One student came with a Darth Vader dog toy tagged, "Together we can rule the galaxy" and a t-shirt her father had made her with the message, "When the going gets tough ... the tough have a good cry and watch *The Princess Bride*." Another brought a factory-made *Alice in Wonderland* t-shirt announcing, "We're all mad here," and a *Kingdom of Hearts* board game. One student wore a *Jurassic Park* ring; another brought a selection of Batman fan art. Two of the adaptations were explicitly linked to food: a McDonald's plate that restored chickens' faces to its pictures of McNuggets and an Optimus Prime truck designed to hold popcorn and soda. One student displayed a Pokémon Airpod case that she described as a product of "the largest media franchise now," whose reach has overtaken even that of the Disney Corporation; another, indicating his more diverse interests, supplemented his Pokémon Squirtle with a t-shirt sporting a *Great Gatsby* logo, a Bards Dispense Profanity card game, and a Frank Lloyd Wright tote bag—one of hundreds of Wright-inspired designer bags available online, which he described as adapted from the plate glass Wright added in 1895 to his Oak Park home. Another student with varied interests came with a Quagsire Pokémon doll, two funko figures of characters from *Lord of the Rings*, and an image of a Minton *Macbeth* tile designed around 1874 by John Moyr Smith. One last student, stretching the concept of adaptation to a breaking point that would have been rejected by aesthetic theorists but eagerly embraced by industrial theorists, brought a computer sticker with a quotation from Katie Ryan's viral twenty-second Vine video of her young daughter: "It's freakin' bats. I love Halloween."

Taking example from Disney, Christopher Anderson considers tie-in adaptations like these as products of "a centrifugal force that guide[s] the viewer away from the immediate textual experience towards a more pervasive sense of textuality, one that encourage[s] the consumption of further Disney texts, further Disney products, further Disney experiences" (Anderson 155). Paul Grainge, by contrast, considers the "interlocking products and services" (Grainge 47) as creating a centripetal force. Kamilla Elliott takes an even more comprehensive view:

> Corporate intertextual incorporation operates both centrifugally and centripetally. On the one hand, through franchise licensing, corporations disperse branded company characters, images, diction, and soundscapes through as many affiliate companies and across as many platforms as they can to reach the widest possible markets. On the other hand, franchise tie-in merchandise operates centripetally, as dispersed intertextualities return to the corporation where they are reincorporated not only as profits, but also as representations pointing and returning to their corporate point of origin. They are dispersed only to be tied in more tightly to the corporation.
>
> (Elliott 193–94)

For Elliott, fictional characters are more central than either world-building or performance to the corporate branding that turns tie-in merchandise into "incorporealization" (Elliott 201). And she sees the necessary gap between specific examples of tie-in merchandise and the media products to which they are tied as an advantage rather than a disadvantage because "[c]omplete dissatisfaction would drive away customers" and "[c]omplete satisfaction would equally put an end to consumption," but "dissatisfied customers … remain hungry, eager to consume more" (Elliott 207–8).

Because Elliott argues that tie-in merchandise allows consumers to act as if they were characters, she sees the gap between tie-in merchandise and the corporate properties to which it is tied as an invitation to consumers to close the gap by turning themselves into active performers embodying the characters and roles the merchandise features. In doing so, this merchandise restores the individual agency to consumers that intertextual approaches to adaptation might have seemed to limit, as players of franchise-themed videogames can attest. But this agency, already conferred on critical consumers when Murray announced that "we are ourselves agents in the system we seek to analyze" (Murray 7), is sharply limited by the affordances of specific media and the implied imperative to be faithful to the franchise—even perhaps more faithful than the tie-in merchandise itself.

These performances are widely dispersed over agents that only begin with Murray's six groups of stakeholders. Ian Fleming, author of the James Bond novels, was originally skeptical about the casting of Scottish ex-bodybuilder Sean Connery as the implacably suave British secret agent in *Dr. No* (1962), the first feature film to be based on a Bond novel. But he was so impressed by the film's success that he wrote Connery's backstory into the franchise, indicating in his 1964 novel *You Only Live Twice* that Bond's father was a Scot from Glencoe. Christopher Reeve, who memorably played Superman in four blockbuster films, seemed determined to embody the moral values he found in Superman offscreen and insisted that they be written into *Superman IV: The Quest for Peace* (1987), which took strong positions on issues from nuclear disarmament to family farms. Innumerable movies have been publicized by reputed romances between their stars, even when these romances have no basis in fact. As audiences and movie stars grow old together, audiences' ideas about those stars can undergo significant transformations whether or not they keep up with their recent movies. Even within specific households, different generations of audiences may have very different visions of stars from Henry Winkler to Julie Andrews.

Still another turn in tie-in merchandise is indicated by retailers like Hot Topic, which specialize in branded merchandise tied in to many different franchises, from t-shirts to costume jewelry to insulated mugs. Visitors to Hot Topic who are intrigued by copies of Andrea Waggener's *Five Night's at Freddy's: The Official Movie Novel* (2023), a tie-in to Scott Cawthorn's series of videogames and their spinoffs, can find a long series of other volumes: the *Five Night's at Freddy's Graphic Novel Trilogy Boxed Set* (2023), the *Five Night's at Freddy's Official Character Encyclopedia* (2023), the *Official Five Night's at Freddy's Coloring Book* (2021), the *Five Night's at Freddy's How to Draw* (2022), and the *Official Five Night's at Freddy's Cookbook* (2023)—all of them duly labeled "Official." Some of these volumes take off explicitly from the videogames; others from the 2023 film; still others from the users' identification and aspiration to participate more actively in the franchise. What is especially noteworthy about Hot Topic is its appeal not only to fans dedicated to acquiring merchandise tied to a specific franchise of their choice, but to browsers looking for branded merchandise not tied to any franchise in particular. This cohort, which suggests that at least some consumers place a positive value on branding as such, implies an appetite for meta beyond meta: the value isn't in the particular brand, but in the act and status of branding themselves.

This last example suggests that industrial approaches to adaptation can be used not merely to challenge but to invert the aesthetic model that defines adaptations as inferior copies of canonical texts by focusing on technologies that promise a series of ever-superior products. Especially notable among these readaptations are remakes of movies like *King Kong* (1933); rereleases, prequels, and sequels to *Star Wars* (1977) that use improved makeup and prosthetics, advanced audiovisual technologies, and computer-generated special effects to make canonical monsters scarier and more convincing; and successive generations of videogames like *Grand Theft Auto*, which present themselves as clearly superior to the texts on which they draw, demoting those texts from canonical originals to earlier entries in the franchise, dress rehearsals for the latest version.

Should remakes, prequels, and sequels be considered adaptations? Frank Kelleter and Kathleen Loock—who carefully distinguish these practices from each other and from spin-offs, revisions, spoofs, re-imaginings, franchises, reboots, and "the more expansive remaking practices of 'genres' and 'cycles' "—acknowledge that "[t]he catalogue of these terms is not systematic because it cannot be systematic": the definition of each of them is constantly evolving in response to changes in remaking practices and in the resulting redefinitions of the other practices (Kelleter and Loock 138). All these practices, they conclude, operate as "a method of *cinematic self-historicization*: cinema writes its own history with remakes, sequels, or prequels—and it does so within the evolving network of expectations, recognitions, allusions, variations, and reinterpretations that makes these iterations possible and keeps them in circulation" through what they call "*second-order seriality*: ongoing narratives about (and through) ongoing narratives" (Kelleter and Loock 134, 144). However rigorously and systematically we attempt to define the relation between adaptation and these other practices, two constants remain: they are all industrial practices designed to sharpen audiences' appetites for further versions of a familiar story; and they all operate by "lay[ing] claim to being state-of-the-art" (Kelleter and Loock 142), even as they position themselves—as Elliott has said of tie-in merchandise—as not quite the earlier text, requiring the production of still further texts. Constantine Verevis, going still further, argues that "all films—originals and/as remakes—invest in the repetition effects that characterise all films, all of cinema itself" (Verevis 177).

It would be easy to infer from Kelleter, Loock, Verevis, and other scholars of cinematic sequels, prequels, and remakes that these practices were limited to, or at least quintessentially represented by, the commercial practices of film industries from Hollywood to Bollywood. But it is important to remind observers who celebrate or deplore new installments, remakes, or techno-logically updated rereleases of *Back to the Future* (1985), *The Matrix*, or *The Lord of the Rings* (2001–3)—this last planned as a pair of feature films that rapidly expanded to three, based on a 1954–55 trilogy J.R.R. Tolkien had first written as an unplanned sequel to *The Hobbit* (1936)—that these practices are much older than the movies. Aeschylus' *Oresteia* (458 B.C.E.), Richard Wagner's *Der Ring des Nibelungen* (1869–76), and Ford Madox Ford's *Parade's End* (1924–28) were all planned as multi-part fictions. Sophocles wrote two prequels to his tragedy *Antigone* (441 B.C.E.) years after it was first staged when he was 55: *Oedipus the King* (429 B.C.E.) when he was 67 and *Oedipus at Colonus* (406 B.C.E.) when he was 90. Two thou-sand years later, the *comedia dell'arte* produced a seemingly endless series of stories about Arlecchino, Pantalone, and other stock characters for the Italian stage. Miguel de Cervantes wrote the second volume of *Don Quixote* (1605/1615) ten years after the first volume. Alexandre Dumas's *Twenty Years After* (1845) and *The Man in the Iron Mask* (1847–50) were originally unplanned sequels to *The Three Musketeers* (1844); Lewis Carroll's *Through the Looking-Glass* (1872) to *Alice's Adventures in Wonderland* (1875); Mark Twain's *The Adventures of Huckleberry Finn* (1884), *Tom Sawyer Abroad* (1894), and *Tom Sawyer, Detective* (1896) to *The Adventures of Tom Sawyer* (1876); and Henry James's *The Princess Casamassima* (1886) to *Roderick Hudson* (1876). The first volume of Laurence Sterne's *The Life and Opinions of Tristram Shandy, Gentleman* (1759) led to eight further volumes; and Anthony Trollope ended up writing five sequels to *The Warden* (1855) and five more to *Can You Forgive Her?* (1865). The fiction factories that arose in the nineteenth century to extend the moralizing adventures of Horatio Alger and dime-novel detective Nick Carter paved the way for the multi-authored twentieth-century franchises of Nancy Drew and the Hardy Boys and the radio serials of the 1930s, many of which made the transition to television to become soap operas like *As the World Turns* (1956–2010) and *The Guiding Light* (radio, 1937–56; television, 1952–2009).

One set of sequels that raises particularly fascinating problems is the sequels to notable detective story franchises. It might seem that of all modern fictional genres, the detective story is the one that most closely follows Aristotle's dictum that "the end is the chief thing of all" (Aristotle 27), pro-viding a definitive closure and meaning to the preceding complications. But the whole business of detective stories ever since Sherlock Holmes is to leave each individual mystery behind as definitively resolved while bringing the detective back for more adventures, like the dozen stories Arthur Conan Doyle collected in *The Adventures of Sherlock Holmes* (1892). The tension between the definitively resolved mystery and the enduring detective informs every detective story, but it rarely rises to the surface except in novels like *Trent's Own Case*, journalist E.C. Bentley's 1936 sequel to his 1912 novel *Trent's Last Case*, which had been designed—as its title suggests—as the detective story to end all detective stories. The relative failure of Bentley's sequel did nothing to disturb the universe of genre fans, who continue to demand an endless series of self-contained puzzles solved by an imperishable detective.

A series of later sequels has raised increasingly challenging questions about exactly what these fans are most invested in. Is it the story of the individual mystery, the longer arc of the detective hero, or the arc of the franchise's storyworld that is seriously threatened by the marriage of hardboiled detective Philip Marlowe in *The Poodle Springs Story* (1962), left uncompleted at Raymond Chandler's death and extended to novel length by Robert B. Parker as *Poodle Springs* in 1989? In most detective stories, this is not much of a problem because neither fictional detectives nor their storyworlds have much of an arc, and when they return for subsequent adventures, fans are looking not for new developments but for more of the same. More recent sequels, however, have made a point of emphasizing the problematic nature of detective-story sequels. Tired of writing about Amsterdam detective Van der Valk, Nicolas Freeling killed him off in *A Long Silence* (1972), then began a new series featuring French detective Henri Castang, interrupted by two novels whose mysteries were solved by Van der Valk's widow Arlette, before reviving his hero for one last case, *Sand Castles* (1989). Authors from Ellery Queen to Stuart Woods and James Patterson have created franchise detectives and then passed the authorship of particular episodes on to other hands. The death of retired jockey Dick Francis did not end his series of horseracing mysteries but turned over their authorial credit to his son, Felix Francis. Other authors' estates have commissioned new adventures for Hercule Poirot, James Bond, and Robert B. Parker's stable of greater Boston detectives—private eyes Spenser and Sunny Randall and Paradise Police Chief Jesse Stone—by other authors.

Some of these posthumous sequels strive for close stylistic fidelity to their franchises. *Where Are the Children Now?* (2023), which carries the bylines of Mary Higgins Clark and Alafair Burke, is a sequel to Clark's first novel, *Where Are the Children?* (1974), which retains the earlier novel's tone and setting as it follows the children of that novel's characters through a new mystery. Others, like Sophie Hannah's books about Hercule Poirot, whom Agatha Christie had killed off in *Curtain* (1976), aim for even greater ingenuity than their models. The Philip Marlowe novels written by Benjamin Black and Denise Mina adopt more frankly revisionist stances that can turn the heroes and their worlds upside-down, raising familiar questions about whether posthumous franchise entries should be more faithful to the franchises they are resurrecting or to modern audiences' assumptions, expectations, and wishes.

Although recent continuations of these detective franchises following the author's (and sometimes the detective's) death may give problems like this new urgency, the problems themselves can be traced back at least as far as Sherlock Holmes. Bored with his prodigiously popular character and determined to devote himself to less frivolous writing, Arthur Conan Doyle sent Holmes and his nemesis Professor Moriarty to their deaths in the 1893 magazine story "The Final Problem," the last story to appear in the darkly titled 1894 collection *Memoirs of Sherlock Holmes*. Fans were so devastated that they insisted Doyle revive their beloved hero. After resisting for eight years, he produced *The Hound of the Baskervilles* (1901), positioning it as a retrospective adventure set in 1889, before Holmes's death. But fans were not satisfied. They wanted not more Holmes adventures, but Holmes restored to life, and Doyle ultimately obliged in 1903 with "The Adventure of the Empty House," which explained that Holmes had improbably faked his own death and gone underground for several years, keeping his survival secret even from his friend and amanuensis Dr. John H. Watson until Moriarty's entire crime ring was brought down. The question of who controlled Sherlock Holmes—the author or his public—was further complicated by a lawsuit the Holmes estate threatened against the publication of Ellery Queen's 1943 anthology *The Misadventures of Sherlock Holmes*, which collected 33 parodies and pastiches of Holmes. After the estate succeeded in preventing any reprintings of *The Misadventures of Sherlock Holmes*, Doyle's heirs continued to insist that they—not Arthur Conan Doyle or his fans, adapters, and imitators—were the true owners of the franchise and did everything they could to keep his latest adventures under copyright. It was not until 2014 that the U.S. Supreme Court ruled that Sherlock Holmes had entered the public domain and that adaptations, sequels, prequels, pastiches, and parodies of the Holmes stories could be freely produced without any payment to the Doyle estate.

Whether or not we choose to call these franchise continuations adaptations of specific texts, they are surely adaptations of the franchise and its characters. It is especially noteworthy that among the hundreds of detective stories that adapt franchises begun by other authors, hardly any of these stories apart from *Where Are the Children Now?* return to their original mysteries to offer new solutions; instead, they focus on adapting detective heroes rather than the mysteries they solve. This emphasis is further illuminated by considering the unique nature of fictional detectives. Unlike superheroes and villains like zombies and Count Dracula, they do not live forever; unlike monsters like Godzilla and Frankenstein's creature, they do not die and then return to life; unlike soap-opera characters like Erica Kane of *All My Children* and Luke and Laura Spencer of *General Hospital*, their romantic and interpersonal relationships do not continue to develop in an endless series of complications. Instead, they provide a reassuringly stable ballast, a defense against the impenetrable mystery of death that their investigations repeatedly render logically understandable. In the world of Sherlock Holmes and his descendants, death is both commonplace and unthinkable. The indefinite deferral of endings many commentators see as a specifically postmodern development is not an addition to the detective genre; as the Holmes franchise shows, it is baked into the genre from the beginning because the detective story is defined by the tension between the impenetrable mystery of death and the imperishable detective who fathoms it. The apparent paradox of posthumous detective story sequels, which demonstrate the ways this most end-oriented of all fictional genres allows for the most indefinite extension of the franchise, turns out to be a dialectic, for each term—universal mortality that amounts to an unfathomable mystery and an omniscient and omnipotent detective who will never die—requires the other for its potency.

Questions

- What do sequels to detective story franchises suggest about possibilities for other successful sequels?
- How do the responsibilities and opportunities for promoting a franchise shift when its authorhood shifts?
- On what basis do fans especially prize posthumous sequels? Is it ever for their imaginative infidelity?
- How does the experience of reading (or viewing or listening to) an authorized sequel compare to the experience of reading an unauthorized sequel?
- What is the relation between authorized sequels and authorized adaptations?
- How closely do these cases resemble the (divergence) culture of the Marvel Universe? How closely do they resemble the "Secret Lives of Batman" and other "imaginary tales" of superheroes? In what ways do they encourage us to distinguish different forces of different endings? In what ways do they encourage us to distinguish different degrees of fictionality and metafictionality?
- If, despite what Aristotle maintains, the end is not the most important thing, just what importance does it have?

Who should speak for the adaptation industry?

The study of industrial approaches to adaptation would be incomplete without some consideration of television adaptations, especially since the age of streaming video has ushered in what Simon Shaps, former Director of Television at UK television network ITV, has called "not merely … a golden age of television drama" but "a golden age of adaptation" (Shaps). The explosive growth of streaming services—like the explosive growth of Hollywood movie studios a century earlier—has generated an insatiable demand for new material, and "[g]iven a choice between a blank page and a book to build on, the book often wins out" (Shaps).

In light of this development, Christopher Hogg's study of television adaptations departs from the pioneering approaches of Sarah Cardwell and Shannon Wells-Lassagne, who emphasized the textual analysis of long-form television adaptations, to focus on the industrial processes behind television adaptations. Hogg concludes his monograph by summarizing the most prominent theme across all of this book's interviews [as] the recognition of the importance of professional and creative adaptation when working in television drama production of any kind. Thus, in this context, what has often been seen as a weakness to television's identity in cultural and artistic terms, its reliance upon the adaptation of skills and content from other, more prestigious forms, is instead revealed here to be a defining strength which ensures that television survives, and thrives, whatever the odds. Television drama has always drawn from other artforms, as have—in turn—the artforms from which it draws.

(Hogg 238)

Hogg's argument against dismissing television adaptations as merely "'pre-sold' commercial entities" (Hogg 238) on the grounds that all television dramas, whether or not they are labeled adaptations, depend on the practices and techniques of adaptation in the same way as the avowedly more original stories on which they draw amounts to a remarkable double inversion of the aesthetic case against television adaptations. Even so, the single most telling word in this conclusion apparently has nothing to do with either adaptation or aesthetic evaluation. That word, *interviews*, refers to the evidence Hogg assembles in support of his view that the television industry depends at every level on adaptation: a series of interviews with television writers, directors, showrunners, producers, casting directors, and other collaborators. Although Hogg often raises pointed questions about the positions these collaborators take, they never come across as disinterested analysts themselves. For example, when "the interviewee's insights work to undermine more cynical assumptions regarding the contemporary prevalence of television adaptations as 'easy options' in production terms" (Hogg 239), that is only to be expected of collaborators who would surprise everyone if they described their work as easy and their productions as second-rate imitations.

The perspectives of the industrial collaborators whose interviews Hogg uses as evidence for his conclusion that adaptation is ubiquitous in contemporary culture are inevitably self-serving. But this does not mean that they should be simply dismissed, as Hogg uses them to counter earlier dismissals of television drama as merely derivative. For they raise one last inescapable question about industrial perspectives on adaptation: where is the best place to look for evidence in support of these perspectives? In *Reading the Romance* (1984), Janice A. Radway focused on interviewing readers, not producers, of romance novels to determine what they were looking for and how their reading informed their lives. In their different ways, Simone Murray, who assumes that all parties in the adaptation industry are motivated by the promise of commercial success, and Liam Burke, who cites box-office returns for superhero films, take the opposite tack by following the money. Eduard Cuelenaere has suggested linking questions like "how do audiences define and assess film remakes?" with "production research, looking into the definitions (of, e.g., a film remake itself) held by those who actually produce, distribute, and evaluate film remakes" (Cuelenaere 219). Ruth McElroy and Caitriona Noonan, whom Hogg cites along with Cuelenaere, focus on "the linked ecologies of local, national and global television drama production" (Hogg 9). If, as Murray argues, following Pierre Bourdieu, "culture [is] always embedded in sociological contexts" (Murray 6), the questions of which contexts to emphasize and how to weigh different contexts against each other become paramount.

In this context, it is refreshing to give the last word on the subject to *Barbie*. If Greta Gerwig's film is indeed an adaptation, it is clearly an adaptation of an industrial product that seeks to extend its franchise empire beyond dolls, outfits, and accessories to the cinema. Along the way, the film goes out of its way to reflect on its own status as an industrial artifact, from its opening sequence showing Barbie mysteriously appearing in a landscape out of *2001: A Space Odyssey* (1968) to its scenes featuring Ruth Handler (Rhea Pearlman), the cofounder of the Mattel Corporation who first created Barbie as an alternative to baby dolls she thought directed the girls who played with them too narrowly toward fantasies of motherhood, and the CEO of Mattel, who is intent on containing the damage threatened by Barbie's escape from Barbieland even as he seeks to wring every possible dollar from the franchise. Although Kate McKinnon's Weird Barbie aptly tells Margot Robbie's stricken Stereotypical Barbie, "Don't blame me. Blame Mattel. They make the rules," casting the comedian Will Ferrell as the Mattel CEO goes far to reassure the audience that even though the film, like its heroine, is an industrial product aimed at making money, the corporation behind the film is willing to be gently ridiculed. This ridicule reaches a climax at the end of the film when Gloria (America Ferrara)—the Mattel employee whose daughter Sasha (Ariana Greenblatt) owns the Barbie that has caused the trouble the corporation is determined to tamp down—proposes a new product, Ordinary Barbie, to complement Stereotypical Barbie. The CEO initially rejects Ordinary Barbie until one of his underlings confides in him, "It'll sell," and he instantly changes his mind. In the process of unmasking and demystifying the agents behind the franchise, the film is actually remythologizing their economic imperatives in the best Marvel tradition by assigning them to fictional characters whose motivations it makes light of within the context of the fictional story. It continues to walk this tightrope even in its end credits, which run alongside contemporaneous illustrations of Mattel's initial rollouts of Barbie, Ken, Midge, Allan, Skipper, Teresa, Nikki, and Barbie Video Girl, zooming in to this last character's embedded screen to display the rest of the credit crawl.

It would be naïve to assume that the mixed commercial success of recent Disney and superhero adaptations could be reversed by the proliferation of more industrial adaptations as self-conscious as *Barbie*. The film's staggering commercial success—it grossed $1.446 billion, "set[ting] the record for any film that was not a sequel, remake, or superhero property" ("*Barbie* (film)")—would be as hard to duplicate as its tone, which deftly manages to be both a satirical critique of its founding corporation and a valentine to it, extending Mattel's franchise even as it deconstructs it. But the film does indicate some promising ways in which adaptations can embrace adaptation as an industrial process without forcing their audiences to dehumanize themselves or compromise the enjoyment it is the business of every franchise to promise.

Questions

- Shannon Wells-Lassagne contends that in the contemporary mediascape, "originality is no longer a matter of source material, but of delivery" (Wells-Lassagne 189). How does this shift change the larger notion of what it means to be original?
- If, as Murray claims, the "now-dominant third [intertextual] wave of adaptation studies has come at a price" (Murray 10), does the industrial approach Murray advocates also have a price—and if so, what exactly is that price?
- What do industrial engagements allow or reveal about adaptations that other engagements don't?

References

Anderson, Christopher. *Hollywood TV: The Studio System in the Fifties*. U of Texas P, 1994.

Andrew, Dudley. "Adaptation." *Concepts in Film Theory*. Oxford UP, 1984, pp. 96–106.

Aristotle. *Aristotle's Theory of Poetry and Fine Art*. Translated by S.H. Butcher. Dover, 1951.

"*Barbie* (film)." *Wikipedia*. https://en.wikipedia.org/wiki/Barbie_(film).

Bazin, André. "Adaptation, or the Cinema as Digest." Translated by Alain Piette and Bert Cardullo. *Bazin at Work* (1997). Rpt. in *Film Adaptation*. Edited by James Naremore. Rutgers UP, 2000, pp. 19–27.

Best Seller to Box Office. https://www.bs2bo.com/#.

Burke, Liam. *The Comic Book Film Adaptation: Exploring Modern Hollywood's Leading Genre*. UP of Mississippi, 2015.

Conner, Amanda. "Introduction." Cooke, Darwyn. *Ego and Other Tails* (DC Comics, 2017), https://readallcomics.com/batman-ego-and-other-tails-deluxe-edition-part-1/.

Cooke, Darwyn. *Ego and Other Tails* (DC Comics, 2017), https://readallcomics.com/batman-ego-and-other-tails-deluxe-edition-part-1/.

Cuelenaere, Edward. "Towards an Integrative Methodological Approach of Film Remake Studies." *Adaptation*, vol. 13, no. 2 (2020), pp. 210–23.

Elliott, Kamilla. "Tie-Intertextuality, or, Intertextuality as Incorporation in the Tie-in Merchandise to Disney's *Alice in Wonderland* (2010)." *Adaptation*, vol. 7, no. 2 (2014). pp. 191–211.

Gordon, Ian. *Comic Strips and Consumer Culture: 1890–1945*. Smithsonian Institution P, 1988.

Grainge, Paul. *Brand Hollywood: Selling Entertainment in a Global Media Age.* Routledge, 2008.

Harmetz, Aljean. *The Making of The Wizard of Oz: Movie Magic and Studio Power in the Prime of MGM—and the Miracle of Production # 1060.* Knopf, 1981.

Harrison, Spencer, Anne Carlsen, and Miha Škerlavaj. "Marvel's Blockbuster Machine." *Harvard Business Review* July–Aug. 2019, https://hbr.org/2019/07/marvels-blockbuster-machine.

Hogg, Christopher. *Adapting TV Drama.* Palgrave Macmillan, 2021.

Hutcheon, Linda, with Siobhan O'Flynn. *A Theory of Adaptation.* Second ed. Routledge, 2012.

Jeannelle, Jean-Louis. "Adaptability: Literature and Cinema Redux." Translated by Margaret C. Flinn. *Studies in French Cinema*, vol. 16, no. 2 (2016), pp. 95–105.

Jenkins, Henry, Sam Ford, and Joshua Green. *Spreadable Media: Creating Value and Meaning in a Networked Culture.* New York University P, 2013.

Kelleter, Frank, and Kathleen Loock. "Hollywood Remaking as Second-Order Serialization." *Media of Serial Narrative.* Edited by Frank Kelleter. Ohio State UP, 2017, pp. 125–47.

Meikle, Kyle. "Rematerializing Adaptation Theory." *Literature/Film Quarterly*, vol. 41, no. 3 (2013), pp. 174–83.

Miller, Frank, and David Mazzucchelli, with Richmond Lewis. *Batman: Year One.* DC Comics, 2007.

Murray, Simone. *The Adaptation Industry: The Cultural Economy of Contemporary Literary Adaptation.* Routledge, 2012.

Parody, Clare. "Franchising/Adaptation." *Adaptation*, vol. 4, no. 2 (Sept. 2011), pp. 210–18.

Ray, Robert B. "The Field of 'Literature and Film.'" *Film Adaptation.* Edited by James Naremore. Rutgers UP, 2000, pp. 38–53.

Ridgely, Charlie. "Zack Snyder Explains Why DC Movies Can't Be Like Marvel Movies." *ComicBook*, Dec. 24, 2020, https://comicbook.com/movies/news/zack-snyder-dc-movies-vs-marvel-movies/.

Ryan, Mike. "Why Marvel Movies Continue to Succeed and DC Just Can't Seem to Get It Right." *Uproxx*, Apr. 30, 2015, https://uproxx.com/movies/marvel-movies-dc-movies-avengers-age-of-ultron/.

Shaps, Simon. "The Golden Age of Adaptation." *Royal Television Society*, Aug. 29, 2018, https://rts.org.uk/article/golden-age-adaptation.

Stam, Robert. "Beyond Fidelity: The Dialogics of Adaptation." *Film Adaptation.* Edited by James Naremore. Rutgers UP, 2000, pp. 54–76.

Verevis, Constantine. *Film Remakes.* Edinburgh UP, 2005.

Wells-Lassagne, Shannon. *Television and Serial Adaptation.* Routledge, 2017.

4 Biological engagements
Adaptation as evolution

The evolution of adaptation

In some ways, a biological engagement with adaptation may seem the most obvious approach of all, since the analogy between textual and biological adaptation is built into the very term "adaptation" as it is most often used these days. And indeed, any number of scholars have imported concepts from Charles Darwin's *On the Origin of Species* (1859) in their attempts to define the nature of aesthetic pleasure, critical theory, and textual evolution. Joseph Carroll has identified four general principles behind his understanding of literature. First, "the relation between organism and environment is a matrix concept" that logically precedes "all social, psychological, and semiotic principles." Second, "the human mind is organized through innate psychological structures ... that have evolved through an adaptive process of natural selection." Third, "inclusive fitness is the ultimate principle that has governed evolutionary adaptations." Fourth, "literature is a form of cognitive mapping" (Carroll, *Literary* 152). Taking exception to psychologist Steven Pinker's view that "[k]nowledge might be adapted, but the pleasure afforded by art ... is merely a nonadaptive exploitation of adaptive sources of pleasures," he describes "art, music, and literature" as "important means by which we cultivate and regulate the complex cognitive machinery on which our more highly developed functions depend" (Carroll, *Literary* 64, 65; see Pinker 524). Carroll's conviction that the pleasures of art play formative roles in human development and survival leads him to conclude that "the principles of organization within specific literary works or within literary history cannot conflict with the larger principles of evolution" (Carroll, *Evolution* 461–62).

Pushing this argument further, David Sloan Wilson argues that "the human mind is constructed to think in terms of stories" (Wilson xxiv). Surprisingly, however, few scholars adopting an evolutionary perspective on literature have shown much interest in literary adaptations themselves. As its title suggests, Brian Boyd's monograph *On the Origin of Stories: Evolution, Cognition, and Fiction* (2010) uses biological adaptation as a metaphor for

DOI: 10.4324/9781003438410-5

the cultural production and transformation of all texts. Calling art "a specifically human adaptation, biologically part of our species," Boyd suggests that "it is from play, widespread across the animal world, that ... art evolved in humans" as a specifically human manifestation of the impulse to play common to many species (Boyd, *On the Origin* 1, 4). Defining "adaptation" as "any trait modified by natural selection that enhances fitness, the capacity to survive and produce viable offspring" (34), Boyd cites biologist Richard Dawkins, who calls Darwin's account of evolution "*not* a theory of random chance. It is a theory of random mutation *plus* non-random natural selection" (Boyd, *On the Origin* 34, 33; see Dawkins, *Selfish* 66). So for Boyd, "[t]he key elements of adaptation are *design* for some *function*" (Boyd, *On the Origin* 37). Art is designed for a specific function essential to the human community: "We come into this world prepared especially to learn from and share with each other—and that ... offers a powerful start for art" (*On the Origin* 40).

Boyd borrows four questions the field of evolutionary psychology poses for any behavior that he seeks to apply to cultural adaptation:

> [W]hy? (fitness: what is its ultimate function?); *how?* (mechanism: how does it operate, what stimuli cause it to occur?); *whence?* (phylogeny: what are its evolutionary predecessors, what did it evolve from?); and *when?* (ontogeny: when does the adaptation develop and change in the individual?).
>
> (Boyd, *On the Origin* 41)

But the principal texts he analyzes–Homer's *Odyssey* and Dr. Seuss's *Horton Hears a Who* (1954)—are not adaptations themselves, and he is more interested in the varied adventures of their reception than in particular adaptations that have been based on them. Neither *On the Origin of Stories* nor *Evolution, Literature, and Film: A Reader*, the collection of essays Boyd coedited with Joseph Carroll and Jonathan Gottschall that same year, discusses what Linda Hutcheon calls "adaptation proper" (Hutcheon 171).

Like the many general discussions of literature and film, or of music and painting, that preceded the recent explosion of work in adaptation studies, these discussions of the evolutionary nature of literature might be considered prologues to analyses of textual adaptation itself as an evolutionary process. Boyd adopts this way of talking about adaptations within a larger evolutionary context in "Making Adaptation Studies Adaptive" (2017), which uses a pair of playfully self-reflexive texts—Vladimir Nabokov's novel *Ada* (1969) and Spike Jonze's film *Adaptation.* (2002)—to illustrate the ways in which "[a]daptation looks two ways, toward retention or fidelity and toward innovation or fertility" (Boyd, "Making" 595–96). In the meantime, Linda Hutcheon partnered with her brother, the late biologist Gary R. Bortolotti, to produce a more sharply focused essay examining the relation between biological adaptation and what Boyd calls "artistic adaptation."

Drawing on Dawkins's influential analogy between "cultural and gen-etic evolution" (Dawkins, *Selfish* 204), Bortolotti and Hutcheon propose "a homology—not an analogy, not a metaphoric association … between biological and cultural adaptation," both marked by "a similarity in struc-ture that is indicative of a common origin: that is, both kinds of adaptation are understandable as processes of replication" (Bortolotti and Hutcheon 444). Defining "adaptation" as "descent with modification" (Bortolotti and Hutcheon 444), they consider successful adaptations those that display the strengths Dawkins had ascribed to the most successful memes: "longevity, fecundity, and copying-fidelity" (Dawkins, *Selfish* 208). They see narratives, like genes, as the "replicators" that transmit this information through adaptive mutations as they work to ensure what Darwin had called the sur-vival of the fittest. Using an analogy from the history of biological study, Bortolotti and Hutcheon make a point of distinguishing these narratives or stories from the specific adaptations that embody and transmit them:

> There is a popular misconception in the lay understanding of biology today (and, in fact, this is what plagued early evolutionary biology) of *whose* survival adaptations are for. They are to ensure *not* the survival of the group or the individual organisms, but instead the "relevant replicators themselves."
> (Bortolotti and Hutcheon 447; see Dawkins, *Extended* 84)

Just as "[o]rganisms act as vehicles for genes," adaptations "are the vehicles of narrative ideas" whose survival and "thriving" (Bortolotti and Hutcheon 447, 450) they work to ensure. The study of "memetics" that followed Dawkins's lead defined successful cultural mutations in terms of "numbers of copies," which reflected "how many people were aware of a narrative" (Bortolotti and Hutcheon 450). To the numbers of copies that indicate a given adaptation's success—which they distinguish specifically from its fidelity to the texts it adapts and "artistic evaluation" generally—they add two other factors: "persistence," which "involves evaluation over the long term"; and "diversity" in being "adapted into many different media" or cultures because it "reduces the probability of chance or other events causing the demise of the narrative" (Bortolotti and Hutcheon 454, 450, 451).

The "phylogenetic," or evolutionary, model of adaptation these commentators share is marked by several limitations. One, which Bortolotti and Hutcheon acknowledge, is the difference between the random mutations Darwin proposed as driving biological adaption and the intentional changes that drive cultural adaptation. The fact that "adaptations influence cul-ture and culture influences the nature of adaptations" seriously complicates questions of agency and causality in cultural adaptation, in which "it is people who change stories and do so with particular intentions" (Bortolotti and Hutcheon 453). Another, which they do not, is their model's bias toward adaptations descending in linear fashion from canonical works. This bias, which makes the model much more suitable for analyzing Virgil's *Aeneid* (19 B.C.E.) as an attempt to refashion Homer's *Iliad* and *Odyssey* as a Roman epic than Joyce's *Ulysses* (1922) as a radically hybrid epic that mixes the features it borrows from Homer with references to hundreds of other texts, carries distinctly hierarchical overtones indicated by the ways in which Boyd uses the word "normal"—for instance, in his remark that "in our own species the impulse to art develops reliably in all normal individuals" (Boyd, *On the Origin* 7). Prizing the survival of the fittest might be taken as authorizing a cultural equivalent of the racist eugenics that sought to identify and exterminate culturally inferior material from the gene pool. And reserving art to human creators endorses the binary between nature and culture that labeling art as a natural activity seems to undermine.

Questions

- In what ways are cultural adaptations most like biological adaptations, and in what ways are they most different?
- Is cultural adaptation better described as an analogy or a homology of biological adaptation?
- If cultural adaptations, like biological adaptations, are designed to ensure the survival of the fittest, what exactly is it that survives—the individual text under adaptation, the story that text tells, the ideas behind the text and story, the community that shares the story and its adaptation, or something else?
- Would defining adaptations in terms of networks or rhizomes challenge the hierarchy behind the family-tree approach Boyd shares with Bortolotti and Hutcheon?

The problems of *Adaptation*

These problems spring to life in *Adaptation.*, which Boyd, like Bortolotti and Hutcheon, cites as an inspiration, an exemplary adaptation, and an illuminating commentary on adaptation. From its opening monologue, in which screenwriter Charlie Kaufman (Nicolas Cage) frets over a black screen about how he really ought to change, Spike Jonze's dizzyingly witty film-about-a-film makes adaptation seem both quintessentially normal and deeply disruptive. Readings of the film, which has unsurprisingly prompted many reactions from adaptation scholars, usually take off from a contrast between two kinds of adaptations. One is the normal-seeming adaptation of Susan Orlean's 1998 nonfiction book *The Orchid Thief* that Charlie hopes to write: an adaptation that is "true to the book," an adaptation that "just *happens*, rather than being plot-driven," like the unreflective process by which insects pollinate flowers that look like them, continuing the life of insects and plants alike. The other kind of adaptation is the kind that Charlie's twin brother Donald Kaufman (also played by Cage) ends up producing: the kind with sex, drugs, and car chases. Donald's preposterous adaptation of Susan's book is more normal than the apparently normal adaptation the blocked Charlie dreams of but can't write in at least three ways. It is highly compatible with the description movie executive Valerie Thomas (Tilda Swinton) proposes to Charlie: "We thought she [Susan] might fall in love." It's an adaptation of a sort students of Hollywood are extremely familiar with. And it's the adaptation Jonze's film actually turns out to be in the end.

Figure 4.1 As Charlie Kaufman (Nicolas Cage), right, struggles to come to terms with Susan Orlean's book *The Orchid Thief,* his brother Donald (Cage), left, relaxes by taking in the lessons of Robert McKee's screenwriting manual *Story*

It might seem that the reason Charlie has such a hard time with adaptation is that he is trying to adapt someone else's material. As he tells his agent, Marty Bowen (Ron Livingston): "I can't adapt this. I should've stuck to my own stuff." The joke here, however, is that sticking to his "own stuff" would not have helped him because Charlie finds it just as impossible to adapt himself. Nor is that entirely surprising because, as the film makes clear, self-adaptation, which may seem perfectly normal, is even more problematic than adapting someone else's stuff because successful self-adaptations end with the disappearance or displacement of the pre-adapted self. As Bortolotti and Hutcheon contend, evolution is designed to ensure the survival of the replicator they compare to "a core narrative idea" (Bortolotti and Hutcheon 447), not the survival of the individual or the group that embodies or transmits that idea. Or, to put it another way, once a biological species has successfully mutated to a species better able to survive, the original species vanishes. This is perhaps the most distinctive departure of cultural or textual adaptation, which creates supplemental copies of the texts it adapts, from biological adaptation, which creates replacement copies of the organisms that transmit their genetic material. That is why Susan (Meryl Streep) tells orchid hunter John Laroche (Chris Cooper), "Adaptation is shameful. It's like running away," and that is why she mourns his death with her last line in the film: "I want my life back. I want it before it was all fucked up."

As Charlie lies in bed awake, he imagines Susan first making love to him, then addressing his writer's block and his fear of letting her down by telling him: "Just whittle it down. Find one thing that you're passionate about, and then write about that." But even passion, which you might think would be the most natural experience in the world, is a problem for the movie's Susan, who lies awake herself troubled by her deepest unfulfilled desire: to know what it's like to feel as passionate about anything as Laroche feels about orchids. Ironically, the scene immediately following this one makes it clear that Laroche's passion for orchids has simply replaced a series of earlier, equally arbitrary passions: tropical fish (his first love), turtles, fossils, and resilvering antique mirrors. In the end, the movie makes it seem that every passion—whether it is Charlie's passion for creating the perfect adaptation, Laroche's passion for orchids, or Susan's passion for passion itself—is just one more transaction, one more mutation, in a life that is inevitably full of passions that are incomplete, unfulfilled, or not all that passionate.

Perhaps the most radical question the movie raises is one so far outside its story that its commentators have generally overlooked it: why did Charlie Kaufman, the real-life screenwriter of *Adaptation.*, introduce his fictitious brother Donald as a foil for his own fictionalized persona in the first place? What does Donald bring to the project that wouldn't be there otherwise? What problems does he solve or dramatize? It is obvious that Donald's facility contrasts with Charlie's writer's block, but that writer's block has already been established in the opening five minutes of the film. Nor does the movie need Donald to introduce its self-reflexive meta-reflections on the problems of adaptation, since Charlie is obsessed with worrying about them before Donald ever turns up. As the story unfolds, it becomes clear that Charlie and Donald are meant to dramatize fundamentally different approaches to adaptation. For Charlie, adaptation is a necessary evil, a harmful transformation of a book he loves and wants to preserve. For Donald, adaptation is a transaction, a job he's eager to take on, and the book is so much raw material. Charlie is passionate, but his passion makes it impossible for him to adapt himself or anything else. Donald is dispassionate, like a hired gunslinger, so he is able to keep adapting himself and thinking about adapting everything else in ways that shock and horrify Charlie.

Charlie's checkered journey along the road to adapting Susan's book is directed by several competing forces: his heartfelt desire to "show people how amazing flowers are"; his wonder at the mysteries of biological evolution; the serious case of writer's block he develops in response; the professional pressures of his job; his growing intimacy with the author; his rivalry with his ruthlessly transactional brother; and his climactic adventures, which are at once wildly unrealistic and eminently predictable by movie-trained audiences. All these forces combine with his closing determination to memorialize the brother who was killed during those climactic adventures. In the end, the adaptation-in-progress that unspools in the film's final shots seems to flow out of him as effortlessly as the natural adaptations that so impressed him earlier that they left him paralyzed and unable to write. But the apparent ease and naturalness of this last adaptation are anything but natural and easy. They are products of the peculiar problems posed by Susan's book, which is not exactly obvious material for adaptation; of Charlie's tortured and traumatized psyche; of the challenges to his vocation embodied by his more commercially minded brother; and of the desires of audiences and the imperatives of popular entertainment. If the adaptation that survives the conflicts among all these forces is indeed the fittest, its fitness is defined by very specific psychological, cultural, and commercial mandates.

Questions

- In what ways does *Adaptation.* operate as an adaptation of Susan Orlean's book *The Orchid Thief*?
- How successful is the film as an adaptation of the book?
- On what terms does it succeed, and on what terms does it fail?
- What does its success or failure suggest about successful adaptations, and the process of cultural adaptation in general?
- Which adaptive product, Charlie's or Donald's, seems more natural?
- Which adaptive process, Charlie's or Donald's, seems more natural?

Who's in charge here?

Scholars who have adopted biological approaches to adaptation have without exception taken their cue from Charles Darwin, whose leading contribution to the debate over biological adaptation is the proposition that the mutations that lead individual species to evolve over time are random, not planned or ordered by a divine providence, and the consequent implication that the course of the evolution of individual species and biological history generally is governed by the ability of individual mutations to adapt to a changing world. Hence Darwin's celebrated phrase "the survival of the fittest" refers not so much to a competition between individual species marked as predators and prey as to a competition between individual mutations within a given species for survival and replication. Despite their invocation of Darwin, most adaptation scholars continue to regard textual adaptation, by contrast, as a purpose-driven activity directed by human agents: creators, publishers, commentators, audiences—a model that effectively restores the divine forces Darwin had specifically sought to banish by speaking of texts not as *adapting*, but as *being adapted by* someone for some purpose and in effect returning to earlier theorists of biological adaptation like Jean-Baptiste Lamarck, whose purpose-driven model of adaptation Darwin had specifically contested.

Whose model, Darwin's or Lamarck's, is more useful in adaptation studies? Although Darwin is invoked far more often by adaptation scholars exploring the analogies between biological and textual adaptation, Lamarck may provide a more precise analogy to scholars' own practice, since most of them assume that adaptations are shaped and brought to birth by human creators who stand in for Lamarck's divine presence rather than adapting randomly under their own agency. So it is well worth considering, at least as a hypothetical exercise, the implications of adopting each one of these models. A transitive, Lamarckian model in which people *adapt* texts to new versions, media, and purposes ascribes the power in forming, shaping, and altering all texts, whether or not they are explicitly marked as adaptations, to human creators who exercise absolute power over their creations—at least until they enter a marketplace full of other creators and their creations. This transitive model (A adapts B) is the one most casual observers of adaptation have followed without identifying it as such. A Darwinian approach that removed divine providence from adaptation, by contrast, would produce an intransitive model (B adapts [itself]) that would require fundamental changes in the ways we thought about several crucial aspects of adaptation.

The most obvious of these is "a changing notion of *agency and intention*" (Leitch, "To Adapt" 95). Even if we granted that particular paintings or dramatic performances or musical scores were shaped by the intentions of their creators, it would not follow that "culture itself intends evolutionary changes … Whether the agency and intentionality of culture in general is more like that of nature in general or of particular authors and adapters remains arguable" (Leitch, "To Adapt" 96). Equally important would be "a changing notion of the *process* of adaptation. Under a transitive model, adapters *make* adaptations"; "under an intransitive model, it might be argued that adaptations are both subject and object of the process," but "it seems more reasonable … to conclude that they do not make anything, not even themselves; what they do instead is *change*" (Leitch, "To Adapt" 96). An intransitive model of adaptation would encourage new ways of thinking about "the *motives* for adaptation" (Leitch, "To Adapt" 97). In addition, a "shift from a transitive to an intransitive model of adaptation involves a changing notion of *teleology*" because biological adaptation—oriented toward success in the future, not fidelity to the past—raises the pointed question: "When has a mutating organism reached its definitive form?" (Leitch, "To Adapt" 98, 100). Since an answer to this question borrowed from Darwinian thinking about biological evolution would clearly be "Never," an intransitive model of adaptation invites us to think in new ways about the "*substance and identity*" of both canonical texts, since there is no definitive *Romeo and Juliet*, and "species of adaptations," especially the notion of "what makes a species a species" rather than simply the newest mutation of an existing species (Leitch, "To Adapt" 100, 101). Pursuing this line of reasoning inevitably subordinates "the noun *adaptation* ... to the verb *adapt*" (Leitch, "To Adapt" 102).

Some of these changes are likely to sound familiar. Patrick Cattrysse's Descriptive Adaptation Studies urges a forward-looking perspective on the roles adaptations play in their target cultures, and Robert Stam's dialogical approach to adaptation emphasizes the process of adapting over the products of adaptation. The most important implication of these changes, therefore, is not their novelty but their consistency with Darwinian approaches to adaptation. A truly Darwinian model suggests that texts are not adapted but adapt (themselves), generating numberless mutations, only a few of which will survive and flourish in present and future cultures with limited archives and even more limited attention spans.

Pursuing this approach to its logical conclusion raises still more radical questions about agency, motive, and identity. Taking off from Pier Paolo Pasolini's provocative observation that a screenplay is a "structure that wants to be another structure," (Pasolini 187), we could ask whether texts are capable of the kinds of agency we ordinarily reserve to their creators. Interestingly, we often speak of them as if they were—for example, when readers say that the novel they are reading makes them feel exhilarated or sad, or when authors say that that they had planned for their novel to go a certain way until the characters took over and demanded that it go quite differently. Most commentators, however, have declined to accept the more general implications of these observations. Richard Dawkins—who approvingly cites N.K. Humphries's observation that "when you plant a fertile meme in my mind you literally parasitize my brain, turning it into a vehicle for the meme's propagation"—warns that "we must not think of genes as conscious, purposeful agents" (Dawkins, *Selfish* 207, 210). It may well be true that

> [a]dopting a view of agency that is less anthropomorphic, less centered on individual control and ownership, less driven by a categorical distinction between active and passive roles, would have the salutary effect of decentring human agency in a world whose survival depends more and more clearly on a global rather than a merely human ecology.
>
> (Leitch, "What" 173)

However we ultimately resolve it, the question of whether textual adaptation is transitive or intransitive has far-reaching implications for textual and cultural studies generally, carrying the power to illuminate areas apparently far beyond the boundaries of adaptation studies.

Questions

- Is textual adaptation transitive or intransitive? Do texts adapt themselves, or are they adapted by someone or something else?

- If Boyd's discussion of the nature and motives for storytelling contrasts humans with animals, what other contrasting communities might illuminate the nature and motives for adapting?
- In order for cultural or textual adaptations to be successful, do they have to thrive or merely survive?
- If all textual production is an adaptive behavior, what role does what Hutcheon calls "adaptation proper" have within the domain of adaptive human behaviors?
- Given the obvious etymological relationship between biological adaptation and textual or cultural adaptation, why hasn't a biological model been the dominant one in adaptation studies?
- Given the broad allegiance to aesthetic, intertextual, or industrial theories of adaptation, what features of a biological approach might you urge to encourage its wider adoption? What features might sell it to prospective buyers?
- What does the study of textual or cultural adaptation suggest about biological adaptation?

This is your brain on adaptations

It is unsurprising that many commentators have declined the invitation toward a radical reassessment of adaptations' agency, intention, process, teleology, substance, and identity that biological approaches to adaptation encourage. Perhaps the most thoroughgoing critique of these approaches is that of Tomas Elliott, who takes exception to adaptation studies' embrace of both Dawkins—whose model contains "significant problems" that have been exposed by "theorists from across the disciplines of philosophy, media studies, the history of science, and evolutionary biology itself"—and *Adaptation.*, whose "evolutionary themes (and, indeed, the theory of evolution itself) are not in and of themselves natural," but rather "clearly historicizable, being entangled in a value system coterminous with (post)-industrial capitalism and based primarily on a logic of survival, domination, dissemination, and growth" (T. Elliott 321). Elliott warns that the film's

> account of a protagonist who changes from being a seemingly "unproductive" member of the human species to someone who finds his place in a heteronormalized version of "evolutionary society" represents a fantasy of evolutionary progress that has less to do with any so-called ontological truth about how adaptation functions in nature and more to do with the formal structures of Hollywood narrative and the conventions of the marriage plot.
>
> (T. Elliott 321)

This basis in capitalistic and generic fantasy, he argues, makes the film an unwise choice for biological theories of adaptation that fail "to historicize either the evolutionary narrative that it employs of the wider implications of that narrative for an ecocritical approach to adaptation" (T. Elliott 329).

In his attempt to "unpack what is at stake in using 'biological ideas' to study adaptation in art," Elliott is particularly critical of Dawkins, whose "ideology ... clearly affects both his idea of the meme and the subsequent theories of adaptation that scholars have derived from it" (T. Elliott 321, 322). The scholars he identifies as having swallowed Dawkins's ideology along with his biological metaphor include Bortolotti and Hutcheon, who borrow Dawkins's "insistence on material literalism"; Kamilla Elliott, whose discussion of biological evolution in *Theorizing Adaptation* (2020) reflects the "widespread inclination among adaptation scholars to reach for the discourse of evolutionary biology to explain cultural change" and "to express a desire for the same kind of positivist certainty that is (typically though not always) found in the natural sciences"; and Brian Boyd, whose presentation of "adaptation as a fertile, fecund, or primarily generative process" overlooks the gendered labor childbirth requires of women, "risk[s] obscuring the material imbalances of fertility and reproduction across both nature and art," and broadly implies that "art is never anything more or less than the most efficient tool for survival within a hostile biocultural marketplace" (T. Elliott 323, 324, 328). In place of these uncritical adoptions of biological concepts and terminology from Dawkins, Spike Jonze, and Charlie Kaufman, he recommends

> a more promising ecological or biological approach to adaptation studies [that] would involve how cultural adaptations like Kaufman and Jonze's film can mobilize certain biological metaphors, narratives, and story arcs to naturally historically circumscribed forms of cultural and sexual (re-)production (such as, e.g., those that are associated with fertility, growth, dissemination, and more). By unpacking these naturalizations, rather than borrowing them for a biologically inflected poetics that views adaptations in terms of their ability to succeed, survive, and thrive, adaptation theorists might be able to challenge some of the expansionist and heteronormative logic that seems to underlie several evolutionary methodologies, a gesture that seems all the more important in our moment of ecological decline.
>
> (T. Elliott 333)

An obvious way to respond to Elliott's critique would be for adaptation studies to reflect more critically on Darwinian (or Lamarckian) theories of evolution instead of simply borrowing and repurposing them—for example, by recognizing, along with Joseph Carroll, that

> [t]he development of modern genetics is not preconstituted by Darwin's theory of natural selection, but it joins the whole complex network of interlocking disciplines that mutually support each other and that together

provide an ever-increasing density of confirmation for the theory of natural selection.

(Carroll, *Evolution* 465)

In "The Adaptation of Adaptation: A Dialogue Between the Arts and
Sciences," Kamilla Elliott has proposed "a dialogue between genetic theories
of adaptation in the sciences, social sciences, and humanities" that recognizes
their interdependence and adaptation studies' aptness for "helping cultural
studies to survive" (K. Elliott 155, 152). Adaptation scholars, she suggests,
should participate in this ongoing dialogue in the hope of "opening up
new research questions and directions ... through interdisciplinarity, not
to conform them to scientific models" and "evolving to challenge our *own*
prevailing theories and beliefs—leading the way instead of following either
scientific or social scientific theories or clinging to our own decades-old theories" (K. Elliott 158, 159).

Another way to respond to Tomas Elliott's critique is to consider adaptation in frankly scientific terms, as a phenomenon that can fruitfully be
studied through the methods of experimental science. Instead of simply
advancing theories about the nature of what Kyle Meikle has called "the
adaptation experience" (Meikle, "A Theory"), Dennis Cutchins and several
of his graduate students at Brigham Young University (BYU) conducted a
controlled experiment in 2019 that was designed to compare the different
effects of "order of exposure, medium, and the passage of time" on audiences
who read "Misery," a short story by Anton Chekhov, and then watched
Heartache, a film BYU students Justin Partridge and Anthony Peterson
produced in 2000 based on the story, to the experiences of audiences who
watched the film before reading the story. Dividing their 97 participants into
six groups, the investigators asked Group A to read the story, wait a week,
watch the film, and then answer a series of 22 questions about their memories of the two, focusing on certain key details that were different in the
story and the film. Group B reversed this procedure, first watching the film,
then waiting a week before reading the story and taking the survey. Group
C read the story, watched the film, and took the survey, all within an hour,
and then took the survey again one week later. Group D watched the film,
then read the story, and then took the survey immediately and once again a
week later. Group E read the story, then watched the film, but waited a week
before taking the survey. And Group F watched the film, then read the story,
and took the survey a week later.

The results were more conclusive in some ways than in others. Apart
from the first two groups, which served as controls, all the other groups had
stronger memories of the more recent version they had encountered than the
first version. But "neither primacy nor recency is the only influence in these
datasets," and the reasons why are not clear. Cutchins is confident of one
conclusion—that "regardless of any *absolute* notion of originality, the *perception* of originality does impact the way subjects remember and respond

to adaptations"—and expresses another more tentatively: "[E]xperiencing the two texts within minutes of each other encouraged the formation of a new, single, gestalt-like memory ... created from some combination of the two texts" (Cutchins, "An Exploratory" 23, 25). For better or worse, he notes, "[n]one of the factors we tried to isolate—order of exposure, medium, or time—seem to operate independently. Indeed, all of these factors (as well as a few unpredicted others) seem to operate *inter*dependently in a multi-dimensional give-and-take" (Cutchins, "An Exploratory" 27). Finally, "primacy and recency do not seem to be opposed, as we originally assumed. Rather, they operate simultaneously" (Cutchins, "An Exploratory" 27). For all these reasons, Cutchins urges further experiments that attempt to measure different audiences' experiences of adaptations.

Questions

- How persuasive, and how useful, do you find the results of Cutchins's experiment to determine which versions of stories audiences remember the best?
- What other experiments can you imagine that would provide scientific evidence about how people experience adaptations?
- What other experiments can you imagine that would provide scientific evidence about how people create adaptations?

From corpse to corpus: adapting bodies

In addition to exploring the effects of experiencing adaptations on audiences' brains, scholars have examined the biological implications of the variously adaptive physical transformations embodied or implied by a wide range of texts in different media. This approach was pioneered by Julie Grossman, whose *Literature, Film, and Their Hideous Progeny: Adaptation and ElasTEXTity* roots its analysis in Mary Shelley's 1818 novel *Frankenstein; or, The Modern Prometheus*. As both her subtitle and her epigraph from Milton's *Paradise Lost* suggest, Shelley's novel is already an updated version of the myth of Prometheus, and it has spawned in turn innumerable adaptations ranging from nineteenth-century plays like Richard Brinsley Peake's 1823 *Presumption; or, The Fate of Frankenstein* to the canonical 1931 Universal horror film and its sequels to hundreds of other movies, radio and television productions, novel sequels, comic books, toys, games, and Halloween costumes.

Despite Shelley's title, which has been largely retained in the countless adaptations of her novel, her central character is not the scientist Victor Frankenstein but the nameless creature he constructs from scavenged parts of corpses, a creature who has often taken the name "Frankenstein" in popular culture. If Frankenstein is the adapter in Shelley's novel, the creature, who remains largely sympathetic in Shelley, is his adaptation whose fearsome appearance, uncivilized behavior, and occasional outbursts of violence cause Frankenstein to regard him as a monster. This notion of adaptation as a monstrous activity is what inspires Grossman, who follows Shelley in labeling the creature Frankenstein brings to life and kindred adaptations as " 'hideous progeny,' 'monsters' birthed with difficulty," who "change not only the *way* we view but also our ideas about *what* we are viewing":

> [A]ny adaptation might be considered "monstrous," that is, isolated from its predecessors because it is born of new concerns, new desires to express ideas in a different medium, with a changed-up narrative reflecting shifting cultural priorities. Because of these altered contexts, adaptations are often born resisting the original desires of their sources. A provoking figure for reanimations of their earlier source texts, "monstrous" describes the shocking violation of original and organically pure matter when adapted or reshaped in new contexts.
>
> (Grossman 1, 2)

Grossman coins the term "elastextity" to describe "the state of being for sources and adaptations that are indivisibly connected" and "a way of thinking about texts as extended beyond themselves, merging their identities with other works of art that follow and precede them" (Grossman 2). This merging of identities may sound abstract, but what makes adaptation monstrous for Grossman is its creation of what initially seem like grossly distorted bodies—in the case of *Frankenstein*, bodies based on literal bodies—capable of provoking physical revulsion.

Grossman's novel approach is firmly rooted in earlier scholarship. Her emphasis on bodily responses echoes and develops Robert Stam's observation that films

> are more directly implicated in bodily response than novels. They are felt upon the pulse, whether through the in-your-face gigantism of close-ups (which shocked Griffith's contemporaries), the visual impact of "flicker effects," or the vertiginous effect of Cinerama-style roller-coaster sequences, or the bodily register of jiggly, hand-held camera movements or "thrill cam" plunges.
>
> (Stam, "Introduction" 6)

And Grossman's emphasis on the monstrous nature of adaptations harks back to Mikhail Bakhtin's concept of the grotesque, which he saw as a foundational property of adaptation. As Dennis Cutchins observes:

> Stam explores Bakhtin's concept of the grotesque body in *Subversive Pleasures*, and his explanations are useful, but they remain fixed in a rather literal understanding of the term ... Bakhtin's notion of the grotesque, more broadly applicable and more metaphorical, suggests why we

perceive some texts as adaptations more readily, and why some texts seem to invite adaptation more often than others.

(Cutchins, "Bakhtin" 81–82; see Stam, *Subversive* 159–60).

Every adaptation of Shelley's novel raises inescapable questions about who is doing the adapting, who or what is the adapted creature within the text, what makes the creature monstrous, and how the adapter's positioning changes our understanding of *Frankenstein* and of adaptation generally. Shelley's sympathetic portrayal of the creature—which makes it clear that his monstrosity is physically and socially constructed by people whose characterization of him he is powerless to control—has been followed by many other film adaptations, from *The Bride of Frankenstein* (1935) to *Young Frankenstein* (1974), that make him sympathetic and often pitiable. These questions are given poignant contemporary relevance by an adaptation that takes an unexpected form: Susan Stryker's "My Words to Victor Frankenstein Above the Village of Chamounix: Performing Transgender Rage," a textual adaptation of a performance piece first staged in "genderfuck drag" (Stryker 237). The text—operating at once as a critical reading of *Frankenstein*, a rage-filled autobiography, a political manifesto in favor of transsexual adaptation, and a self-performance of gender identity and gender deconstruction—begins by announcing:

> The transsexual body is an unnatural body. It is the product of medical science. It is a technological construction. It is flesh torn apart and sewn together again in a shape other than that in which it was born. In these circumstances, I find a deep affinity between myself as a transsexual woman and the monster in Mary Shelley's Frankenstein. Like the monster, I am too often perceived as less than fully human due to the means of my embodiment; like the monster's as well, my exclusion from human community fuels a deep and abiding rage in me that I, like the monster, direct against the conditions in which I must struggle to exist.
>
> (Stryker 238)

Recalling the case of Filisa Vistima—a pre-operative transsexual woman who took her own life at 22 soon after "the Seattle Bisexual Woman's Network announced that if it admitted transsexuals the SBWN would no longer be a woman's organization"—and writing in her journal, "I wish I was anatomically 'normal' so I could go swimming ... But no, I'm a mutant, Frankenstein's monster," Stryker asks, "Did Filisa Vistima commit suicide, or did the queer community of Seattle kill her?" and urges her audience: "[W]ords like 'creature,' 'monster,' and 'unnatural' need to be reclaimed by the transgendered" (Stryker 240, 239, 240). Following Peter Brooks's suggestion that "whatever else a monster might be, it 'may also be that which eludes gender definition,'" she argues that Shelley's story raises inescapable questions about the limits of human agency in determining identity—"rather than demonstrate

Frankenstein's power over materiality, the newly enlivened body of the creature attests to its maker's failure to attain the mastery he sought"—and adds: "Transsexual embodiment, like the embodiment of the monster, places its subject in an unassimilable, antagonistic, queer relationship to a Nature in which it must nevertheless exist" (Stryker 241, 242, 242–43; see Brooks 219).

By borrowing and capitalizing on the figure of Frankenstein's abjected monster uplifted and galvanized by rage, Stryker seeks to transform and empower herself as monstrous rather than being fashioned as a monster by someone else—a quest that complicates the relations between transitive and intransitive models of adaptation, which Stryker sees as no more mutually exclusive than the categories male and female. This relation is further complicated by another surprising *Frankenstein* adaptation: Tyler the Creator's 2019 album *Igor*. Tyler the Creator—born Tyler Gregory Okonma—is a rapper, record producer, singer-songwriter, and co-founder of Odd Future, an online music collective and performance group. His earlier music is often sexist, homophobic, and violent. But when *Igor* was named Best Rap Album at the 2020 Grammy Awards, many members of his audience realized for the first time that Okonma is bisexual. Although he had been out for some time, the album's narrative, which follows the adventures of Igor, a closeted bisexual Black man as he navigates a love triangle, suddenly turned Okonma's identity into headline news.

In the course of *Igor*'s dozen songs, supplemented by "Boyfriend," a thirteenth song added to the cycle a year after its release, Tyler sings, "I think I've fallen in love. This time I think it's for real" (in "I Think"); wonders, "Are you livin' in pretend" (in "Running Out of Time"); demands total commitment from his new love ("I want a hundred of your time, you're mine"); and threatens to kill his former partner ("She's gonna be dead, I just got a magic wand," both in "New Magic Wand"). More pointedly, he wonders what the nature of his new relationship is and how it affects his own identity ("I am Santa, where is Rudolph? You're parasitic, I do not have self-control," in "Puppet"), before deciding to break off the relationship ("Thank you for the love, thank you for the joy, But I don't wanna fall in love again," in "Gone, Gone/Thank You"). After "I Don't Love You Anymore"—sung in the strained, high-pitched voice Tyler had used for "Boyfriend"—he admits, in the last line of the final song, "Are We Still Friends?" that he "can't say goodbye, goodbye," presumably because he cannot detach his own identity from his lover's.

Tyler's performance of Igor and Okonma's performance of Tyler raise a wide range of new questions. Is there a creature within the 13 songs of *Igor*? Is this creature Igor—and if so, why does Tyler choose the name of Frankenstein's assistant in the Universal films rather than identifying with Frankenstein's creature? Or is the album itself the creature, stitched transgressively together by Tyler as Frankenstein? Has the bisexual monster Igor been self-created, or has he been created by Tyler or someone else? Is it appropriate to equate Igor with Tyler the Creator, or Tyler with Okonma, or should distinctions between them be upheld? Does Okonma seek to emphasize or minimize these distinctions? If the authenticity of the album's songs depends on Tyler's lived experience, what does it mean for a performance to be authentic or inauthentic? And if assuming the persona of Igor allows Okonma to performer Tyler as a bisexual Black man, what makes those qualities the most important ones to perform?

Pamela Demory suggests that we might approach questions like these by considering any "adaptation—particularly a stage adaptation—a kind of drag" whose "[p]erformers use costume, makeup, wigs, and mannerisms to perform identities that may or may not align with their own gender expression" (Demory, "Queer Adaptation" 154). In her Introduction to *Queer/ Adaptation* (2019), Demory follows other scholars in broadening the notion of "queer" beyond homosexual, bisexual, transsexual, or gender-nonconforming. She cites Harry M. Benshoff's suggestion that queering "disrupts narrative equilibrium and sets in motion a questioning of the status quo" (Demory, "Queer/Adaptation" 2; see Benshoff 5)—a program that offers obvious parallels to the decentering possibilities of adaptation. The dozen essays Demory collects in *Queer/Adaptation* take three overlapping but distinct approaches to the intersections between adapting and queering, which Demory calls "parallel theoretical constructs that can both orient or think about a given text or texts" (Demory, "Queer/Adaptation" 1). Some of Demory's contributors seek to unmask specific adaptations as queer by outing them or analyzing their queerness. Others explore the ways queer adaptations depart from the norms of what might be called "straight adaptations" and offer new ways of thinking about adaptation in order to propose new theories about queering and adapting. Still others argue that the act of adaptation as both a productive and a receptive process is inseparable from queering, so that all adaptations are queer, just as all queer behavior is adaptive, in order to out adaptation itself. To adapt J. Hillis Miller's well-known remark that "[d]econstruction is not the dismantling of the structure of a text but a demonstration that it has already dismantled itself" (Miller 341), queering a given adaptation, or adaptation generally, demonstrates that the adaptation has already queered itself with respect to both the text it has adapted and the expectations its audience has brought to it.

In *Embodying Adaptation: Character and the Body*, Christina Wilkins broadens the arguments about performance left implicit in Frankenstein's monster and Tyler the Creator and made explicit in Demory by arguing that

> the adapted body is a way to understand our place in the world, and that considering the hierarchical relationship between actor and character, and possibly reconfiguring that [relationship], raises useful parallels with the field of adaptation—namely what seems to be "original" or "true" is to be viewed as more valuable.
>
> (Wilkins 6)

Like Demory, Wilkins assigns central importance to performance in understanding both adaptations and bodies, and like Demory, she argues that "the physicality of the body itself is crucial to understanding the nature of adaptation" (Wilkins 6). In Wilkins's view, the physicality of bodies as actors play characters less authentic than they are reveals the way "adaptation implements a hierarchy that is mistaken for something fixed"—an error that may be addressed, for example, by "say[ing] that it is the character that is primary, and rendering the actor's self secondary, a vessel to be used" (Wilkins 71, 75). She raises questions about whether actors playing themselves, like John Malkovich in *Adaptation.* and *Being John Malkovich* (1999), are playing characters to complicate this relation in other ways, noting that even though actors may seem to have priority over characters, "[o]ur encounters with the body are *as* a particular character, which arguably should foreground them over the actor" (Wilkins 78). Given the difficulties in disentangling actors from characters, performances from roles, adaptation from adapted texts, Wilkins proposes the term *charactor*, which can describe "the represented and constructed form a character takes when embodied by an actor and is then subsequently engaged with and received by the audience" (Wilkins 86) without relying on any hierarchies between actor and character.

Questions

- If the Frankenstein story requires a Faustian creator, an abject creature, an isolated setting, and a certain number of obligatory set pieces, how many of these elements could be eliminated without returning the story to its roots as another Promethean myth?
- If another trans performer delivered Susan Stryker's monologue, would it still be about Stryker? Would it be possible for a straight cis performer to do Stryker's monologue justice?
- If someone else produced a cover album of *Igor*, would still be about Tyler the Creator? If so, does it follow that cover albums cannot be authentic, or only that they are meta-performances?
- If it weren't for its title's reference to Frankenstein's assistant, many listeners would probably find it harder to identify *Igor* as an adaptation. Apart from operas, can you identify any musical adaptations that can readily be identified as adaptations by their musical elements alone?
- Do you think of characters as basically written or basically performed?
- Who creates characters—writers, directors, performers, audiences, or someone else?
- Which contexts are most important for creating and understanding characters—star personas, genres, earlier appearances of the character, earlier versions of the story being adapted, or the status of a given character as an adaptation?
- Is character a product of creation, or performance, of perception and interpretation, or of all three?

- When biographers write about real-life people, do they treat them as characters, and do their readers think of these people as characters?

Ecocriticism and ecodaptation

The much-adapted figure of Frankenstein's monster suggests that although many biological adaptations are widely recognized as successful, others are failed, abortive, dangerous, or downright malign. The many mutations of COVID-19—itself a genetic adaptation also called the "novel coronavirus" that has spawned several generations of further adaptations aimed at resisting therapies designed to eliminate the infection—are an obvious example. Although viral mutations are not always dangerous to humans or other animals, these mutations raise the possibility of considering adaptation itself a plague.

This position has often been taken by defenders of traditional art who consider textual and cultural adaptation menacing or harmful. Although Virginia Woolf stops short of calling adaptations of *Anna Karenina* a plague, she condemns their status as derivative and parasitic, their ability to desensitize mass audiences to the subtleties of Tolstoy's novel, and their challenge to traditional aesthetics by the implication that the texts they adapt are themselves a series of performances, not an archive of timeless classics. In fact, ekphrastic studies—the analysis of artworks based on other artworks—arose precisely from the attempt to elevate the representational claims of poetry by comparing it to the older and more established medium of painting.

As *Adaptation.* reminds us, there are some stakeholders in every adaptive transaction who accept and even welcome the new adaptation and others who oppose the adaptation, or maybe any adaptation. Inside and outside adaptation studies, the virtue of adaptability, the ability to generate new adaptations, is routinely set against the virtue of integrity, the ability to remain true to oneself. Moral philosophers and champions of the Western literary canon like E.D. Hirsch and Harold Bloom typically prize integrity over adaptability. Adaptability is prized above integrity in the world of fashion, an industry sustained by implanting the desire for more or less unnecessary wardrobe purchases that aren't motivated by any practical necessity, as in the production number "Think Pink" in the 1957 movie *Funny Face*. Bodybuilders and gym coaches urge their followers to change themselves until they reach their ideal specs, then urge them to avoid changing by maintaining their target weight and muscular ability through a routine that demands strict attention to their diet and physical activity.

Does maintaining your fitness once you have reached your goals require adaptation or integrity? The fact that this question is hard to answer indicates the tricky relationship between these two values, which can be surprisingly close. The same homeowners who use their heating and air-conditioning systems to maintain a consistent temperature usually have a more ambivalent attitude toward feeding and watering their lawn, since they want to encourage the grass to grow every year, but they still weed and mow the lawn in order to maintain a highly unnatural monoculture. More to the point, adaptability is preached by Hollywood agents and dealmakers who live off new movies, and by writing teachers working to help their students adapt models like the five-paragraph essay to their own expressive or argumentative uses.

One of the foundational debates in contemporary adaptation studies is between the champions of integrity, who frown on adaptations generally and prefer them faithful, and the champions of adaptability, who want to do whatever they can to make a thousand flowers bloom. Different positions in this debate can readily be traced to different stakeholders in the adaptation community. Since the rise of copyright law, authors have usually been pleased when their novels, plays and stories are adapted for television, film or theater—even if they like to retain tight control over them, as J.K. Rowling has done, or if they disapprove of specific adaptations, as Daphne du Maurier did of the 1939 film *Jamaica Inn*. And authors who don't want to be adapted—like J.D. Salinger, Sara Paretsky, and Thomas Pynchon—can easily take measures to avoid it. Screenwriters and filmmakers of every sort prefer to be able to adapt established properties instead of being obliged to invent their own. Fans eagerly await the latest iterations of Spider-Man, *Emma* (1815), or *Lord of the Rings* (1954–55), even if they end up trashing specific adaptations online. Adaptation scholars, once united in denigrating adaptations as derivative, have softened this stance, as Bluestone did, or reversed it, as Bortolotti and Hutcheon do.

The stakeholders most likely to be scandalized by particular adaptations or adaptation generally are academics—especially literature teachers—who don't happen to be adaptation scholars, and movie reviewers who aren't academics. Academics, of course, are famous defenders of canons because their livelihood depends on maintaining them, and reviewers are always eager to demonstrate that they are superior to the material they review. But it doesn't follow that we should prize adaptability over integrity—only that in assessing particular adaptations, and adaptation in general, we should consider which cohorts we represent, how our views compare to our cohorts' interests, and what arguments can reasonably be advanced against them.

Adaptation scholars themselves continue to debate the wisdom of approaching adaptation as a biological process or through biological homologies. Tomas Elliott warns that biological evolution is hierarchical and heteronormative, and that it prioritizes what Bortolotti and Hutcheon have called "success" in ways textual and cultural adaptation do not. Nor are these debates limited to adaptation scholars. For better or worse, biologists themselves do not agree about some of the fundamental principles of biological evolution. Science reporter Carl Zimmer has noted that "biologists cannot agree on what a species is. A 2021 survey found that practicing biologists used 16 different approaches to categorizing species" (Zimmer D1; see also Stankowski and Ravinet). The question of what counts as a species—that is, which characteristics have led which groups of plants and animals to develop in measurably different directions—has become far more urgent in what scientists have called the "Anthropocene Era": the historical period during which human technologies and social activities have had a measurable effect on our planet's biosystem. Instead of asking, "What is it that survives?", scientists have increasingly been asking, "What is it that we most want to survive?" and "Who gets to decide what counts as success?"

These questions have provided a foundation for the emerging field of ecocriticism: the study of the ways literary texts represent the natural world. The term, which first appeared in William Rueckert's 1978 essay "Literature and Ecology: An Experiment in Ecocriticism," has since expanded to include non-literary texts like paintings, songs, comics, movies, and television programs, and sharpened to focus on the role of human agency in shaping the future of the ecosphere—the natural environment that only begins, or ends, with human beings. Alexa Weik von Mossner speaks for many commentators when she defines "environmental narratives" as "any type of narrative in any media that foregrounds ecological issues and human-nature relationships, often but always with the openly stated intention of bringing about human change" (von Mossner 3).

Kyle Meikle—whose examination of the screenplays Ishmael Reed had based on his novels *The Free-Lance Pallbearers* (1967) and *Yellow Back Radio Broke-Down* (1969) led him to conclude that "[i]n a networked model of adaptation, projects do not die—they drift to Kickstarter" (Meikle, "Towards" 266)—has proposed a program of "reorienting adaptation studies to the present moment" of ecological crisis through three "policy recommendations":

1. The study of adaptation needs to be joined with the study of political ecology in the age of climate change ...
2. The study of adaptation needs to be joined with the study of climate change in contemporary media studies ...
3. The study of adaptation needs to be joined with the study of sustainable design.
   (Meikle, "Is Adaptation Studies Sustainable?" 265, 267, 269)

Following Meikle, Robert Geal has called for an ecocritical adaptation studies that situates human agency and the wellbeing of individual humans and communities in a broader environmental context and added several more specific recommendations to Meikle's program. He urges complementing ecocriticism's focus on texts like Rachel Carson's *Silent Spring* that "have the potential to challenge ecologically harmful ways of thinking" by "analysing how adapted texts communicate negative attitudes towards the environment" through "ecophobia" (Geal 5). He suggests:

Adaptation studies can ... help address the fundamental ecocritical question—what is it about our culture(s) which cause(s) us to endanger our own survival by treating the biosphere with such contempt?—by outlining how human attitudes towards the environment, and cultural expressions of these attitudes in the form of various kinds of texts, are adapted through time, across cultures, between texts, and so on.

(Geal 6)

He goes on to observe:

[I]n addition to a broader analysis of the different ways that, say, Biblical narratives, Ancient Greek myths, Renaissance paintings, and Romantic poems represent rural locations and human experiences within these locations, adaptation studies can draw out the historically and culturally specific development of more particular threads which inform and support those broader contexts ... [enabling more specific theories] about how and why certain intertextual components replicate, proliferate, recur, mutate, and so on.

(Geal 7, 8)

In short:

[I]f any field can analyse how specific components of memes like Hesiodic and Biblical nostalgia for a lost Eden mutate through time and across cultures as they appear in media as diverse as myth, literature, biography, painting, sculpture, print media, theatre, film, television, music, video games, and beyond, then that field is adaptation studies.

(Geal 8)

Agreeing with Geal that "the ecological crisis and the climate crisis are not topics are restricted to investigations in the natural sciences or that solutions to the crisis can be reduced to technological solutions" (Bruhn and Salmose 35), Jørgen Bruhn and Niklas Salmose expose another aspect of the relations between adaptation and ecocriticism in *Intermedial Ecocriticism* (2023) by focusing on the ways information and recommendations about the ecosphere are disseminated through different media. Because these media inevitably inflect the information they communicate, "the data from scientific investigations must be considered impure, or, rather, mediated"—whether the media in question are "poetry, science fiction novels, feature films, and art exhibitions" or "[n]ewspapers, political science journals, and documentaries" (Bruhn and Salmose 8, 9). "[T]o obtain experience from media products," they observe, "we must somehow be able to trust the people or institutions involved in their production, and therefore most media types are framed by a set of gatekeeping procedures that assert a media product's credibility" (Bruhn and Salmose 78).

Invoking related developments in actor network theory and new materialism, Bruhn and Salmose note:

By questioning the ontology of concepts like "nature" and "wilderness" and the inherent dichotomy between "humans" and "culture," [these orientations] illustrate how agency can be described as a force rather than an action. The related field of multispecies studies discusses how multispecies relations work by focusing on networks that exist between [human and non-human] entities.

(Bruhn and Salmose 37)

Their own definition of "ecological agency"—"broadly understood as the possibility not only to understand but also to act upon the climate crisis"—stands in sharp contrast to Meikle's and Geal's accounts of ecocritical agency:

Ecological agency should not be confused with how agency in environmental humanities is sometimes discussed (in subcategories such as speciesism and multispeciesism), where the basic idea is that all non-human entities have an agency of their own, not only insects or viruses but also natural phenomena such as oceans and trees. Ecological agency ... is a way to define and discuss how environmental and ecological communication—ecomedia—impact its [sic] receivers and how such ecomedia afford human agency in many different forms.

(Bruhn and Salmose 165, 40)

Because an important implication of this definition is that "ecological agency is ... dependent on the specific potentials of different media types and products" (Bruhn and Salmose 9), Bruhn and Salmose spend most of their monograph comparing the different claims to authority made by particular novels, film adaptations of those novels, graphic novels, advertisements, and scientific papers, and the different ways texts in these different media work to establish their authority.

Julie Grossman's analysis of Anne Washburn's *Mr. Burns: A Post-Electric Play*, a black comedy first produced in 2012, pushes notions of ecocritical adaptation close to their breaking point. In some ways, *Mr. Burns* is a natural text for ecocritical study, since it is an adaptation of "Cape Feare"—a 1993 episode from the fifth season of animated television series *The Simpsons* (1989–) based on two films, *Cape Fear* (1962) and *Cape Fear* (1991), that are themselves adaptations of John D. MacDonald's 1957 novel *The Executioners*. But *Mr. Burns*—which explores the dangerous conditions of making art and adaptations in a post-apocalyptic world—is by any possible definition a very free adaptation of "Cape Feare" that is perhaps better described as a mashup of this particular episode, moments and characters from other *Simpsons* episodes and other monuments of popular culture, and the fraught and fractured cultural history behind these elements. The play's first act presents half a dozen survivors of an apocalyptic holocaust huddled around a fire sharing their memories of scenes and snatches of dialogue from the television episode. Its second act, which takes place seven years later, shows these characters—now members of a theatrical troupe that specializes in *Simpsons* adaptations—as they present a dramatized version of "Cape Feare" that departs still further from the episode. By the time of the third act, 75 years later, the episode—which has assumed mythic proportions—is presented as a musical, climaxing in a duel to the death between Bart Simpson and Homer Simpson's malevolent boss Mr. Burns, now conflated with Sideshow Bob, the villain in "Cape Feare."

At what point does *Mr. Burns* stop being "Cape Feare" and become something else? The already imperfect and incomplete memories the survivors present in Washburn's first act would seem to make it an involuntary adaptation intended to inspire a new communal energy by memorializing the past. The performance in the second act is punctuated by a commercial for Pret à Manger and a discussion in which Jenny criticizes the commercial for mentioning the obscure wine Shiraz, since "[t]he point of a Commercial is to create a reality which is *welcoming*, not challenging," and Gibson recalls "that whole other thing commercials used to do, like, there always used to be that question of identity. Like, it's not just what is the desire, it's *who has* the desire. I think people are ready for Status again" (Washburn 53). Passages like this make it clear that by adapting episodes of *The Simpsons*, the troupe is attempting to adapt (themselves) to their post-apocalyptic world by adapting cultural texts they recall, however marginal and insubstantial these may have seemed at the time. In this sense, the Pret à Manger commercial, like *Mr. Burns* itself, isn't selling anything; it is revealing social utopian desires. Post-apocalyptic thinking both mourns and critiques what has come before, even as it seeks to create new memories like the Simpson mythology that emerges in the play's third act.

For Grossman, *Mr. Burns*—which "see[s] capitalism and consumerism (symbolized by the greedy *Simpsons* character Mr. Burns) as the causes of civilization's decay"—simultaneously "suggests the vital role adaptation can play in crafting a future in which our real and imagined worlds merge" (Grossman 181–82, 177). This role shifts in important ways from act to act. In the first act, "memory serves to memorialize lost family members and friends in the reading of their names" (Grossman 183). In the second act, "memory has become a traded commodity, as the troupes buy lines from those they encounter who can remember episodes, or persons coming forward with lines" (Grossman 183). By the time of the third act, "the play has moved far away from its 'source,' such that the characters have now *become* the Simpsons figures they have been playing" (Grossman 187). These three imagined historical moments and the modes of memory they invoke, which pose far more questions than they answer, present a rich tapestry of the uses of adaptation for its creators and audiences.

Questions

- Why are some people so much more receptive to the plague of adaptation than others?

- Why isn't everybody against adaptation, which *Mr. Burns: A Post-Electric Play* makes sound like the zombie apocalypse?
- Just as there are COVID-19 deniers, are there adaptation deniers?
- What are the hallmarks of a receptive adaptation host?
- Are there asymptomatic adaptation transmitters?

The evolution of Barbie

After pursuing eco-adaptation to the future frontiers of civilization in *Mr. Burns*, it is deeply reassuring to return for a brief biological take on *Barbie*. A running joke in the film is that Barbie, who has arched feet designed for no purpose other than fitting into high-heeled shoes, and Ken, who (despite his repeated assertions to the contrary) has no penis, just as Barbie has no vagina, are not biologically adapted to the real world; they are adapted to allow Barbie's target clientele of pre-teen girls to undress them without provoking sexual questions or fantasies.

These biological affordances are linked to other affordances Michael McShane finds in Barbie's Dreamhouse, which was originally designed as an apartment without a ceiling and later expanded to a three-level house without exterior walls so that Barbie's owners could move her easily from outside to inside or from one room to the next. As McShane puts it:

> Even if the Dreamhouse has historically kept Barbie at the center of its design, that does not mean the structure was designed *for* Barbie as much as it was designed *around* Barbie. Following Marxist logic, Barbie is a toy, and her central purpose as a commodity is her own exchange-value, whether that be some form of economic capital, how much money she is worth as a product; or cultural capital, what she signifies about womanhood as a so-called feminist icon. As Marx theorized in his namesake text *Capital*, "If commodities could speak, they would say this: our use-value may interest men, but it does not belong to us as objects. What does belong to us as objects, however, is our value. Our own intercourse as commodities proves it. We relate to each other merely as exchange-values."
>
> (McShane 7–8; see Marx, vol. 1, 176)

In Greta Gerwig's film, the absence of exterior walls becomes for McShane a sign of Barbie's essential sociability—in contrast to Ken, who immediately installs exterior doors when he converts the Dreamhouse to Ken's Mojo Dojo Casa House and incorrectly assumes that other characters standing directly outside the house will be unable to hear anything he says inside.

The biological roots of these toys specifically adapted to a certain kind of play assume menacing overtones when Barbie asks her friends, "You guys ever think about dying?", stopping their daily party in its tracks because Barbieland has no room for mortality. Barbie's involuntary reflection, coupled with the flattening of her feet and the advice she gets from Weird Barbie, drives her to go in search of the girl she belongs to. The ultimate success of this search is signaled by her wish to her creator Ruth (Rhea Perlman): "I want to be part of the people that make meaning. Not the thing that's made. I want to do the imagining. I don't want to be the idea"—a wish that is presented as the film's climactic insight, the defining quality of human beings. And it is humorously capped and confirmed by the film's last line of dialogue, when Barbie tells a medical receptionist, "I'm here to see my gynecologist."

Questions

- Does Barbie in Gerwig's film need to adapt intransitively, or is she adapted by others?
- Does the film's addition of ceilings in the Barbie Dreamhouse reflect Barbie's agency to move around on her own or simply transfer that agency to her performers in the film?
- What do biological engagements allow or reveal about adaptations that other engagements don't?

References

Benshoff, Harry M. *Monsters in the Closet: Homosexuality and the Horror Film.* Manchester UP, 1997.

Bortolotti, Gary R. and Linda Hutcheon. "On the Origin of Adaptations: Rethinking Fidelity Discourse and 'Success': Biologically." *New Literary History*, vol. 38, no. 3 (2007), pp. 443–58.

Boyd, Brian. *On the Origin of Stories: Evolution, Cognition, and Fiction.* Harvard/Belknap, 2010.

Boyd, Brian. "Making Adaptation Studies Adaptive." *The Oxford Handbook of Adaptation Studies.* Edited by Thomas Leitch. Oxford UP, 2017, pp. 587–606.

Brooks, Peter. *Body Work: Objects of Desire in Modern Narrative.* Harvard UP, 1993.

Bruhn, Jørgen and Niklas Salmose. *Intermedial Ecocriticism.* Lexington, 2023.

Carroll, Joseph. *Evolution and Literary Theory.* U of Missouri P, 1995.

Carroll, Joseph. *Literary Darwinism: Evolution, Human Nature, and Literature.* Routledge 2004.

Cutchins, Dennis. "Bakhtin, Intertextuality, and Adaptation." *The Oxford Handbook of Adaptation Studies.* Edited by Thomas Leitch. Oxford UP, 2017, pp. 71–86.

Cutchins, Dennis. "An Exploratory Study of the Cognitive Experience of Adaptation." Unpublished essay, 2023.

Dawkins, Richard. *The Selfish Gene.* Oxford UP, 1976.

Dawkins, Richard. *The Extended Phenotype: The Gene as the Unit of Selection.* Freeman, 1982.

Demory, Pamela. "Queer Adaptation." *The Routledge Companion to Adaptation.* Edited by Dennis Cutchins, Katja Krebs, and Eckart Voigts. Routledge, 2018, pp. 146–56.

Demory, Pamela. "Queer/Adaptation: An Introduction," *Queer/Adaptation: A Collection of Critical Essays.* Palgrave Macmillan, 2019, pp. 1–13.

Elliott, Kamilla. "The Adaptation of Adaptation: A Dialogue Between the Arts and Sciences." *Adaptation and Cultural Appropriation: Literature, Film, and the Arts.* Edited by Pascal Nicklas and Oliver Lindner. De Gruyter, 2012, pp. 145–62.

Elliott, Tomas. "'A Movie about Flowers?' Notes on the Ecological Turn in Adaptation Studies." *Adaptation* vol. 17, no. 2 (2024), pp. 320–37.

Geal, Robert. "Towards an Ecocritical Adaptation Studies." *Adaptation*, vol. 16, no. 1 (March 2023), pp. 1–12.

Grossman, Julie. *Literature, Film, and Their Hideous Progeny: Adaptation and ElasTEXTity.* Palgrave Macmillan, 2015.

Hutcheon, Linda, with Siobhan O'Flynn. *A Theory of Adaptation.* Second ed. Routledge, 2012.

Leitch, Thomas. "To Adapt or to Adapt to: Some Problems in Defining Adaptation Intransitively." *Studia Filmoznawcze*, no. 30 (2009), pp. 91–103.

Leitch, Thomas. "What Movies Want." *Adaptation Studies: New Challenges, New Directions.* Edited by Jørgen Bruhn, Anne Gjelsvik, and Eirik Frisvold Hanssen. Bloomsbury, 2013, pp. 155–75.

McShane, Michael. "Too Many Hands in the Playhouse: Gender, Space, and Excess in *Barbie.*" Conference paper, Northeast Modern Language Association, March 2024.

Marx, Karl. *Capital: A Critique of Political Economy.* Translated by Ben Fowkes. Penguin, 1990.

Meikle, Kyle. "Towards an Adaptation Network." *Adaptation*, vol. 6, no. 3 (2013), pp. 260–67.

Meikle, Kyle. "A Theory of Adaptation Audiences." *Literature/Film Quarterly*, vol. 45, no. 4 (2017), https://www.jstor.org/stable/10.2307/48678529.

Meikle, Kyle. "Is Adaptation Studies Sustainable?" *Adaptation*, vol. 14, no. 2 (Aug. 2020), pp. 260–73.

Miller, J. Hillis. "Stevens' Rock and Criticism as Cure, II." *Georgia Review*, vol. 30, no. 2 (Summer 1976), pp. 330–48.

Orlean, Susan. *The Orchid Thief: A True Story of Beauty and Obsession.* Random House, 1998.

Pasolini, Pier Paolo. "'The Screenplay as a 'Structure That Wants to Be Another Structure.'" Pasolini, *Heretical Empiricism.* Edited by Louise K. Barnett. Translated by Ben Lawton and Barnett. Indiana UP, 1988, pp. 187–96.

Pinker, Steven. *How the Mind Works.* Norton, 1997.

Stam, Robert. *Subversive Pleasures: Bakhtin, Cultural Criticism, and Film.* Johns Hopkins UP, 1989.

Stam, Robert. "Introduction: The Theory and Practice of Adaptation." *Literature and Film: A Guide to the Theory and Practice of Adaptation.* Edited by Robert Stam and Alessandra Raengo. Blackwell, 2005, pp. 1–52.

Stankowski, Stan and Mark Ravinet. "Quantifying the Use of Species Concepts." *Current Biology* 31.9 (May 10, 2021), org/10.1016/j.cub.2021.03.060, https://www.cell.com/current-biology/fulltext/S0960-9822(21)00433-4?_returnURL=https%3A%2F%2Flinkinghub.elsevier.com%2Fretrieve%2Fpii%2FS0960982221004334%3Fshowall%3Dtrue.

Stryker, Susan. "My Words to Victor Frankenstein Above the Village of Chamounix: Performing Transgender Rage." *GLQ: A Journal of Lesbian and Gay Studies*, vol. 1 (1994), pp. 237–54.

von Mossner, Alexa Weik. *Affective Ecologies: Empathy, Emotion, and Environmental Narrative.* Ohio SUP, 2017.

Washburn, Anne. *Mr. Burns: A Post-Electric Play*. Oberon, 2014.

Wilkins, Christina. *Embodying Adaptation: Character and the Body*. Palgrave Macmillan, 2022.

Wilson, David Sloan. "Introduction: Literature—a Last Frontier in Human Evolutionary Studies." *The Literary Animal: Evolution and the Nature of Narrative*. Edited by Jonathan Gottshall and David Sloan Wilson. Northwestern UP, 2005, pp. xvii–xxiv.

Zimmer, Carl. "What Is a Species, Anyway?" *New York Times*, Feb. 19, 2024, Section D, p. 1.

5 Sociological engagements
Adaptation as border crossing

Emigrants, immigrants, migrants

Whether or not Simone Murray's economic engagement with the institutions serving as gatekeepers to adaptation and adaptation studies discussed in Chapter 3 is more broadly sociological, it has still left plenty of room for more targeted sociological engagements with adaptation. Since adaptations are by definition texts that cross borders between different languages, genres, or media, it makes sense to compare them to human migrants, whose status is also defined by the borders they cross and the ways they cross them. Scholars who have combined elements of Robert Stam's analysis of postcolonial adaptations of canonical Anglophone texts with recent political discussions of human migrants have laid the groundwork for a variety of new ways to engage with adaptation.

Like the mutations behind biological evolution, the experience and affordances of border crossing provide a metaphor that is both suggestive and problematic. When we speak of human migration across borders, most of us assume that the borders in question are national, political, and geographical. But as Hamid Naficy points out:

> Journeys are not limited to those that take exilic and diasporic subjects physically, psychologically, or metaphorically out of home countries and deliver them elsewhere or return them to their points of origin. There are also "journeys of identity" that displaced people inevitably undergo once they arrive in the new lands. Like other journeys, these internal journeys are composite and serial, since most exilic conditions involve multiple motivations and evolutions. Displaced individuals and uprooted communities may enter the host country with one status—as exiles, refugees, asylees, émigrés, students, or illegal aliens—but they do not remain in that status for long, especially if they arrive with significant cultural, racial, educational, class, and other capitals.
>
> (Naficy 237)

DOI: 10.4324/9781003438410-6

Following this analogy, adaptations can cross many additional kinds of borders—medial, linguistic, temporal, cultural—changing their status in the process. In their quest to speak at once to and for different audiences— citizens of different nations, adherents of different political beliefs, audiences who identify with different genders or ways of thinking about gender— adaptations can cross borders without leaving a single room. So in addition to asking how these borders compare to the borders human migrants cross, it is important to ask how the processes of adaptation compare to the processes of human border crossing. Engaging with adaptations as textual versions of biological mutations in Chapter 4 raised pointed questions about the agency involved in textual and cultural adaptation. Who makes adaptations? Do they become adaptations through the ways they are formed or through the ways they are perceived? Are they better described as new creations or as the latest in an endless series of mutations?

Engaging with adaptation in sociological terms, as an activity defined by border crossing, does not resolve these questions but reframes them in often urgent ways shaped by at least four elements Edward W. Said has identified as the set of circumstances under which a given text was created, the dis- tance it has traveled, the conditions under which its new culture accepts or resists it, and its transformation in the context of its new time and place (Said 226–27). Of all the questions these elements raise, the most obvious concern agency. Do adaptations cross borders themselves or does someone arrange for them to cross? More particularly, who exactly is complicit in facilitating or inhibiting adaptations as they cross borders, and what are the roles of these different agents?

This question generates fundamentally different responses depending on whether we define adaptations as emigrants (texts defined by their host cultures, as emigrants are defined by their birthplaces); as immigrants (texts defined by their target cultures, as immigrants are defined by a process of cul- tural and legal naturalization); or as migrants (texts defined by their propen- sity for crossing borders in general, with no special weight attached to any particular borders or movements in any particular direction). The most per- vasive of these ways sees adaptations as unauthorized immigrants—outlaw texts that remain marginalized in the more desirable places they have sought to enter. This perspective, rooted in both reverential views of the aesthetic canon and national pride and suspicion of outsiders, has been turbocharged in recent years by an analogous development: the increasingly intense oppos- ition to the illegal or even legal immigration of economically deprived newcomers in many countries around the world, especially the United States, which has defined itself intermittently as a nation of immigrants. But this is not the only way to think of adaptations as migrants. A second perspective, which remains so far largely hypothetical because it has rarely been explored by adaptation scholars, would treat adaptations as authorized immigrants— texts with a green card supplied by identifiable gatekeepers like acquisi- tion editors, translators, publishers, film producers, reviewers, and teachers for specific motives: cultural imperialism, cosmopolitanism, tokenism, or a heartfelt desire to expand the boundaries of a culture that welcomed renewal. A third perspective would define adaptations as emigrants from host cultures rather than immigrants to target cultures that defined themselves largely in opposition to this influx. High-school English teachers who help their students negotiate long and challenging novels like Henry Fielding's *Tom Jones* (1749) and Thomas Hardy's *Tess of the d'Urbervilles* (1891) by showing them film adaptations of those novels are treating these adaptations as emigrants, reconfigured versions of foundational texts that establish those foundational texts' identity even more securely. Even though these teaching experiences are primarily informed by an aesthetic approach to "literature on screen" that defines adaptations as copies of canonical works, this perspective can be broadened to emphasize the ways migrating adaptations invite their audiences to cross borders, expanding their boundaries by taking to heart stories and ideas from outside the more comfortable cultures that have conferred them a sense of who they are to give them a potentially more global or transnational, though not a universalized, identity. So a primary question raised by sociological engagements with adaptation is whether adaptations are more like immigrants, emigrants, or migrants—and what the implications are of choosing each of these labels.

This last question reveals the inescapable political implications of sociological engagements with adaptation that begin by asking who defines adaptations as emigrants or as immigrants, and on what grounds. English teachers who define adaptations as emigrants by using film adaptations to ease their students into more culturally remote literary works are showing the films in question specifically because of their similarities to the novels they adapt. In this view, adaptations are first and foremost citizens of the republic of literature who have wandered away into other languages or media, often shedding many of the hallmarks that made Virginia Woolf prize Tolstoy's *Anna Karenina* above any possible film version.

A much more impressive array of gatekeepers has lined up to define adaptations as immigrants, creatures defined by their target cultures rather than their host cultures. These begin with the indispensable pillars of the adaptation industry—"working adapters like translators, screenwriters, producers, and performers"—along with positively facilitating gatekeepers—"agents, publishers, editors, publicists, reviewers, and critics"—and "negative facilitators like police officers, censors, and linguistic medial purists" (Leitch 16), all of whom play gatekeeping, curatorial, and preservationist roles comparable to those Murray assigns publishing houses, magazines, movie studios, archives, libraries, and museums. They include what we might call "adaptation hardware," or the differing capabilities of different languages and media that have helped adaptations make themselves comfortable on nineteenth-century stages, in twentieth-century movies, and on twenty-first century social media from podcasts to TikTok. Since human immigration has been much more closely policed than emigration throughout history, it stands to reason that the adaptation police will also be more suspicious of adaptations that present themselves as immigrants than of those that present themselves as emigrants.

It might seem that emigration and especially immigration are both so politically fraught that it would be more prudent to define adaptation simply as migration. And there are certainly advantages to this strategy. But it comes with costs as well, for it opens up a whole new series of problems. Because there are institutional gatekeepers for adaptations seen as either emigrants or immigrants but none for adaptations seen as migrants, it is not clear who gets to define this much larger group of migrants, whose movements may be as temporary as those of tourists, as cyclic as those of snowbirds traveling south every autumn and north every spring, or as random as those of picaresque heroes like Lazarillo de Tormes and Don Quixote, whose adventures stubbornly refuse to take the form or a straight or predictable line. Since, as the metaphorical term "snowbirds" suggests, some migrants may never cross national borders and may not even be human, it is not clear whether adaptations are more like human or non-human creatures. Nor is it clear whether human migrants themselves are active or reactive. Since some migrants cross borders independently, they presumably have the agency to determine their own fate. But other migrants rely on agents from tour guides to human traffickers to ferry them across borders, making them arguably slaves to their handlers.

Questions

- In your view, are adaptations more like emigrants or immigrants?
- Can adaptations cross borders on their own, or does someone have to help them across?
- It may well be that one reason why migrants are much more loosely defined than emigrants and immigrants is precisely that there are no migrant police, for no one has any particular stake in defining them. If adaptation scholars decided that they had such a stake, how might they define migration in ways that resonated beyond their field?

What do adaptations want?

Considering adaptations as migrants rather than immigrants or emigrants subordinates the legal implications of border crossing to the experience of border crossing, a process Cristina Della Coletta has examined in detail. Della Coletta draws on the work of several earlier adaptation scholars, most notably Robert Stam, whom she echoes in her assertion that "a literary work has no exclusive mode of existence and no unique and more or less extractable essence" (Della Coletta 5). But her primary theoretical grounding is the hermeneutics of Hans-Georg Gadamer. Inspired by Gadamer's rejection of both relativism and categorical certainty in the search for knowledge, she defines adaptation as dwelling in "an *agoraic* domain," a "bounded enclosure" and "a place of free commerce" that "engages the notion of *interpretive plurality* in the ongoing production and interpretation of meaning" (Della Coletta 2). For Della Coletta, adaptations are "encounters across media—fiction and film primarily—and across cultures and traditions" (Della Coletta 3). Like "all dialogic encounters," adaptations "simultaneously inspire and challenge understanding" (Della Coletta 3). Because they are "concrete vehicles for cross-cultural dialogue" that involve "a journey from one communicative environment to another," adaptations are better "viewed as ... *events* than as stable and normative entities" (Della Coletta 9, 6). So it is entirely logical that Della Coletta emphasizes "travel" as "a structuring device, the objective correlative of narrativity itself" (Della Coletta 22). In a formulation which marries Gadamer to Bakhtin, she concludes: "Adaptation from a literary text to a film takes place in a domain of *neither excess nor reduction* but in one of mutual displacement, of sustained estrangement, which has a 'generative' power on both aesthetic and hermeneutical grounds" (Della Coletta 21).

Della Coletta's account of interpretation as "always a collective endeavor" (11) uses Gadamer's notion of a horizon—which he defines as "the range of vision that includes everything that can be seen from a particular vantage point" (Gadamer 302)—to argue that "[u]nderstanding a different horizon does not involve crossing over into alien worlds unconnected in any way with our own but, rather, achieving that fusion of horizons that allows us to see the world from a larger perspective" (Della Coletta 11, 14). When stories travel across national, linguistic, generic, or ideological borders, Della Coletta sees them as expanding their audiences' horizons rather than substituting one horizon for another—a process she regards as incessant and inevitable. Although she notes that for Gadamer, "*agreement* is the logical outcome of the hermeneutical encounter" (Della Coletta 14), this happy ending is never achieved without often turbulent complications: "Every encounter involves the experience of a tension between a text and the present" (Gadamer 306). Nor is this ending really an ending, for its resolution is "never final but the intermediate goal in a persistently renewed process" (Della Coletta 15). Stories, like their audiences, are always on the road.

Irina O. Rajewsky approaches questions about border crossing by focusing on media borders rather than political, cultural, or ideological borders. Noting that "the crossing of media borders has been defined as a founding category of intermediality" (Rajewsky 52), she distinguishes three intermedial practices (Rajewsky 55). The first of these—adaptation, or "medial transposition"—raises "genetic" questions about "the way in which a medial configuration *comes into being*" (Rajewsky 56). The second—hybrid forms like "visual poetry, illuminated manuscripts, Sound Art, opera, comics, multimedia shows, [and] multimedial computer 'texts' or installations" that depend on "media combination"—and the third, "intermedial references" like allusion, both raise questions about identity, "playing around" in ways that depend on some "*cross-over* moment" implicit in "*the reference itself*"

(Rajewsky 55, 58, 59). Observing that every act of intermedial crossing both reifies medial domains and reveals their limitations, Rajewsky echoes Della Coletta in her own very different terms in her injunction that discussions of media borders—which she prefers to call "border zones"—"should be shifted from taxonomies to the dynamic and creative potential of the border itself" (Rajewsky 64–65).

Like multiculturalists who support the easing of regulations on political borders, both Della Coletta and Rajewsky celebrate textual border crossing as an activity that makes textual generation and interpretation more vibrant and inclusive. The twist they add to contemporary political arguments for open borders is their shared position that texts will always cross borders, will always raise problems when they do, and will always lead ultimately to broader and more generous perspectives that grapple with these problems in constructive ways instead of seeking to ignore them by building higher fences.

Whether we consider adaptations as migrants, immigrants, or emigrants, emphasizing their status as travelers inevitably focuses our attention on the motives of all the parties to any adaptive journey. What do adaptations, which a sociological account defines precisely as texts that cross borders, want, and what do the adaptation police who seek to define, limit, and control them want? The most widely documented motive for restricting border crossing in contemporary culture is xenophobic and nativist politicians' full-throated demand, duly enforced by immigration officials and likeminded citizens, to keep aspiring aliens away in order to maintain the integrity of a national population by maintaining the integrity of its borders, through either purification or selective improvement of the race or nation. The immigration police are dedicated to maintaining their target culture's purity, repelling aspiring conquerors or challengers who might pollute the nation's genetic or economic pool, and unmasking and punishing fraudulent plagiarists or violators of international copyright laws. The emigration police, by contrast, are devoted to preventing defections from authoritarian regimes, protecting authors from copyright violations, preserving the canonical status of unadapted texts, and more generally preserving categorical assumptions about media specificity by promoting the idea that novels like *Tristram Shandy* (1759–67) and *À la recherche du temps perdu* (1913–27) are unadaptable. Their practice is like that of the gatekeepers of police states that forbid defections, like the Eastern European countries that spent the 45 years after the Second World War intent on keeping their citizens behind the Iron Curtain. Like the designers of the Berlin Wall, the adaptation police are more invested in regulating emigration than immigration, more likely to focus on keeping texts within existing borders in order to celebrate their uniqueness or their canonical status as untranslatable and unadaptable than in preventing them from entering new domains by posting bans or threatening penalties.

The motives of the agents responsible for border control typically conflict with the motives migrants have for making the journeys they do.

Migrants deliberately cross borders for many reasons. Temporary migrants may be fueled by the invitations of friends and relatives living abroad, the quest to discover their roots by returning to the lands of their ancestors, the promise of enjoying the novel experiences marketed to tourists, the advantages of the educational opportunities offered by student visas, or the call to act as diplomats seeking to broker peace among warring factions. Some migrants who do not plan to return to the culture they are leaving may be returning from the diaspora to a homeland to which they feel they belong, or may be enticed by the cosmopolitan benefits of dual citizenship in both the country they have left and the country they are entering. Still others, hoping to escape from economic hardship, racial or ethnic persecution, or government hostility, seek better lives in places whose streets are reputed to be paved in gold. Even the most innocuous of these experiences can have an unexpected edge, as Dean Armitage (Bradley Whitfield) reveals when he observes to Chris Washington (Daniel Kaluuya) in the 2017 film *Get Out*, "It's such a privilege to be able to own something from someone else's culture." His remark, apparently a casual reference to a souvenir sculpture he has brought home from Mali, has deeper and more troubling implications for audiences who know how this particular story will turn out. That edge can sharpen to a breaking point when involuntary migrants are forced against their will to cross borders by legal tribunals that exile them from their homeland, courts that extradite them to venues where they are accused of having committed crimes, or human traffickers intent on profiting from their misfortune.

Adaptations are shaped by an equally varied set of motives that are hard to map onto the motives of human migrants. Some adaptations, like stage adaptations of well-known novels, seek to supplement the texts they adapt. Others, like Hollywood remakes of films from *King Kong* to *A Star Is Born*, seek to replace earlier texts they aim to render obsolete. *Romeo and Juliet* has been repeatedly reworked across many media—cinema, radio, television, ballet, symphonic music, and innumerable stage productions—to appeal to new audiences. Just as novels like James Joyce's *Ulysses* (1922) and D.H. Lawrence's *Lady Chatterley's Lover* (1928) were published in English-language versions by French publishing houses while they were still banned in their home countries, and Boris Pasternak's *Doctor Zhivago* was smuggled out of Russia, where Pasternak feared its publication would be forbidden, and first published in 1957 in an Italian translation, film adaptations from *Forever Amber* (1947) to *Lolita* (1962) have crossed cultural borders erected by censoring boards by presenting variously sanitized versions of scandalous novels, implicitly joining *Ulysses* and *Doctor Zhivago* in challenging the legal institutions that censored them in the first place. The "dual citizenship" (Leitch 18) these adaptations have sought in order to make themselves at home in both host and target cultures indicates the closest similarity between the motives of human and textual migrants: the desire and determination to speak in multiple tongues, whether or not these take the form of new lexical languages in order to speak to a wider range of audiences on behalf of a wider range of viewpoints and cultures whose voices would otherwise go unheeded and unheard. The most successful border crossing operations are those that manage to escape or resolve the conflicts between migrants and the people and institutions that seek to police them, from more cosmopolitan or openminded tourists to adaptations that reveal or encourage productive new attitudes toward both their host and their target cultures.

Although theorists commonly assume that adaptations cross borders for a much more narrowly defined range of reasons, they differ among and even within themselves over one paramount question of motive: whether adaptations, like translations, should be treated as supplements to or substitutes for the texts they adapt. A surprising number of theorists from George Bluestone to Brian McFarlane have begun by theorizing adaptations as supplements designed to return audiences to the texts they adapt, like tourists returning home with an enlarged store of treasured memories and potentially illuminating new perspectives, and then have proceeded to analyze their individual case studies as variously successful substitutes that seek to replace those texts by providing an arguably equivalent experience that renders any direct consumption of those texts unnecessary, like the experiences of immigrants packing their bags in preparation for an arduous one-way trip from which they have no plans to return. Hutcheon's attempt to thread this needle by pronouncing adaptations "inherently double- or multilaminated works" that are "haunted at all times by their adapted texts" suggests that the processes of creating and perceiving "adaptations *as adaptations*" (Hutcheon 4), in Hutcheon's terms, are both informed, as Della Coletta might say, by a combination of adventure and nostalgia—like the perspectives of refugees who have strong reasons for crossing borders but still miss the land they called home.

All these considerations of motive depend on a highly problematic analogy between adaptations and migrants. The title of W.J.T. Mitchell's 2005 *What Do Pictures Want?* raises a question adaptation studies, even more than image studies, has been slow to reckon with. Can adaptations, or indeed pictures, want anything at all? Whether or not texts have agency, their creators sometimes act as if they did—as showrunner Damon Lindelof, who collaborated with Tom Perrotta in adapting Perrotta's 2011 novel *The Leftovers* for television, acknowledged of the series' fictional characters: "You think this person is a supporting character in your story, but you're a supporting character in theirs" (Lindelof C4). Even more frequently, audiences impute motives to texts whether or not they are adaptations, as when we recall times that we meant to put down a book or to walk away from a streaming movie or television episode that wouldn't let go of us. So whether or not adaptations can want anything in particular, we often act as if they could, and our experience of them is inseparable from that belief.

All of the perspectives that arise from approaching adaptation as immigration focus on transnational and transcultural adaptations, which have been largely neglected in adaptation studies as it is practiced in Anglophone countries. Whether we think of adaptations as authorized or unauthorized immigrants or, like *Doctor Zhivago*, as refugees from the cultures that gave them birth, approaching adaptation as migration invites us to think more critically about what Benedict Anderson has called the "imagined communities" forged by national, cultural, and political boundaries; about the sources of power behind their gatekeepers and their police; about the structural racism, orientalism, and xenophobia that define some people as insiders by differentiating them from outsiders held to be inferior; and about the many ways texts, creators, and citizens have been marginalized and may possibly be recentered.

Every adaptation crosses borders in both its production and its reception. But the most obvious kinds of border-crossing adaptations, the ones most clearly entitled to that label, are the transnational adaptations that are produced when a text from one national host culture is adapted into another text aimed at a new target culture. These adaptations throw a new light on both adaptation and nationality because, as Richard White observes, "[o]nly in particular circumstances is nationality self-consciously and actively imagined, usually in circumstances where the borderlines between 'us' and 'them' can be not only marked but negotiated and brought into being" (White 109). Everyone can identify examples of this practice, from Antonin Dvorak's "New World" symphony (1893) and Nikolai Rimsky-Korsakov's *Capriccio Espagnol* (1887) to Salvador Dalí's studies of the paintings of seventeenth-century Dutch artist Jan Vermeer to Japanese *anime*, which Gatu Narita, the Disney Corporation's executive director of original content for Japan, has said is "increasingly becoming a borderless form of mass entertainment" (Brzeski). Even the meaning of *anime* involves border crossing, since in Japan the term refers to all animated entertainment, while outside Japan it has come to mean hand-drawn, computer-generated animation produced in Japan.

In the film industries of nations like Turkey, Iran, and India that are not signatories to the Berne Convention, transnational adaptation is even more ubiquitous because adapters are not legally obliged to pay anything to the creators whose work they are adapting or acknowledge them in their credits. This practice has begun to change in India, home to the largest and most diverse filmmaking industry in the world, although well over half of the films released in India every year are still unacknowledged adaptations of older material. It might be assumed that when the film industries in these countries produce adaptations of Hollywood films, the results would be easily identifiable as American-inflected for the same reasons that *anime* is widely recognized as Japanese. Iain Robert Smith has criticized the use of overbroad models of "cultural hybridization" based on "Americanization" or "cultural imperialism" (Smith 18) to describe such transnational adaptations because they involve adapting cultural norms and habits as well as specific textual features. Smith notes Ien Ang's observation that

[i]t would be ludicrous ... to try to find a definitive and unambiguous, general theoretical answer to [the question of cultural globalisation] precisely because there is no way to know in advance which strategies and tactics different people in the world will invent to negotiate with the intrusions of global forces in their lives.

(Smith 23; see Ang 143)

Smith goes on to ask:

Why is one form of adaptation proliferating within a specific context? How do governmental policy and industrial conditions affect the modes of adaptation used? How does this relate to tensions in global copyright agreements? What meanings do these adaptations have in their contexts of production and reception?

(Smith 32–33)

Smith reviews "four key modes of absorption" Paul S.N. Lee "characterizes utilising biological metaphors" (Smith 27). The Parrot holistically adopts "foreign cultural forms and contents" by swallowing themes whole; the Amoeba "keeps the content but changes the form"; the Coral "keeps the form but changes the content"; and the Butterfly "absorbs and indigenizes foreign cultures to an extent that one can hardly distinguish the foreign from the indigenous" (Smith 27, 28). And he cites an "alternative taxonomic model" proposed by Tom O'Regan, which proposes "five stages that a national cinema must go through in order to move from being a receiving culture to a transmitting culture": "The texts coming from outside keep their 'strangeness'"; "the imported text and the home culture ... restructure each other"; "the home culture's product is re-evaluated 'in a situation of assumed international comparison'"; the receiving culture "assimilates the imported matrices making them entirely its own"; and "the receiving culture ... changes into a transmitting culture" (Smith 28, 29, 30; see O'Regan 220, 221). Smith's own model of transnational adaptation is drawn, like many biological models of adaptation, from Richard Dawkins's idea of the meme as "the unit of cultural transmission, or a unit of imitation" (Smith 31; see Dawkins 206, which italicizes "imitation"). Smith takes Dawkins's model seriously but not literally, using it as a metaphor for cultural transmission, border crossing, and survival rather than as a scientifically established phenomenon. Although he concedes that Henry Jenkins and others have "criticized the notion of the meme for stripping aside the concept of human agency," he suggests that "this concept of the meme is already more attentive to agency than this critique allows for" (Smith 32).

In her account of the Yeşilçam remakes of Hollywood films like *Young Frankenstein* (1974) produced in Turkey between 1960 and 1980, Seda Öz argues:

[W]hen marginal cinemas speak indirectly under political orthodoxies, their industrial choices in recycling texts … turn … the act of border crossing into dialogic moments in which journeys between source and adaptation, original and remake, or culture A and culture B do not take linear routes, but instead chaotically oscillate.

(Öz)

She identifies an entirely different industrial motive behind films like *Sevimli Frankenştayn* (*My Friend Frankenstein*, 1975):

[These r]emakes were produced not in order to capitalize on the success of the films they were remaking but in order to avoid the resistance that would more likely greet more original Turkish films because of the political unrest caused by the 1960 and 1980 *coups d'état*, a tension that revolves around nationalistic borders.

(Öz)

No matter how closely these films copied the films they remade—and Öz presents abundant evidence that *My Friend Frankenstein* borrowed its story, its characters, much of its dialogue and visual design, and even many individual shots from *Young Frankenstein*—their Turkish audiences did not experience them as remakes because they had no awareness of the films they remade or, in this case, of the Universal *Frankenstein* films or Mary Shelley's novel, which had yet to be translated into Turkish. Hence "the fact that these texts are crossing geographical borders does not necessarily make them transnational as the term is generally used" (Öz). By showcasing the wide divergences in different audiences' reception of remakes in particular and adaptations in general, Öz's analysis raises inescapable questions about which borders count as borders and which crossings count as crossings.

Questions

- How much of Della Coletta's and Rajewsky's arguments are applicable to human migration, and vice versa?
- How do the values immigrants provide the cultures that welcome them (taking low-paying jobs, enriching cultural experience for all) compare to the values adaptations provide their target cultures (raising/spotlighting questions about cultural identity and border-crossing practices)?
- What can adaptations do better than other texts?
- Does focusing on memes allow for a more sophisticated account of (individual and collective) human agency than models driven by political agendas?
- How might Smith's analysis change if it focused on adaptations that immigrated to the United States instead of emigrating from it?

- How much of Öz's argument about Yeşilçam Turkish remakes can be applied to transnational adaptations generally, or indeed to all adaptations?

The many journeys of *Persepolis*

These questions are sharpened by a consideration of Marjane Satrapi's *Persepolis* (2000–3) precisely because it involves so many different journeys. *Persepolis*—whose title, referring to the Persian capital city founded in the sixth century B.C.E. by Darius I that flourished as a powerful model of its kind until it was destroyed by Alexander the Great 1,000 years later, may be freely translated as "City of Persians"—is a memoir of the coming of age of its author, whom it follows from 1980 to 1994, between the ages of ten and 24. It is also a story of her journey from her native Tehran to Vienna and back home again and her vacations along the way to other points in Europe before what she calls "my definitive departure" (Satrapi 340) for Paris. Along the way, Satrapi recounts the effects of the Islamic Revolution that motivated her two departures from Iran—the first on her parents' initiative, the second on her own—and her attempts to come to terms with the cultural changes they produce by adapting to or rebelling against them (another form of adaptation here, as it is for Robert Stam). Her development is largely shaped by her rebellions against the Iranian school she attends as a child and the French nuns whom she accuses of being former prostitutes, along with the gradual deepening of her friendship with her roommate Lucia, who speaks neither Persian nor French, and her complicated relationship with her friend Reza, who becomes in turn her lover and husband before their estrangement, then a professional colleague with whom she works closely and successfully before their divorce.

Although no officials try to prevent Satrapi's journeys between countries and cultures, her memoir is everywhere informed by the internalized pressures on the journeys that define her and raises crucial questions about them. Are they journeys toward or away from the City of Persians the title indicates? What do they have to do with each other? How fruitful is it to talk about each one of them as a journey? Which borders that Satrapi crosses are most important to her story and her life, and what are the relations between these borders and these crossings?

These questions are further complicated by the borders *Persepolis* continued to cross after its initial publication. Satrapi's graphic memoir was first published in two volumes in French as *Persepolis 1* and *Persepolis 2* in 2000 and 2001. Two sequels, *Persepolis 3* and *Persepolis 4*, also published in French, followed in 2002 and 2003. The first two volumes, widely translated, were first combined and published in English as *Persepolis 1: The Story of a Childhood* in 2003; the third and fourth volumes first appeared in English translation as *Persepolis 2: The Story of a Return* in 2004; and all four volumes, combined into a single work, were translated and published as *The Complete Persepolis* in 2007. This last date coincided with still another border crossing: the theatrical release of *Persepolis*, an animated feature film based on Satrapi's memoir and written and directed by Satrapi and French comic-book writer Vincent Paronnaud. In this regard, it followed a long-established pattern whose distant ancestor was the *Classics Illustrated* comic-book adaptations that followed the release of, and often took their visual cues from, movies based on their sources—a series that includes *The Three Musketeers, A Tale of Two Cities, Robin Hood, The Adventures of Huckleberry Finn, Great Expectations, The Prisoner of Zenda, A Midsummer Night's Dream, King Solomon's Mines, Hamlet,* and *Mutiny on the Bounty.* So questions about the relations between the many journeys within Satrapi's memoir can be productively expanded to include questions about the journeys the memoir itself has made in traveling from a single publication to a series of four publications to collections of pairs of these publications to a reworking as an award-winning feature film.

Adaptation scholars assessing books that have been turned into films typically begin by comparing the thematic and textual features of those books and films. In the case of *Persepolis*, this exercise is particularly challenging because the film follows both the events and the visual style of Satrapi's graphic novel so closely. Like most films of longer narratives, *Persepolis* omits many episodes of Satrapi's memoir—the posters of Kim Wilde and Iron Maiden her father smuggles into the country at her request, her expulsion from her first school, her surprisingly close friendship with her flatmate Lucia, her mother's visit to her in Vienna, her brief career as a drug dealer, her partnership with her estranged husband Reza in creating a theme park, and her climactic announcement, "I can't take it anymore! I want to leave this country!" (Satrapi 128–29, 143, 161, 200–6, 222–25, 328–31, 337). It adds a much smaller amount of new material and reorders a few other incidents. And it adds a great deal of additional dialogue, prunes back Satrapi's third-person commentary accordingly, and adds music and sound effects to its images.

These images themselves mark border crossings that are especially interesting because the close resemblance of the film's visuals to the memoir's is the product of a conscious series of decisions. The film's producers, Marc-Antoine Robert and Xavier Rigault of 2.4.7. Films, initially wanted to make a live-action adaptation because of the technical complexities of animation. But Satrapi resolutely opposed this idea because "[w]ith live-action, it would have turned into a story of people living in a distant land who didn't look like us. At best, it would have been an exotic story, and at worst, a 'third-world' story" (Hetherington). The film, already distinguished from other autobiographical films by its animated style, is set apart from other animated films by being shot almost entirely in black and white in order to mimic more closely the visuals of Satrapi's graphic memoir, which is itself set apart from other graphic novels in at least two ways: by the nonfictional story it tells, which makes it a memoir rather than a novel; and by its black-and-white format, which separates it from most other graphic volumes (though not of course from the comic strips daily newspapers run). It is inspired in both these regards by *Maus*, Art Spiegelman's second-hand Holocaust memoir serialized from 1980 to 1991 and published in two volumes in 1986 and 1991. Although Satrapi does not follow Spiegelman's much-discussed decision to turn his human characters into cats, pigs, and mice, she is deeply influenced by his visual style. Like *Maus*, *Persepolis* presents a world in starkly contrasting black and white, with even more limited use of the gray scale—for example, in the presentation of the Baba-Levys' ruined house (Satrapi 142)—than Spiegelman. Although the film is shot mostly in black and white and set in spaces that take their cue from Satrapi's resolutely two-dimensional spaces, its much more frequent use of grays and its use of muted colors to set the present day apart from the flashbacks in which most of the film's (though not the memoir's) events are contained subtly naturalize its material even as they emphasize its visual stylization. In addition, the film, by using color for the present and black and white for the past, suggests that its heroine herself is partly responsible for seeing her childhood in black and white.

Figure 5.1 Marjane Satrapi's uncomfortable stroll in the 2007 film adaptation of *Persepolis* adds textured grays and other three-dimensional cues mostly absent from Satrapi's even more black-and-white graphic memoir

This last decision is especially crucial because the most important borders *Persepolis* crosses as both memoir and film are between the historical past, the remembered past, and the present in which Satrapi must live with her country's recent past and her memories of it. In talking about her memoir—or, as she calls it, her novel—Satrapi emphasizes its universality: "The novels have been a worldwide success because the drawings are abstract, black-and-white. I think this helped everybody to relate to it, whether in China, Israel, Chile, or Korea" (Hetherington). Despite its departures from the memoir's visual style, the film captures the persistent contrast the memoir establishes between its two most pervasive visual elements: the whiteness of individual characters' faces and the blackness of the *hijabs* Iranian women are compelled to wear by the male clerics who run their government.

The visual style of both the memoir and the film, borrowing freely from Japanese *manga*, is at once universalized and abstracted from the particular life it chronicles, whose events presumably unfolded in color. This tension between the particular, the abstract, and the universal is so well established in autobiographical memoirs that it may be described as a foundational trope of the genre. Memoirists like Augustine of Hippo have recorded the stories of their lives because they thought they incorporated universal patterns (in Augustine's case, the movement from sin to repentance and conversion) their audiences might benefit from understanding and imitating. For this reason, Augustine's *Confessions* and the many spiritual autobiographies that follow it combine recollections of the authors' earlier experiences, frequent citations of Scripture, and prayers of gratitude and praise to the God who called Augustine to conversion. Memoirists like Jean-Jacques Rousseau, by contrast, have emphasized the uniqueness over the typicality of their lives, as Rousseau makes clear in his opening announcement: "I am unlike anyone I have ever met; I will even venture to say that I am like no one in the whole world. I may be no better, but at least I am different" (Rousseau 17). The single most remarkable achievement of Satrapi's memoir and the film based on it is their ability to use this tension between individuality and universality as the basis of so many of the author's journeys—her journey from childhood to adulthood; her journey from loving her homeland to feeling increasingly estranged from it; and her troubled journey through European cultures and equally troubled journey back to Iran—which ultimately lead her to embrace her chosen status as a voluntary exile who never feels truly at home wherever she lives, an exile who is both a sharply defined individual and a prototypical member of a much larger community of Iranian women determined to speak for these women, who have been persistently marginalized both in their own country and abroad.

Satrapi's leading quest as she grows from child to adult is defined by her father, who tells her, "Don't ever forget who you are," and her grandmother, who advises her, "Always keep your dignity and be true to yourself" (Satrapi 148, 150). The central question of *Persepolis* is what it means for migrants and exiles to be true to themselves. This question surfaces whenever Satrapi refers to her culture, since she is writing about her repeated resistance to revolutionary changes in Iran's culture. Along with raising questions about what it means to be true to yourself, Satrapi's memoir is itself already an adaptation of her memories of her journey from childhood to adulthood and from native to exile that is both a critique of her Iranian identity and a valentine to it. "I AM IRANIAN AND PROUD OF IT!" she shouts at European schoolmates she overhears gossiping about her (Satrapi 197). *Persepolis* repeatedly raises questions about what counts as a border crossing. Clearly Satrapi's journeys to Austria and France cross important borders. But how about her vacations within Iran or Europe, or her movement from one unsatisfactory apartment to another, or the two months she spends living literally on the streets of Vienna (Satrapi 240)? When Satrapi smokes her first cigarette and "kisse[s] childhood goodbye" at 14 (Satrapi 117), is she crossing a border? Do life decisions, developmental or biological changes, or the decision to wear or remove a *hijab* cross borders? More generally, if your homeland undergoes a revolution but you don't move, does that count as a border crossing? If you change instead to accommodate yourself to the new regime, does that count as a border crossing?

One last way to frame the many questions about border crossing Satrapi raises is to ask who her target audience is. Is she more intent on reaching fellow citizens inside her native culture or outsiders she wants to educate about that culture? And if it is the latter, as the production and reception history of *Persepolis* would suggest, then what exactly does Satrapi want to tell non-Iranians about contemporary Iranian culture? Despite the many honors that greeted both Satrapi's memoir and its film adaptation, these controversies have continued past their release. By 2014, *Persepolis*—presumably because of its unusual frankness about sex, drugs, and gender identity—had become one of the most challenged comic books in public libraries across the United States. So the resolution and embrace of a single stable cultural identity Satrapi learned to stop seeking have continued, for better or worse, to elude her memoir as well.

As its title suggests, the many links between adaptation and migration are the focus of Nafiseh Mousavi's 2021 dissertation, *The Art of Repeating Oneself: Migratory Self-Adaptation: Media Transformation and Authorship in Persepolis and The Patience Stone*, which explores the screen adaptations of both *Persepolis* and Franco-Afghan novelist Atiq Rahimi's *The Patience Stone* (2008). In Mousavi's view,

> the two concepts of adaptation and migration raise various connotations in one another. Adaptation can convincingly be understood as migration of transmedial elements (or media content and media form) among different media, especially when viewed from the viewpoint of authorship and production. From the other side, migration commonly relates to various connotations of adaptation, namely change, acceptance, integration, acculturation, and survival in the new environment.
>
> (Mousavi 40)

She sees Satrapi's memoir as a public performance, "a narrative of witnessing" required by the fact that "[a] migrant learns very soon to prepare a condensed autobiography formed around the journey of migration" in anticipation of questions that will inevitably be raised by others. In response to these questions, Satrapi's performance adopts an explicitly political agenda: "*Persepolis* ... was published with a need to clarify and dissociate the Iranian people, including—and more urgently—the Iranian diaspora, from the acts of the government" (Mousavi 128, 146, 74).

Satrapi's public performance of border crossing is also, for Mousavi, inevitably a self-performance because "migrant authorship, in its broadest sense, is *a practice which emerges at the intersection of the life experience of displacement (across cultures), at individual and/or collective levels, with 'the diasporic desire', or obligation, to communicate*" (Mousavi 28). Just as "[m]igratory self-adaptation is repetition with difference, not only of a narrative, but, more broadly, of the baggage which does not ever seem to stop burdening the migrant author," Satrapi's authorial self-adaptation

> seems to oscillate between two drives, one being the desire to control the life of one's work, and the other the inevitable necessity for the less-visible and less-audible—here the migrant—to shout and repeat to be heard and seen.
>
> (Mousavi 7)

So Satrapi adapts herself to her changing circumstances and the choices she makes in response to them in order to allow her sense of sanity and dignity to survive; to clarify and transform her identification with her culture of origin and her adopted culture; to construct a narrative that can respond to questions she is asked about her identity; to present this narrative in a public space in the form of an achieved and completed journey; and, along the way, to chart the development of the many different selves she has devised and inhabited in pursuit of this identity.

As this last process suggests, Mousavi sees adaptation as an incessant process for the same reason that migration is: because it is these processes, not any final destination, that ends up conferring an identity on Satrapi as both subject and author. Borrowing the term "bordering" from Chris Rumford, she notes that "[t]he constant negotiation of borders redefines migratory self-adaptation as bordering and then re-bordering" (Mousavi 10; see Johnson et al. 67). The identities of both adaptations and their authors arise from this constant process of re-bordering: "[A]utobiographicality is perhaps the immediate consequence of considering the works as contributors to the performance and transformation of the author's identity as a migrant" (Mousavi 23). And the criteria for their ultimate success are less a function of the author's intention than of the author's migratory transformation: "The point is not to see if the works have achieved the author's goals but ... to look at what migratory self-adaptation has done to the narrative and to the authorship of the author" (Mousavi 55).

Pushing this argument further, Mousavi argues that adaptation is not a product of memories but a "Remediation of Memories": "[M]ediation, specificities of different media, and transformation of media, shape the mnemonic practices in migratory self-adaptation. Furthermore, ... through memory work, the *self* of the self-adaptation is linked to the collective *identity*" (Mousavi 122). This process, common to all migrants, is particularly emphasized when their memories, which "need ... repetition, or in more technical terms, *rehearsal*, to stay alive, be remembered, and to stick," are further transformed by their adaptative performances in different media, for "remembering in comics proves to be quite different from remembering in film" (Mousavi 136, 134). The need to keep remembering and re-bordering

> can be geared towards survival and extension of the life and visibility of what is being repeated. With a frame of repetition, migratory self-adaptation materializes numerous urges of survival coming together: the urge to save a memory from oblivion; the impulse to extend the life of a narrative; or the necessity of surviving as a stranger.
>
> (Mousavi 147)

As a result of her journeys from childhood to adulthood, from Iran to Europe, from page to screen, from embracing to rejecting her own earlier selves, and between different ways of identifying with different national and cultural communities as she seeks to maintain a constant identification with her family,

> Satrapi shows us the state of being in memory (as opposed to a singular act of recall) by triangulating between the different versions of herself as represented on the page. She shows us, then, the visual and discursive process of "never forgetting".
>
> (Chute 144, quoted by Mousavi 130)

Mousavi urges that

> the focus on memory works shows how important it is to speak of *adaptations* in plural, rather than a singular act of adaptation. Without considering the network of adaptations which frame each or both of the versions of the works, the multiple steps of memory work, or broadly the process of migratory self-adaptation could not be scrutinized.
>
> (Mousavi 144)

Contending that "[c]itizenship, in relation to cultural productions, needs to be understood beyond the stability and clarity of IDs and passports, and rather in a performative framework," Mousavi concludes:

> In the journeys of *Persepolis* and *The Patience Stone*, the again-ness of self-adaptation and the migrant experience is integrated with the contingencies of access. Like citizenship, adaptation is also a scene for co-occurrence of inclusion and exclusion. It is a scene for conformation to some, and opposition to other existing narratives and norms. When performed across

a cultural trajectory, adaptation becomes as well a synthesis of drives to familiarize and foreignize.

(Mousavi 149, 150)

Mousavi sounds a tonic warning note when she says that "fetishizing mobility" by celebrating adaptability as such "detaches the figure of the migrant from the lived experience of various groups of displaced people for whom migration is as much about being stuck, as it is about movement" (Mousavi 25):

> In the aftermath of the so-called refugee crisis, it has become more difficult to talk about migration and migrants in vague, metaphorical and appropriating ways when the hardships of such lives have finally penetrated the global image of mobilities, and as they are increasingly subjected to everyday and institutionalized xenophobia. The new image of the migrant is a Janus-faced one, triggering sympathy as well as alertness. In this image, migrants and refugees are portrayed as "welcomed guests" as much as they are described as the "swarms" or "hordes" attacking and contaminating the well-kept borders. In such context, it is crucial, more than ever, to talk about migrant agencies in practical and intersectional terms.
>
> (Mousavi 10)

Anyone who wishes to borrow the stressful experience to which migrants have been subjected by using their status as an analogy, or perhaps a homology, for situations that arise in adaptation studies should plan to repay it with interest through newly proactive interventions in the problems of migration that these new perspectives reveal—or at the very least, with formative, liberating, respectful perspectives on human migration as such. Several insights might help repay this debt. Adaptation studies has now progressed to a point at which most practitioners reject the source/copy or source/target binary. It would be encouraging if discussions of migration, informed as well by border studies, could do the same, rejecting in particular the assumption that migrants invariably leave homes for non-homes and more general binaries like native/interloper, legal/illegal, and citizen/immigrant. These binaries are always unnecessarily reductive—even, or especially, when they are internalized by people who essentialize their identification with a single privileged or vilified community instead of thinking of themselves as simultaneously members of nuclear families, extended families, school or workplace communities, neighborhoods, cities, provinces or states, countries, continents, the planet, and the universe. Even immigrants who announce proudly that they are done with binaries often acknowledge ruefully that binaries—heuristic, legalistic, and tribal—aren't done with them. Although it may be beyond the power of adaptation studies to resolve these binaries, it can provide models that can go far to help manage them. One possible place to begin would be to use examples of adaptations as relatives of the texts they adapt to open the notion of *family*, and eventually *community*, to more critical scrutiny. Another would be to shift, as Mousavi recommends, from talking about how a particular adaptation crosses a particular border to talking about adaptations, bordering, rebordering, and performances that take border-crossing selves as both their subjects and their objects.

Questions

- What makes some lives worth memorializing in books?
- What do you think encouraged Marjane Satrapi to write her memoir in the form of a comic book?
- Is it easier or harder to adapt a novel that already includes visual elements?
- Although she has written many other things since 2003, Satrapi hasn't written any additional installments of *Persepolis*. Does this mean that the story of her life, or at least of its most interesting chapters, is over? How surprised would you be to see a new chapter appear?
- If you wrote your own memoir, what borders would it most likely cross and where would it end?
- Is it possible to establish yourself without repeating yourself? Is just being yourself sufficient to establish yourself, or do you need to cite or perform yourself at least once—maybe more than once—to confirm your identity as an identity and not simply a quality?
- What ethical and existential dimensions does the charge to be true to yourself imply?

Border skirmishes

The act of crossing borders—whether they are political, cultural, or textual—always has moral and ethical implications that frequently disturb the borders in question. The chapter has examined some of these, especially those concerning agency (who is responsible for carrying texts across borders and identifying them as emigrants, immigrants, or migrants?). A few others deserve at least brief consideration.

The most obvious of these is plagiarism, the borrowing of material from earlier texts without acknowledgment or payment to the creators of those texts. In *Adaptation and Appropriation*, Julie Sanders considers at length the case of *Last Orders*, Graham Swift's 1996 account of "four male friends transporting the ashes of their late friend, the butcher Jack Dodds, to scatter off the end of Margate Pier," which scholar John Flow accused of copying the plot and some of the most striking stylistic elements of *As I Lay Dying*, William Faulkner's 1930 novel about "a Mississippi family group transporting the corpse of their dead wife/mother to the town of Jefferson for burial" (Sanders 33). The question of whether *Last Orders* should be considered an "homage" to Faulkner, as Swift described it, or an unauthorized copying of *As I Lay Dying* may seem to have little to do with border crossing, but the connection is clarified and strengthened by cases of cultural appropriation—adaptations of texts from another culture by adapters seeking to exoticize or universalize or otherwise complicate or subvert their earlier cultural import.

The borders these appropriations cross need not be national, and they may involve reception as well as production, as Alfred L. Martin, Jr. demonstrates in his analysis of the contemporaneous reception of *The Wiz* (1978), Sidney Lumet's celebrated all-Black film adaptation of *The Wizard of Oz* and "the first black-cast blockbuster" (Martin 56). Martin contends that the reputation of the film, whose failure to recuperate its $23 million budget discouraged Hollywood studios that had enjoyed repeated success with low-budget Blaxploitation films throughout the 1970s from launching any big-budget Black films for another ten years, as a failure "cannot simply be reduced to the lack of attention paid to its financials. It is also racially inscribed" (Martin 57). Because the overwhelming majority of the reviewers on which the film counted for its success were white, it had to navigate a "delicate balance ... between universality for white (re)viewers and its particularity for Black (re)viewers" (Martin 68). More specifically, the film's association with the 1939 film *The Wizard of Oz* "prevented some white reviewers from regarding *The Wiz* as a standalone text and judging it on its own merits" (Martin 73). Martin quotes an anonymous reviewer in *New York* as an example of "how mainstream press inextricably linked *The Wiz* and *The Wizard of Oz*": "All it has to do is the following: (1) surpass the [L. Frank Baum] book; (2) surpass the musical; and (3) surpass Judy Garland's *The Wizard of Oz*" (Martin 74; see "Made in New York" 79). Even though *The Wiz* was based on a live-action musical that was in turn based on Baum's 1900 novel, white reviewers judged it, reflexively and generally unfavorably, as a Black appropriation of the 1939 film adaptation, "too Black for white audiences and yet not Black enough" (76), which served as a privileged and racialized context for its reception by reviewers who could not "shake the phantom of *The Wizard of Oz* as the referent by which to judge *The Wiz*" (Martin 76, 75), ignoring along the way the fact that the earlier film had been a financial failure as well.

Both *Last Orders* and *The Wiz* dramatize the ethical questions that arise not simply in comparing adaptations to their sources, but in choosing to identify any particular texts as sources. Which texts count as sources for recent Black adaptations like the live-action film *The Little Mermaid* (2023) or Studio Ghibli adaptations like *The Boy and the Heron* (2023) or James Joyce's omnivorous novels *Ulysses* and *Finnegans Wake* (1939), and who gets to decide which of them should be perceived and taken most seriously as sources? These questions take still another turn for anyone who contemplates the relation between adaptation and translation. Noting that "[m]igrant communication can be understood as what Ted Striphas formulates as 'communication as translation' (2006) in which, not coherence and mutual understanding, but differences and blockages of understanding be [sic] the normal status of communication" (Mousavi 29; see Striphas), Mousavi asserts: "In these processes of rebordering, it is not only media transformation which is at work but multiple practices of language change and translation" (Mousavi 103).

Even more obviously than adaptation, translation is a process of crossing borders that are typically both linguistic and national, as Johann Wolfgang von Goethe observes in an 1813 essay on Wieland:

> [T]here are two maxims in translation: one requires that the author of a foreign nation be brought across to us in such a way that we can look on him as ours; the other requires that we should go across to what is foreign and adapt ourselves to its conditions, its use of language, its peculiarities.
>
> (Translated by Lefevere 39)

Academic research in translation studies is so rich, varied, and voluminous that no brief summary could do it justice. But it is worthwhile to focus on a single aspect of it that is particularly appropriate to adaptation studies in general and this chapter in particular: the longstanding feud between adaptation scholars and translation scholars about which of them should have greater authority in analyzing the way texts cross borders. Despite, or because of, their obvious parallels, adaptation studies and translation studies, like Marjane Satrapi and Iran, have yet to find a comfortable way to get along.

Translation scholar Lawrence Venuti announces that "translation theory can advance thinking about film adaptations by contributing to the formulation of a more rigorous methodology for studying them" (Venuti 41). In place of the fidelity discourse that treats adaptations as generally inferior copies, or the intertextual approach of Robert Stam, in which "the film [adaptation] is not compared directly to the literary text, but rather to a version of it mediated by an ideological critique" which itself becomes the privileged context in which it should be analyzed, Venuti proposes a third approach based on the "interpretants" he identifies as a foundational basis for the parallels between the two disciplines:

> An interpretation is inscribed through the application of a category that mediates between the source language and culture, on the one hand, and the translating language and culture, on the other, a method of choosing the source text and transforming it into the translation. This category consists of *interpretants*, which can be either formal or thematic. Formal interpretants may include a relation of equivalence, such as a semantic correspondence based on dictionary definitions of philological research, or a particular style, such as a lexicon and syntax characteristic of a genre. Thematic interpretants are codes: an interpretation of the source text that

has been articulated independently in commentary; a discourse in the sense of a relatively coherent body of concepts, problems, and arguments linked to a genre and housed in a social institution; or values, beliefs and representation affiliated with specific social groups.

(Venuti 28, 31)

Adaptation scholars have chafed under Venuti's dismissive description of Stam's intertextual approach to adaptation as informed by an ideological position "which the critic applies as a standard on the assumption that the adaptation should somehow inscribe that and only that ideology," or of Patrick Cattrysse's translation-inspired approach to adaptation as one more "version of the discourse of fidelity" whose norms are "too narrowly defined and too simply applied to encompass the multiple factors that enable and constrain film production" (Venuti 28, 32). More generally, they have resisted the proposition that adaptation studies would improve to the extent that it adopted the terms and methodologies of translation studies. Laurence Raw, arguing that "adaptation studies should not be treated as a subaltern discipline operating in translation studies' shadow," has suggested bringing adaptation studies and translation studies together under the banner of psychologist Jean Piaget, whose theory of knowledge acquisition in each childhood "offers a credible model for understanding how individuals make sense of the world, and how adaptation and translation are intrinsic to that process" (Raw 495, 499). Katja Krebs suggests that "theatre offers an abundance of case studies that blur the distinction between adaptation processes, as well as products" (Krebs 45). Susan Knutson, drawing on the work of "theatre practitioners and scholars in Québec," proposes "tradaptation"—a term both combining and straddling the two processes—as "a word for the future" (Knutson 112). More recently, Johannes Fehrle and Mark Schmitt have observed:

[A]n approach that brings into contact the disciplines of adaptation and translation studies reveals not only that the boundaries between translation and adaptation are highly diffuse and dependent on historical and cultural contexts. It also means that many of the questions and methods developed in the respective fields are, in fact, compatible and can be fruitfully brought into contact.

(Fehrle and Schmitt 3)

Fehrle and Schmitt "propose the concept of cultural 'translation'" as a way of uniting "adaptation and translation as both lenses and metaphors to explore the traveling of cultures, discourses, and concepts across a wide array of fields" (Fehrle and Schmitt 2).

In her analysis of the borders *Persepolis* and its author cross, Mousavi considers adaptation and translation as indispensable and interrelated processes. Like adaptation, Mousavi contends, "[t]ranslation is performative in the three senses in situations of migration in general, and in migratory self-adaptation in particular: 1- it *does* things, 2- it includes processes and relations, and 3- it shapes identities" (Mousavi 105). She cites Moira Inghilleri's distinction "between two understandings of translation in the migratory context as 'dialogue about difference' and 'dialogue across difference'" (Mousavi 106; see Inghilleri 12).

One last set of moral questions about adaptation as border crossing is raised by the transformative journeys of Barbie and Ken. The plot of *Barbie* assigns pivotal importance to border crossings between Barbieland and the Real World. Weird Barbie (Kate McKinnon) first advises Barbie (Margot Robbie) to make this trip as an immigrant seeking to get in touch with her roots in the community between Barbie and Sasha (Ariana Greenblatt), the young woman who owns her, in the hope of discovering the source of the intimations of mortality that have so disturbed her equilibrium. After her sadly unrewarding reunion with Sasha and her much more illuminating reunion with Sasha's mother Gloria (America Ferrara), Barbie, shocked that "I thought that Barbie had made the Real World better, but the Real World is forever and irrevocably messed up," returns to Barbieland only to discover that Ken (Ryan Gosling), who made the trip with her, has learned all about the power of patriarchy in the Real World and resolved to bring patriarchy back home with him. He has renamed Barbieland Kendom and taken over her Dreamhouse, which he's renamed the Casa Ken Mojo Dojo House and turned into a male-governed fortress that lacks the social transparency of the Dreamhouse. Even this house makes border crossing into an important issue, for Ken, convinced that Barbie can't see him from outside his doorway even though the house has no walls, treats its boundaries as a good deal more impregnable than the film does. After the patriarchal motion to change the constitution of Barbieland is defeated when all the Barbies distract all the Kens from voting so that they can cast the deciding votes themselves, a weeping Ken opens the door of the Mojo Dojo House and disappears inside, only to be followed a moment later by Barbie, who seeks to console him by entering the house through the open space left by the nonexistent wall next to the door.

To these there-and-back-again journeys the film adds the journeys of Sasha and Gloria and the Mattel executives determined to reassert proprietary control over Barbie. If *Barbie* weren't a pastel fantasy about dolls, the questions raised by these journeys would be deeply troubling. Who should rightfully be in charge of Barbieland (or Kendom)? What is the proper relation of women (dolls) to men (dolls)? Who owns Barbie, and who has the right to control her thoughts and her behavior? Would Barbieland lose its appeal if its males and females wielded equal power? As it is, the journeys that begin as quests for solutions to specific problems in the film's fantasy world end up being mutually informing and enriching for all parties and lands without ever resolving those problems. As in *Persepolis*, the kinds of transformation fostered by crossing borders turn out to be formative.

Questions

- What are the relations between the ways adaptations and other texts cross borders?
- Are there adaptations that don't cross any borders?
- Are there texts of any kind that don't cross any borders?
- When we consider the ethics of adaptation as a border-crossing practice, which rights should be paramount—those of emigrants, immigrants, producers, source cultures, or target cultures?
- How would adaptation studies change if we prioritized adaptation as a process of migration regulated but not produced by laws over adaptations as a series of entities that are defined by the laws governing emigration and immigration?
- Should adaptation scholars seek to naturalize, problematize, or construct and defend borders between adaptations and other textual and human practices that involve border crossings?
- What do sociological engagements allow or reveal about adaptations that other engagements don't?

References

Anderson, Benedict. *Imagined Communities: Reflections on the Origin and Spread of Nationalism*. Revised ed. Verso, 2006.

Ang, Ien. *Watching Dallas: Soap Opera and the Melodramatic Imagination*. Routledge, 1989.

Brzeski, Patrick. "How Japanese Anime Became the World's Most Bankable Genre," *Hollywood Reporter*, May 16, 2022, https://www.hollywoodreporter.com/busin ess/business-news/japanese-anime-worlds-most-bankable-genre-1235146810/.

Chute, Hillary. *Graphic Women*. Columbia UP, 2010.

Dawkins, Richard. *The Selfish Gene*. Second ed. Oxford UP, 1989.

Della Coletta, Cristina. *When Stories Travel: Cross-Cultural Encounters between Fiction and Film*. Johns Hopkins UP, 2012.

Fehrle, Johannes and Mark Schmitt. "Introduction: Adaptation as Translation: Transferring Cultural Narratives." *Komparatistik Online*, 2018.

Gadamer, Hans-Georg. *Truth and Method*. Translated by Joel Weinsheimer and Donald G. Marshall. Continuum, 1995.

Hetherington, Janet. "'Persepolis' in Motion." *Animation World Network*, Dec. 21, 2007, https://www.awn.com/animationworld/persepolis-motion.

Inghilleri, Moira. *Translation and Migration*. Routledge, 2017.

Johnson, Corey, Reece Jones, Anssi Paasi, Louise Amoor, Alison Mountz, Mark Salter, and Chris Rumford. "Interventions on Rethinking 'the Border' in Border Studies," *Political Geography*, vol. 30, no. 2 (2011), pp. 61–69.

Knutson, Susan. "'Tradaptation *Dans le Sense Québécois*: A Word for the Future." *Translation, Adaptation, and Transformation*. Edited by Laurence Raw. Continuum, 2012, pp. 112–22.

Krebs, Katja. "Translation and Adaptation—Two Sides of an Ideological Coin." *Translation, Adaptation, and Transformation*. Edited by Laurence Raw. Continuum, 2012, pp. 42–53.

Lee, Paul S.N. "The Absorption and Indigenisation of Foreign Media Cultures." *Asian Journal of Communication*, vol. 1, no. 2 (1991).

Lefevere, André. *Translating Literature: The German Tradition from Luther to Rosenzweig*. Van Gorcum, 1977.

Leitch, Thomas. "Adaptation as Migration." *Interfaces*, no. 47 (2022), pp. 10–25, https://journals.openedition.org/interfaces/5304.

Lindelof, Damon. "'The Leftovers' Still Speaks to Loss and Grief." *New York Times*, Aug. 14, 2024, section C, p. 4.

"Made in New York." *New York*, Sept. 18, 1978, p. 79.

Martin, Alfred L., Jr. "Blackbusting Hollywood: Racialized Media Reception, Failure, and *The Wiz* as Black Blockbuster." *Journal of Cinema and Media Studies*, vol. 60. no. 2 (Winter 2021), pp. 56–79.

Naficy, Hamid. *An Accented Cinema: Exilic and Diasporic Filmmaking*. Princeton UP, 2001.

O'Regan, Tom. *Australian National Cinema*. Routledge, 1996.

Öz, Seda. "The Politics of Transnational Remakes: A Turkish *Young Frankenstein*." *Literature/Film Quarterly*, vol. 50, no. 2 (Spring 2022), https://lfq.salisbury.edu/_issues/50_2/the_politics_of_transnational_film_remakes_a_turkish_young_frankenstein.html

Rajewsky, Irina O. "Border Talks: The Problematic Status of Media Borders in the Current Debate about Intermediality." *Media Borders, Multimodality and Intermediality*. Edited by Lars Elleström. Palgrave Macmillan, 2010, pp. 51–68.

Raw, Laurence. "Aligning Adaptation Studies with Translation Studies," *The Oxford Handbook of Adaptation Studies*. Edited by Thomas Leitch. Oxford UP, 2017, pp. 494–508.

Rousseau, Jean-Jacques. *The Confessions of Jean-Jacques Rousseau*. Translated by J.M. Cohen. Penguin, 1954.

Said, Edward W. *The World, the Text, and the Critic*. Harvard UP, 1983.

Sanders, Julie. *Adaptation and Appropriation*. Routledge, 2006.

Satrapi, Marjane. *The Complete Persepolis*. Translated by Anjali Singh. Pantheon, 2004.

Smith, Iain Robert. *The Hollywood Meme: Transnational Adaptations in World Cinema*. Edinburgh UP, 2016.

Striphas, Ted. "Communication as Translation." *Communication as …: Perspectives on Theory*. Edited by Gregory J. Shepherd, Jeffrey St. John, and Ted Striphas. SAGE, 2006, pp. 232–41.

Venuti, Lawrence. "Adaptation, Translation, Critique," *Journal of Visual Culture*, vol. 6, no. 1 (2007), pp. 25–43, https://citeseerx.ist.psu.edu/document?repid=rep1&type=pdf&doi=91133d9b5f299464c6ac9f8d1b6c5f2b8c7a4c81.

White, Richard. "Cooees Across the Strand: Australian Travelers in London and the Performance of National Identity." *Australian Historical Studies*, vol. 32 (2001), pp. 109–27.

6 Participatory engagements

Adaptation as play

Convergence culture

The state of adaptation studies, which had already been shaped repeatedly by reactions against canonical approaches, intertextual approaches, and industrial approaches, was challenged in unprecedented ways by the rapid rise and spread of new digital media at the dawn of the twenty-first century. The new mediascape was distinguished by several factors. One was the profusion of emerging media and media platforms, from videogames to computers to smartphones and the social media they spawned, which marginalized the traditional literature-to-film model of adaptation still further. Another, highlighted by the title of Henry Jenkins's broadly influential 2006 study *Convergence Culture: Where Old and New Media Collide*, was the interactions among these media, which made it possible for Lana and Lily Wachowski, once they had released *The Matrix* in 1999, to use "transmedia storytelling" (Jenkins, *Convergence* 21) to build an impressive range of Matrix fictions across many media, from feature-length film sequels and animated cartoons to fan fiction sites, chatrooms, and message boards, each of which supplied new information about the world of the Matrix that could not be accessed through any other platform, encouraging die-hard fans to hop from one platform to the next in search of the information that would allow them to reconstruct the most comprehensive storyworld possible. A third, indicated by the nature of these last few venues, was the growing ability of fans to participate actively in shaping franchises like *The Matrix* and *Lord of the Rings* (2001–3) through online discussions, suggestions, and demands that established them as a powerful community of stakeholders even the most powerful corporations feared offending:

> If old consumers were assumed to be passive, the new consumers are active. If old consumers were predictable and stayed where you told them to stay, then new consumers are migratory, showing a declining loyalty to networks or media. If old consumers were isolated individuals, the new

DOI: 10.4324/9781003438410-7

consumers are more socially connected. If the work of media consumers was once silent and invisible, the new consumers are now noisy and public.
(Jenkins, *Convergence* 18–19)

An early signal of corporate producers' recognition of the growing power of audiences came in the closing credits of the DVD releases of the three *Lord of the Rings* film adaptations, which included an acknowledgment expressing thanks for the support of all charter members of the Lord of the Rings Fan Club—a hyperextended moment in the credit crawl that lasted for 20 minutes, far longer than all the remaining credits combined.

The transition from a culture of what Roland Barthes called "readerly texts"—those designed to be passively consumed and enjoyed—to a culture of what Barthes called "writerly texts," which encourage and reward active participation, raised many questions about the relation of the new mediascape to the old. Jenkins, who defined convergence as "the flow of content across multiple media platforms, the cooperation between multiple media industries, and the migratory behavior of media audiences who will go almost anywhere in search of the kinds of entertainment experiences they want," viewed this brave new world in terms that invited comparison to Jorge Luis Borges's visionary Library of Babel, an infinite collection that contained not only every book ever written but every book that could possibly be written: "In the world of media convergence, every important story gets told, every brand gets sold, and every consumer gets courted across multiple media platforms" (Jenkins, *Convergence* 2, 3). A crucial difference, however, emerges in the word *important*. Jenkins's convergence culture does not tell every story imaginable, only the most important stories. Although Jenkins leaves undefined the question of what makes a story important (universal themes that speak to audiences across many cultures? Widespread brand recognition? Mammoth sales?), he is certain that the fans, once relegated to the sidelines as mere consumers, now join individual and corporate producers in determining which stories are the most important.

Once "[t]he popping of the dot-com bubble" (Jenkins, *Convergence* 6) made it clear that new digital media were not simply going to replace old media like books and paintings, as Nicholas Negroponte had predicted in *Being Digital* (1990) and Sven Birkerts had feared in *The Gutenberg Elegies* (1994), questions about the new mediascape were supplemented by questions about the old mediascape that no one had thought to ask. Surveying a disruptive historical moment in which "the emerging convergence paradigm assumes that old and new media will interact in ever more complex ways," industry leaders reimagined convergence as "a way of making sense of a moment of disorienting change" (Jenkins, *Convergence* 6). Writing in 2006, Jenkins predicted that "[c]ollective intelligence can be seen as an alternative source of media power ... Right now, we are mostly using this collective power through our recreational life, but soon we will be deploying these skills for more 'serious' purposes" (Jenkins, *Convergence* 4).

Surveying the ever more dramatic encroachments of digital affordances like deepfake photos, AI-generated text, and household appliances like Amazon's Alexa is far beyond the scope of this book. But the impact of convergence culture on adaptation is inextricably linked to many of these other changes, beginning with audiences' changing views of themselves. Jenkins makes no secret of his status as what Alvin Toffler calls a "prosumer" (Toffler 282–305), someone who is both a producer and a consumer of the texts he most loves, adding: "I am not simply a consumer of many of these media products; I am also an active fan" (Jenkins, *Convergence* 12). Jenkins's description of himself as an "acafan" (see Jenkins, "Acafandom") has been widely adopted by many other fans who happen to be academics.

Jenkins complicates this both/and model by observing: "Entertainment content isn't the only thing that flows across multiple media platforms. Our lives, relationships, memories, fantasies, desires also flow across media channels. Being a lover or a mommy or a teacher occurs on multiple platforms" (Jenkins, *Convergence* 17). Calling convergence "both a top-down corporate-driven process and a bottom-up consumer-driven process," he explains that "new media technologies have ... enabled consumers to archive, annotate, appropriate, and recirculate media in powerful new ways. At the same time, there has been an alarming concentration of the ownership of mainstream commercial media" (Jenkins, *Convergence* 18, 17–18). Asking which of these forces—the drive to disperse power enabled by emerging digital technologies or the drive to centralize power at the hands of increasingly monopolistic content providers—is dominant, he decides that "the truth lies somewhere in between" (Jenkins, *Convergence* 18). The battle he describes between corporations determined to retain control of the intellectual property they have commissioned and the prosumers who increasingly regard this property as their own, many of them casting themselves as outlaws fighting the power rather than consumers content to enjoy the nourishment dished out to them, continues apace.

In summarizing his impressions of The New Orleans Media Experience—a 2003 gathering that combined a film festival, a lineup of concerts and theatrical performances, a showcase for new game releases, commercials, and music videos, and a series of panels and discussions with the leaders of HSI Productions—Jenkins lists three takeaways that have come to seem prophetic:

1. Convergence is coming and you had better be ready.
2. Convergence is harder than it sounds.
3. Everyone will survive if everyone works together. (Unfortunately, that was the one thing nobody knew how to do.)

(Jenkins, Convergence 10)

Citing foundational texts on media convergence by Negroponte and Ithiel de Sola Pool, Jenkins observes: "Digitization set the conditions for convergence; corporate conglomerates created its imperative" (Jenkins, *Convergence* 11).

He notes with some amusement that as individual storyworlds like that of *The Matrix* expanded over an ever-wider range of platforms, the technologies required to deliver different updates to those storyworlds stubbornly refused to converge. Seeking to refute "the Black Box Fallacy," which predicted that "all media content is going to flow through a single black box into our living rooms (or, in the mobile scenario, through black boxes we carry around with us everywhere we go)," he concludes from the proliferation of his own hardware—"my VCR, my DVD player, my digital recorder, my sound system, and my two game systems"—that "[w]hat we are now seeing is the hardware diverging while the content converges" (Jenkins, *Convergence* 14, 15). In the years since, the smartphone has inched closer and closer toward the center of this array through its ability to deliver more and more different kinds of material and encourage interactive responses undreamed of by the creators of videotapes and DVDs. Whether or not the smartphone is ultimately crowned as the Black Box to rule them all, its rising popularity and the widening range of uses to which it is put suggest that what Jenkins calls "convergence culture" has morphed into something even broader that Jenkins calls "participatory culture": "a culture with relatively low barriers to artistic expression and civic engagement, strong support for creating and sharing creations, and some type of informal mentorship whereby experienced participants pass along knowledge to novices"; a culture whose "members also believe their contributions matter and feel some degree of social connection with one another (at the least, members care about others' opinions of what they have created)" (Jenkins et al. xi).

Writing in 2006, Jenkins sees convergence as more active in popular culture than in political culture but predicts that although "we are mostly using [our] collective power through our recreational life, ... we will soon be deploying [our] skills for more 'serious' purposes" (Jenkins, *Convergence* 4). Sometimes Jenkins makes convergence culture sound like an enormous gamble: "Welcome to convergence culture ... where the power of the media producer and the power of the media consumer interact in unpredictable ways" (Jenkins, *Convergence* 2). Sometimes he makes it sound like a social utopia: "None of us can know everything; each of us knows something; and we can put the pieces together if we pool our resources and combine our skills" (Jenkins, *Convergence* 4). This utopian view of convergence culture, in which consumers-turned-prosumers wrest unprecedented degrees of control over entertainment culture from the industrial capitalists that have long restricted their roles to either consuming or rejecting it, is echoed in the revised 2012 edition of Linda Hutcheon's *A Theory of Adaptation*. Hutcheon's colleague Siobhan O'Flynn, now credited for the first time as the volume's coauthor, supplies a new Epilogue, the principal addition to the new edition, which answers the question the new edition's Preface poses— "For adaptation studies, is ours a transitional time or are we facing a totally new world?" (Hutcheon xix)—by wholeheartedly embracing the latter of these alternatives. For Hutcheon and O'Flynn, convergence culture is a gamechanger that upends the rules and practices of adaptation in irreversible ways. This question becomes even more urgent if, taking our cue from Jenkins's remark that "convergence refers to a process, not an endpoint" (Jenkins, *Convergence* 16), we expand our focus from a convergence culture of interdependent multimedia to an interactive culture that invites active participation from prosumers.

Questions

- Would you call yourself an acafan?
- Given the contradictions between media centralization and decentralization Jenkins examines, which of these forces do you think is dominant now?
- In the time since *Convergence Culture* first appeared, what evidence do you see that it has migrated from popular culture to political culture, or to culture in general?
- Which label—convergence culture, interactive culture, or participatory culture—best describes your own view of contemporary entertainment, and of social culture?

Living with convergence culture

Adaptation scholars considering the place that what Linda Hutcheon calls "adaptation proper" (Hutcheon 171) has in convergence culture have expressed a wide variety of reactions toward Jenkins's analysis. Despite their acknowledgment that "telling" and "showing" modes do not render their audiences "passive" but invite active engagement (Hutcheon xvi, xx, 16, 22f.), Hutcheon and O'Flynn find something fundamentally different in texts like the iBook adaptation *Our Choice*, Al Gore's polemic urging action against climate change, which "adds a wealth of interactive content to the book's text and images" (O'Flynn 204). The most significant change O'Flynn's Epilogue notes in between the 2006 publication of *A Theory of Adaptation* and its second edition six years later is a shift from a world in which "media conglomerates and IP holders once controlled the production and distribution of adaptations" to a world in which "audiences now claim all aspects of ownership over content that they identify with, immerse themselves in, adapt, remix, reuse, and share," forcing these conglomerates into positions that are *"reactive* to the rapid ebb and flow of changing social phenomena, enabled by new technologies and platforms" (O'Flynn 206, 186).

Unlike Hutcheon and O'Flynn, who agree that convergence culture is a landscape that fundamentally changes the rules and practices of textual production and consumption for the better, Kyle Meikle takes the opposing position, drawing his evidence from

[the] children's books (and adaptations thereof) [that] constitute a disproportionate share of convergence culture: the myriad film franchises

based on comics and young adult properties; the growing popularity of digital and analogue games, many of which are adaptations ... and the growing demand for texts like adult coloring books ... some of which, like Fred Armisen, Carrie Brownstein, and Jonathan Kreisel's *The Portlandia Activity Book*, are film or television tie-ins.

(Meikle, "Adaptation" 546)

Citing O'Flynn's description of Trilogy Studios' 2011 iBook adaptation of Crockett Johnson's 1955 storybook *Harold and the Purple Crayon* as "designed to invite interactivity" by "engag[ing] the reader/player in a different way" (Meikle, "Adaptation" 543; see O'Flynn 202) from the book, Meikle notes: "The innovations in Trilogy Studios' iBook seem somewhat less innovative if we speculate on the original book's uses, or the book's original uses" (Meikle, "Adaptation" 543). Despite repeated invitations throughout the book for readers to use their own purple crayons to supplement and complete the drawings its young hero uses to explore the world and deal with obstacles as they arise, Meikle observes, tech reporter Rich DeMuro

implicitly dismisses the interactivity of a child using a crayon to scribble on *Harold*'s pages as unwelcome, just as O'Flynn dismisses the interactivity of parents reading aloud to—or *with*—their children when she frames the iBook's 'Read to Me' mode as innovative. A text like Trilogy Studios' *Harold* doesn't so much innovate new modes of interactivity as it does make explicit the modes of interactivity that were in place all along.

(Meikle, "Adaptation" 543)

"Rather than asking what's new in new media," Meikle proposes, "scholars should ask what's old in adaptations—that is, how adaptations are and always have been interactive" (Meikle, "Adaptation" 545). Just as Johnson invites his readers to use their purple crayons to complete the story as they wish, Meikle invites his readers to actively consider other adaptations as material objects, things that cannot be reduced to thoughts, emotions, ideas, or economic imperatives, and to think in new ways about the political, economic, industrial, and material forces that drive textual marketplaces. Noting that "O'Flynn focuses far more on how new media make meaning as new media than on how adaptations make meaning as adaptations within the context of those new media," and that "[c]onvergence culture threatens to multiply the objects of adaptation study without multiplying its methodologies," Meikle recommends "[r]ethinking the difference between old and new media as one of degree, not of kind," and in particular "considering not (or not only) what new media can do that old media can't, but, more pressingly, what adaptations can do that other texts can't" (Meikle, "Adaptation" 544, 546, 545).

Lars Elleström and other intermedial scholars who agree that adaptations can do things other things can't but want to reserve space for other intermedial and multimodal practices that can do things adaptations can't have argued that adaptation theory is inadequate to account for the dazzling profusion of new textual practices across multiple media and advocated for the more capacious methodology of intermedial theory instead. No consensual agreement has emerged on where to position adaptation among those other practices, or what the implications would be of installing it as the leading intermedial practice. If, as Regina Schober argues, adaptation "is no longer regarded as the exception but instead represents the rule as to how media products and stories emerge, proliferate, and interact with each other" (Schober 32), it might seem that we are entering the Golden Age of Adaptation. On the other hand, if everything is an adaptation, then it might be argued that adaptation studies is pointless, for nothing is gained by labeling any particular text an adaptation.

Taking still another approach, Kamilla Elliott urges adaptation scholars to join translation scholars, most of whom are also translators, in actively producing the texts they are studying by citing her own classroom practice, which involves a

> creative-critical assignment [that] goes beyond the verbal and the rational and beyond scripts, treatments, and storyboards to nonverbal and nonrational adaptations in all kinds of media, accompanied by a critical essay that interprets the student's own adaptation as a response to the work(s) it adapts.
>
> (Elliott 75)

In response to this assignment, Elliott's students have

> not only made films, they have also adapted media in many other forms: writing, dramatizing, storyboarding, filming, novelizing, graphic-novelising, drawing, illustrating, painting, sculpting, set designing, costuming, staging, scoring, puppeteering, acting, dancing, singing, editing, directing, casting, choreographing, gaming, videogaming, and producing marketing materials, film posters, book covers, news articles, political pamphlets, magazine spreads, scrapbooks, and multimedia installations.
>
> (Elliott 77)

Elliott regards these creations—ranging from a boardgame based on *Gone with the Wind* to a suitcase adapting "Strange Case of Dr. Jekyll and Mr. Hyde"—not as alternatives to analyzing adaptation, but as new ways of engaging adaptation as a practice in which her students, like the prosumers of Toffler and Jenkins, have an active stake. Her approach, which sounds remarkably cutting-edge, is in its own way a return to a much older approach in literary studies, in which teachers of English courses a century ago—in the days before new criticism provided a breakthrough methodology for close reading—asked their students to fulfill assignments not by writing analytical essays about Virgil's *Eclogues* (44–38 B.C.E.) or Shakespeare's sonnets (1609), but by translating one of Virgil's poems or writing an imitation of one of Shakespeare's sonnets themselves.

Elliott's practice suggests still another possible approach to convergence culture: accepting its implicit invitation to reexamine longstanding assumptions about the consumer culture it seems to be decentering or replacing. Although it might seem, for example, that consumer culture has been around forever, in fact it has had a relatively short history itself. As Toffler points out, nomadic and agricultural communities in which "most people consumed what they themselves produced" (Toffler 283) had no room for consumer culture. It was not until a significant fraction of a culture's population had disposable income and a significant number and range of industrial and cultural artifacts and experiences were made available to this potential audience that it would make sense to talk about consumer culture. The great painters and sculptors of the Italian Renaissance worked for aristocratic patrons who offered them financial support in return for the promise of a stream of new works instead of paying individually for those works as consumer goods. In the same way, Johann Sebastian Bach and Franz Joseph Haydn spent most of their careers as employees of churches or aristocratic patrons for whom they served as in-house composers; it was not until the last years of Haydn's life that the impresario Joseph Salomon arranged to bring him to London, where he composed his final 12 symphonies for the enjoyment of paying customers—not long after the rise of the novel and the growing popularity of magazines had made literary careers possible in England. Participatory culture is much older than consumer culture, as both Plato and Aristotle realized in Plato's attack on theatrical productions as twice removed from reality, which Aristotle in turn defended for their ability to arouse the reactions of pity and terror, serving an important civic function by inviting the aristocrats of ancient Athens who had gathered in amphitheaters to share in collective experiences that would make them literally better Athenians.

Observing that Jenkins "explicates the notion of convergence culture in terms of complexity or network theory, without explicitly using those terms," Regina Schober urges a new engagement with adaptation that emphasizes what Werner Wolf calls "function" over aesthetic fidelity or evolutionary success:

Of the various implications the network perspective may have, I would argue that three are particularly relevant. Firstly, convergence culture "as network" focuses more on the process rather than on the result or "art work." Secondly, the decentralized quality of adaptation and convergence urges us to rethink agency and control. Thirdly, adaptation processes display emergent properties that result from complex reciprocal interaction. Taken together, these three principles shift the focus from "fidelity" and "origin" to "function" and enable a scalable, thus multidimensional, approach to the study of adaptation as a shifting configuration of ideas, media, and human actors.

(Schober 44, 46)

This recommendation may sound forbiddingly earnest. After all, what could be more serious than thinking constantly about the function of every adaptation in every context, even as those contexts shimmer and change from moment to moment? In practice, however, participatory communities define adaptations in terms of their functions because they seek and use them for those very functions themselves. Long before massive multiplayer online roleplaying games brought together players who would never meet each other in person, boardgames, card games, and roleplaying games brought together smaller communities who took pleasure in both the gaming experience and the company of others. Long before digital culture made online membership in the Lord of the Rings Fan Club possible, in-person fan clubs met to celebrate Sherlock Holmes' or Frank Sinatra's power to engage members and bring them together in pleasurable ways. Long before Elliott designed the creative-critical assignments that made her courses so distinctive, literature programs typically featured weekly meetings designed to engage students in active discussions of *A Midsummer Night's Dream* or *The Tale of Genji* in order to sharpen those students' skills in literary analysis while also introducing them to the rewards of membership in an intellectual community. When Jenkins notes that "knowledge becomes power in the age of media convergence" (Jenkins, *Convergence* 20), he is updating a bromide that proponents of liberal education had propagated for generations during the age of the book.

Instead of regarding shifts in power from media conglomerates to fan communities as the latest moves in a zero-sum game in which each side's gains must be matched by the other side's losses, it makes sense to look more closely at Jenkins's remark that "the skills we acquire through play may have implications for how we learn, work, participate in the political process, and connect with other people around the world" (Jenkins, *Convergence* 23) in the light of Hutcheon and O'Flynn's observation that "iPads and iPhones have become new sites for adaptive play" (Hutcheon xix). Prosumers can choose to maintain the hierarchies they grew up with or to play with them in ways that share power, and generate new ways of thinking about power, through transformative participation.

Questions

- What becomes of intellectual property claims in convergence culture? How far would you be willing to go in protecting claims about the origin, agency, or ownership of intellectual property?
- Is social knowledge additive or progressive? Does each new development in cultural understanding require a reset that reinvents the wheel?

- Which of the three approaches Schober identifies—through fidelity, success, or function—seems to you more useful in engaging particular adaptations and adaptation in general?
- Of the three broad implications of defining adaptations in terms of network theory—emphasizing process over product, rethinking agency, and emphasizing reciprocality—which is most important and which is most novel? Or have you already seen them all before within different approaches to adaptation?
- Given the obvious downsides of real-world adaptation, is this particular game worth the risk? What sorts of rules would you propose for real-world adaptation that would promote responsible play?

Playing adaptations

Of the many kinds of play that adaptations engage and invite, the most obvious appear in film adaptations specifically based on games. One of the first of these, Jonathan Lynn's 1985 movie *Clue*, provides an especially comprehensive map of the kinds of play these films do and do not permit. The film, based on Waddington's boardgame *Cluedo* (known in the United States as the Parker Brothers game *Clue*), begins with the murder of Mr. Boddy, whose six guests—Colonel Mustard, Professor Plum, Mr. Green, Mrs. Peacock, Miss Scarlett, and Mrs. White—immediately become suspects. The film, like the game, takes the form of a quest to determine which of these six committed the murder and also, rather improbably, what the murder weapon was and where the crime was committed.

Players of the game, whose answers to these questions lie in three unseen cards placed in an envelope in the middle of the board, choose one character they will play as they move from room to room within the house and propose hypothetical solutions to the mystery by consulting the cards they have been dealt, making suggestions to other players, and then narrowing their suggestions based on the cards that other players have shown them. Every time the game is played, the mystery is solved by a process of logical elimination or by an inspired guess. The film makes no attempt to duplicate these affordances. There are no cards that indicate the solution to the mystery; audience members do not choose playing pieces identified with particular characters; and although audience members watching the film are free to make guesses about the solution, they cannot confirm or disconfirm these guesses by consulting other members. Nor is the film competitive in the way the game is: audiences can neither win nor lose as they move toward the solution together.

The film adds several new elements to the game. It adds characters like Wadsworth the butler and Yvette the maid. Its casting of well-known character actors like Madeleine Kahn, Christopher Lloyd, and Martin Mull allows it to play with the stereotypical characters the game presents. It adds a plot in which the characters' quest for clues is supplemented by their suspicions of each other and extended by several other murders of minor characters. And, in its boldest stroke, it includes three different endings presenting three different solutions to the crime. Audiences who watched the film during its first theatrical release saw one of these endings chosen at random; if they returned to a different theater, they might well see a different ending. Home video releases of the film featured all three endings. Yet none of these playful elements encourages the kinds of play the boardgame permits. Viewers of the film cannot rely on other viewers to feed them information; they cannot attempt to deceive other viewers (e.g., by suggesting solutions they know are incorrect) in the hope of beating them to the solution; they can do nothing to control the pace or outcome of the mystery; they can neither win nor lose the game. Although the film incorporates many elements of the game and can be just as playful as the game—or even, in its way, more playful—it is not a game itself. It is clearly less interactive because it necessarily limits the ways in which fans of the game can participate in its mystery. Audiences of the movie can still interact with it by whispering or shouting remarks to fellow audience members like, "It's Yvette! She's not really dead! Wait and see!" or, "They're all in it together!", but these remarks are no more or less appropriate to *Clue* than to any other film or stage production. Given all these limitations, it is no surprise that the 1990 television show based on *Monopoly*, another Parker Brothers boardgame, lasted only 13 weeks even though its game-show format allowed it to be far more competitive and interactive.

The videogames based on *Monopoly* and *Clue* replicate the experience of playing these games more faithfully because videogames allow much more interactive participation than movies, and participation of the same kinds that the boardgames allow. Players who enjoy videogames like *Monopoly*, *Clue*, *Othello*, *Pictionary*, or the countless versions of checkers, chess, dominoes, and solitaire that are available expect to have the same kinds of experiences the boardgames provide, with some added bonuses: they don't have to shuffle the cards or reset the playing pieces in between games, and they can play by themselves or against the computer if no other players are present, as they rarely are on the airline flights that often make these games available.

Videogames are clearly participatory adaptations. Even when they do not adapt boardgames like *Clue*, print texts like the Harry Potter books, or movies like *Monty Python and the Holy Grail* (1975), the later generations of them that designers and fans alike hope will follow are adaptations of their earlier generations. And videogames adapt a dazzling array of different materials. *The Wolf Among Us* (2013) is based on the Fables comic-book series by Bill Willingham. *Never Alone* (2014) constructs a world based on the Iñupiaq stories of Alaska Native cultures. *Breath of the Wild* (2017) incorporates references to fabulous monsters, a century-old curse, and the sword in the stone into the storyworld of *The Legend of Zelda*, first launched in 1983. *Epic Mickey* (2009)—a testament to Disney's boundless ability to reinvent itself by plundering its backlist—is presumably aimed at serious nostalgia buffs with significant investments in Disneyland, the Blot, Oswald the

Lucky Rabbit, the 1937 Mickey Mouse short *Through the Mirror* (1937), and other early manifestations of Mickey before he became less of an upstart and more of a family man.

At the same time, videogames allow many other kinds of engagements with adaptations. Fans are frequently sensitive to their fidelity or infidelity to valued texts like *Pokémon* (1996–) or *Lord of the Rings* (1954–55), even as they use the games to raise questions about how faithful they can or should be to non-game sources. The many generations of games like *Grand Theft Auto* (1997–2021), along with the different versions of games produced for different consoles, allow both repetition and intertextual correction and improvement—a process dramatized and accelerated by "romhacking," in which players get under the hood and modify the read-only memory files of specific games to suit their own tastes. Fans' keen awareness of production companies' economics and politics emphasizes their status as industrial products. Although relatively few videogames emphasize biological processes, the processes of their own gestation and their competition for survival suggest that each of them represents a more or less successfully evolved mutation of some earlier version. And videogames like *This War of Mine* (2014) and *Whisper of a Rose* (2014), which have fostered greater social awareness of sensitive subjects like the costs of warfare and bullying, have reflected producers' and players' increasing investment in sociological engagements.

Despite their differences, all these engagements can be seen as representing diverse aspects of play—if we simply define play broadly enough. Ian Bogost's discussion of videogames borrows one such definition from Eric Zimmerman:

> Instead of understanding play as child's activity, or as the means to consume games, or even as the shifting centers of meaning in poststructuralist though, I suggest [defining play as] "the free space of movement within a more rigid structure." Understood in this sense, play refers to the "possibility space" created by constraints of all kinds. Play activities are not rooted in one social practice, but in many social and material practices.
>
> (Bogost 120; see Zimmerman 159)

Bogost's full-throated defense of videogames builds on James Paul Gee's argument that "when young people are interacting with video games—and other popular cultural practices—they are learning, and learning in deep ways," because "[g]ood video games offer players strong identities"; they "make players think like scientists"; they "let players be producers, not just consumers"; they "lower the consequences of failure"; they "allow players to customize the game to fit their learning and playing styles"; they "encourage players to think about relationships, not isolated events, facts, and skills"; they "encourage a distinctive view of intelligence"; and they "operate by a principle of performance before competence" (Gee 215–18). These defenses both echo and invert Virginia Woolf's ferocious attack on the cinema nearly a century earlier. Bogost explains:

In a video game, the possibility space refers to the myriad configurations the player might construct to see the ways the processes inscribed in the system might work. This is really what we do when we *play* video games: we explore the possibility space its rules afford by manipulating the symbolic systems the game provides.

(Bogost 121)

He goes on to link this broad understanding of play to Kenneth Burke's equally broad understanding of rhetoric, which

extends rhetoric beyond persuasion, instead suggesting "identification" as a key term for this practice. We use symbolic systems like language, says Burke, as a way to achieve this identification ... In addition to expanding the conception of rhetoric, Burke expands its domain. In the tradition of oral and written rhetoric, language remains central. But Burke's understanding of humans as creators and consumers of symbolic systems expands rhetoric to include nonverbal domains known and yet to be invented or discovered.

(Bogost 124; see Burke 19)

Videogames, in Bogost's view, give their players practice in many different kinds of identification—with the characters they are playing, with their opponents, with the issues at stake in a given game, and even with nonhuman agents and the larger world:

Video games are models of real and imagined systems. We always *play* when we use video games, but the sort of play that we perform is not always the stuff of leisure. Rather, when we play, we explore the possibility space of a set of rules—we learn to understand and evaluate a game's meaning. Video games make arguments about how social or cultural systems work in the world—or how they could work, or don't work.

(Bogost 136)

Bogost's argument may seem familiar because it could clearly be made about all adaptations, which invite their readers and viewers and listeners and consumers to play with them, modeling this play on the ways in which the adaptations themselves play with the texts or experiences they adapt. This play may sometimes be frivolous, but it also has the ability to be serious, for "video games are not just stages that facilitate cultural, social, or political practices; they are also media where cultural values themselves can be represented—for critique, satire, education, or commentary" (Bogost 119). This combination of representation and participation allows videogames to "make claims about the world. But when they do, they do it not with oral speech, nor in writing, nor even with images. Rather, video games make argument with *processes*" (Bogost 125)—just as adaptations in any medium do for audiences that are alert to the processes behind both the creation of adaptations and their own participation in them.

If Bogost's account of videogames opens the door to taking their engagement with real-world problems and processes seriously, Alenda Y. Chang leaps through that doorway in her discussion of videogames not as exercises in virtual reality—a term she finds overloaded with "technological, historical, and contemporary baggage"—but as mesocosms, an ecological term that refers to "experimental enclosures intermediate in size and complexity between small, highly controlled lab experiments and large, often unpredictable real-world environments" (A.Y. Chang 39, 17). For Chang, who describes videogames as "environmental text[s]" (32)—a term she borrows from Lawrence Buell (Buell 6):

> games and scientific experimentation are cut from the same cloth ... Describing games as mesocosms is for me the ideal way to characterize the subtle negotiations that take place between human and nonhuman actors and technological assemblages during play, while also taking into account diverse situational and interpretive contexts.
>
> (A.Y. Chang 32, 20)

Unsurprisingly, given this analogy between games and experiments, her account of gameplaying places much less emphasis on play than Bogost's:

> Having been saturated for some time by sometimes amorphous notions of play, narrative, and computation, games are sorely in need of more diverse forms of critical articulation even as they offer particularly fertile terrain upon which to raise questions of environmental representation, knowledge, and ethics—questions that have dogged ecocritical attempts to reconcile the natural and ecological with the literary and artistic.
>
> (A.Y. Chang 24)

Chang's discussion of mesocosms focuses on videogames that are directly concerned with physical environments or ecological problems, like Will Crowther's 1975 text game *Adventure*, also known as *Colossal Cave Adventure*; *Firewatch*, a 2016 game set in a space modeled on Shoshone National Forest; and *World without Oil*, a 2007 game that "simulated a thirty-two-week global oil crisis over the course of thirty-two days, challenging its players (who played themselves) to imagine an alternate reality uncomfortably close to our present times" (A.Y. Chang 53). Although she acknowledges the playful side of videogaming, she subordinates it to the responsibilities these games work to make their players more acutely aware of: "[T]he ideal environmental text produces involvement. It brings the nonhuman world into equal prominence with the human, exposes humanity's moral responsibility to and participation in the natural world, and portrays the environment as fluid process, not static representation" (A.Y. Chang 32).

For Chang, as for Gee and Bogost, play is not an alternative to collective engagement; it is an invitation to a very particular and powerful kind of collective engagement.

By extending invitations parallel to those of What Would Jesus Do? bracelets, videogames can function as hypothetical mesocosms in many different ways. *The Sims* (2000–) encourages players to focus on the mundane economics of maintaining and developing the world the game presents through what Chang calls the "selective fidelity" of "ecomimesis" (A.Y. Chang 37, 24). Since videogames adapt earlier videogames and earlier stories as well as the world outside, their relations to those other texts are varied and often complex. If *Pokémon* (1996–) seems to have little connection to the real world, *World of Warcraft* (2004–) has a much closer connection. The *Legend of Zelda* games (1986–) add ecological urgency to playing the game successfully. Fans of *Fallout* (1997–) have spent a great deal of time on discussion boards commenting on the accuracy of its maps of real-world cities. Even *Super Mario Bros.* (1985–86) refers at some level of abstraction to the real world, as the exaggerated Italian accents of Mario and Luigi indicate. More generally, all videogames heighten and impart urgency to present-day actions since—unlike most novels, for instance—they unfold by presenting an often rapid-fire series of dangers and obstacles players must overcome in their own indefinitely extended present to move to the next level. And the more imaginary worlds players master, the less likely they are to take the problems of their own world for granted.

Of course, not all videogames explicitly invite their players to contemplate ecological issues. Indeed, there are almost as many different ways to play videogames as there are to play games in general. Players can race to finish their favorite games or linger over the increasingly realistic audiovisual worlds these games present. They can focus on competing with other players, either sitting next to them or joining them online from thousands of miles away, for victory. They can compete with themselves, trying to improve their best times as they move from level to level, spurred by their increasing success in adapting their strategies for playing a particular game, or take the time to explore all the highways and byways of each game, deliberately going down unpromising paths in order to see what kinds of dead ends they lead to. Some fans eagerly wait weeks or months for the release of games they can hardly wait to play; others play old favorites to revisit a familiar world from a new perspective. And, of course, countless players cue up videogames on their cellphones to kill time while they are waiting for something else to happen.

The popularity of walkthroughs—video tours posted online or on social media that allow audiences to follow more experienced players as they negotiate the obstacles of specific games and point out opportunities, pitfalls, and Easter eggs—suggests that the experience of videogames may not always be participatory; sometimes prospective players deliberately adopt the roles of audiences looking for introductions and tips to games they are thinking about buying or playing themselves. Many people enjoy watching their friends or partners play games—whether because they hope to learn from these vicarious experiences, because they want to enjoy their sense of superiority to novice players falling into traps the viewers have learned to avoid, or because they want to bond with the players over a shared experience, even if it's an experience of a game they wouldn't particularly want to play themselves. But even these vicarious experiences are interactive in the same ways the experiences of all adaptations are interactive.

Chang pursues this line of reasoning when she asks: "Can games really promote learning, activism, and lifestyle change? The designers of educational games and the broader category of serious games ... would certainly answer in the affirmative" (A.Y. Chang 64). She adds: "As Henry Jenkins and Alexander Galloway have pointed out, however, granting games this ability also renders them susceptible to the criticism of media-effects theories, most prominent among them what Galloway calls the 'Columbine theory' of video game violence" (A.Y. Chang 64), which encourages players who have become desensitized to violence to act out their violent fantasies in the real world. For better or worse, gaming has always had a dark side. Individual players who become addicted to their favorite games can miss other engagements or deadlines, neglect important responsibilities, or become sleep-deprived or physically or mentally exhausted. Players who devote themselves to game-breaking—introducing bugs that render games either unchallenging or unplayable for others—demonstrate a distinctly antisocial behavior that has affinities with equally antisocial behavior in other adaptations (e.g., deliberately bungling your lines during a stage production to throw off your fellow performers). The behavior of gaming communities can be equally antisocial, as when they discourage, ridicule, or expel novice gamers. Newcomers to a given gaming ecosphere can quickly learn that despite its positive overtones, the term "ecosphere" can include a great deal of hostile behavior posing dangers even more consequential, if less visually dramatic, than those represented in the game worlds themselves. Although many of these dangers are specific to videogames, versions of most of them can be found in adaptations of all kinds, for as soon as we grant that play has consequences, we must accept the corollary that some of those consequences may be highly undesirable. For all its strengths, adaptation is never neutral.

Questions

- When you play videogames, do you prefer to experience familiar or unfamiliar worlds? Is it more fun to play a particular videogame the first time or the hundredth time?
- More generally, which has the higher value: the exhilarating novelty of unfamiliar worlds or the experience that makes familiar worlds easier to negotiate?

- Do you and the gamers you know (seek to) experience videogames primarily as adaptations? Does the answer to this question depend on the specific game at hand?
- Is videogame literacy fundamentally passive or active?
- Do games teach you how to play them? If so, are they the only texts that do?
- Are videogames more transmedial than other games? Are they more transmedial than other texts? Does their transmediality automatically make them all adaptations?
- How would you explain "why we should bother to create literature, art, or games that portray people's relationships to their environment" (A.Y. Chang 39)?
- Is videogame literacy as essential to cultural literacy as the mastery of reading and writing?

Playing outside the box

Along with videogames, superhero movies have been the most commercially successful and widely discussed instance of convergence culture—an interactive culture in which the meaning and value of every new production in a given cluster are incomplete. The Marvel and DC Universes have extended their domain across multiple movies that often require the audience's knowledge of earlier installments in the franchise as the price of informed admission. Particularly devoted fans can tap into resources far beyond these movies, actively participating in the franchises by attending conventions like ComicCon, dressing as their favorite superheroes, blogging about their devotion to the franchise, and generating new adventures that they post on fansites and vlogs. These different activities, which have helped to brand convergence culture as participatory culture, emphasize communal interactions over individual responses. Observing that "on its most fundamental level cosplay is adaptation," Liam Burke contends that "cosplay, with its carnivalesque egalitarianism, is the type of vernacular adaptation that might help move adaptation studies forward" because "[a]nalysing cosplays … as adaptations allows many of the key debates that have animated adaptation studies to be revived and proved useful" (Burke 2, 14). Fans' devotion to cosplay "is only one part of a much larger live-action adaptational fabric in which fans enjoin and embody different sources" (Meikle, *Adaptations* 156), including performing musical numbers they have added to *The Hunger Games*, posting point-of-view videos of their experiences on theme park attractions, and donning virtual reality headsets to experience apps and games in uniquely immersive ways that vastly expand the ability of audiences in the groove to play with texts they love.

Although adaptation is often considered a serious business, it is an intrinsically playful activity. For every straight-faced film adaptation of history (e.g., *The Longest Day*, 1962), biography (*Lincoln*, 2012), or current events

(*Spotlight*, 2015), there is an overtly satirical or playful theatrical take on real-world events—like Awkward Productions' *Gwyneth Goes Skiing* and Roger Dipper and Rick Pearson's *I Wish You Well: The Gwyneth Paltrow Ski-Trial Musical*, both staged at the 2024 Edinburgh Festival Fringe festival, provoking laughter over the $3.1 million lawsuit optometrist Terry Sanderson filed against movie star Gwyneth Paltrow after they collided on a ski slope. Satirical productions like these are more common in live theater than cinema because lower production costs allow them to turn a profit from smaller audiences. But it could well be argued that all adaptations in any medium are playful because what they do by definition is play with their material. Political satires from Charles Chaplin's *The Great Dictator* (1940) to Stanley Kubrick's *Dr. Strangelove Or: How I Learned to Stopped Worrying and Love the Bomb* (1964) operate by cloaking serious jabs at real-world targets in wildly exaggerated language or physical hijinks, from the sequence in which Chaplin, as Hitler lookalike Adenoid Hynkel, expresses his dreams of world dominance by blithely tossing an oversized globe around his office to the custard-pie fight in the War Room originally planned to end *Dr. Strangelove*. Just as Barry Levinson's 1997 film *Wag the Dog* plays with Larry Beinhart's 1993 novel *American Hero* in many ways, beginning by changing the target of its satire about starting an imaginary war to create a diversion from problems closer to home from George H.W. Bush to Bill Clinton, William Shakespeare plays with the story of Pyramus and Thisbe in *A Midsummer Night's Dream* (1595), casting its play-within-a-play with proletarian "mechanicals" utterly unsuited to the task and supplementing its setting in ancient Athens with characters like Puck and Nick Bottom clearly drawn from different and comically incompatible universes. The very label "plays" for productions of Molière and Tom Stoppard reminds us that everyone involved with theatrical adaptations—writers, directors, performers, producers, critics, fans, and audience members—is playing with their material.

Everyone knows that news stories are contingent and subject to updating and revision, but the same thing is true of history for the same reasons. In fact, there would be no point in writing new histories of the Roman Empire or the Industrial Revolution if contemporary historians were not convinced that their research gave them something new to say that rendered earlier histories incomplete, inadequate, or mistaken. So when Davinia Thornley introduced a recent collection by announcing, "All these essays are attempting to find new ways of engaging old adaptive questions ... What does it mean for a director to become part of his/her own brand? How do we try to present the *un*representable and—more to the point—should we even try? In aiming for more exact terminology, do we, in fact, lose sight of the humanity at stake in any true event?" (Thornley 4–5), it was perfectly logical that this collection was titled *True Event Adaptation*, for storytellers have often played with true events by adapting them, sometimes to fictional, sometimes to nonfictional, texts. In recent years, we have seen a distinct downside to this impulse revealed in deepfake photos and videos, viral hoaxes, and fake news. But adaptation has always been a risky business. For better or worse, the drive toward adaptive play truly knows no limits.

Many other recent adaptations have been equally playful. The *Choose Your Own Adventure* series of children's stories, told in the second person, allowed readers to select different alternatives that led to many different narrative developments. The series generated 184 titles from 1976 to 1998, when it was discontinued because of increasing competition from videogames. Thinking about this popular series, which a generation grew up with, illuminates the interactive nature of counterfactual histories like Mackinlay Kantor's *If the South Had Won the Civil War* (1961), Philip K. Dick's *The Man in the High Castle* (1962), Margaret Atwood's *The Handmaid's Tale* (1985), and Philip Roth's *American Pastoral* (1997)—all of which play with history despite their often dystopian tone. Most Hollywood biographies, from Alexander Korda's *The Private Life of Henry VIII* (1933) to Sofia Coppola's *Marie Antoinette* (2006), are variously fictionalized stories that play fast and loose with the facts of their subjects' lives. And satirical plays like Barbara Garson's *Macbird!* (1967), which filters John F. Kennedy's assassination through the lens of *Macbeth*, and movies like Franklin J. Schaffner's *The Best Man* (1964), based on Gore Vidal's play, and Mike Nichols's *Primary Colors* (1998), based on the book that reporter Joe Klein originally published anonymously, play with politics by posing the question, "What if …?"

Nor are these interactions limited to a single direction. Just as hundreds of novelizations—from Valentine Davies's *Miracle on 34th Street* (1947) to John Jackson Miller's *Batman: Resurrection* (2024)—have been based on movies and timed to publicize those movies' release, the artist Matt Stevens has created hundreds of vintage paperback covers that adapt visual and plot motifs from movies like *Alien* and *Get Out* and collected them in *Good Movies as Old Books* (Chronicle, 2025). An even stronger and more adventurous branch of participatory culture is represented by the thousands of new stories based on familiar material archived online. The pioneer site for fan fiction, www.fan fiction.net, collected thousands of stories told in words. Many of these stories were slash fiction that introduced sexual elements into the decorous professional relationships between Sherlock Holmes and Dr. Watson or Captain Kirk and Mr. Spock. More recently, websites like www.archiveofourown. org and www.wattpad.com have shifted their focus from archives of lexical stories to archives of images, videos, and social media posts. Fans who once could only wonder how a podcast of *Pride and Prejudice* (1813) might unfold can watch and comment on the 100 episodes of *The Lizzie Bennet Diaries* (2012–13) and its many spinoffs. Users of audiovisual media from YouTube to TikTok have repurposed familiar material, or material by other fans, in provocative new ways.

Beyond these apparently boundless horizons lie still more possibilities for participatory adaptations. One of these is new: audiences with access to Open AI's ChatGPT and its VS Code extension can generate new audiovisual versions of familiar stories by means of a few strategic commands, essentially creating worlds simply by imagining them. Already the recent widely shared image of a five-second video generated by AI in response to the prompt, "Show a cow at a birthday party" (https://www.youtube.com/watch?v=fD6PSh6ToMg) has become dated as other AI platforms have created ever more sophisticated images and videos. Another is as old as listening to stories: audiences routinely fill in gaps the storytellers have left to their imaginations and engage in other activities long accepted as part of narrative literacy. And hard as it may be for students in college English courses to believe, many literary critics approach reading and interpreting as an essentially playful activity. Critics who abandon the readerly approach to texts that Roland Barthes finds characteristic of passive consumers in favor of an actively writerly approach that seeks to rewrite every text they encounter are adapting not only these particular texts but their own assumptions about traditional canons and the norms and practices of scholarship.

Whenever we create and share homemade videos, Snapchat posts, or allusive text messages, we can draw on a rich history of textual productions, from ancient epics to tomorrow's news, in combinations as unlikely as what Elizabeth Coggeshall has called "Dante memes" (Coggeshall). Not even the emerging field of image studies is capacious enough to include adaptations that can combine elements of photographs, videos, soundtracks, emojis, and more extended written, coded, or visually decorative texts. The ever-expanding work of prosumers emphasizes adaptation as an activity that similarly challenges us to think anew about our roles in the textual and metatextual universe, and whatever gaps we may have assumed between writing and reading, thinking and doing. But all these activities, like videogaming and rewriting history, pose dangers of their own. Convergence culture opens the door not only to romhacking, game-breaking, and often toxic online communities, but to the possibilities of cheating, fraud, and the unwitting loss of privacy by players unaware that the personal data they have given in order to enter a storyworld that Jenkins compares to a "Trojan horse" (Jenkins, *Convergence* 8) has been monetized and sold to data collectors. Although it may seem that "participatory culture" is a more precisely descriptive label than "convergence culture," it seems ironically unsuited for affordances that risk compromising players' personal information.

Adaptation studies has yet to generate the comprehensive concepts, methodologies, and conceptual tools that would enable its practitioners to theorize textual amalgams that combine words, images, and music, virtual reality chambers whose users find the experiences they provide indistinguishable from the experiences they simulate, or texts imagined by human beings but made to order by non-humans. These radical new intermedia are so far outside the remit of adaptation studies that the field would have to be fundamentally reimagined simply to contain them, especially since the context in which AI most often surfaces in classrooms is a warning against students using AI without acknowledgment to complete assignments they pass off as their own. The challenge of AI-generated media—which raises profound methodological, ethical, moral, and existential questions—is an unavoidable byproduct of the most up-to-the-minute variation of invisible adaptation yet to emerge from a contemporary mediascape that is bound to keep on changing.

Questions

- Are there any other games that might be especially useful to the exploration of adaptation as play—for example, boardgames, card games, casino games, improvised games, escape rooms? Why, or why not?
- How does your active participation in games compare to your active participation in other adaptations?
- How do you think adaptations would change if they were produced with the assistance of AI?

Playing (with) *Barbie*

It would be unfair to expect adaptation studies, or indeed any scholarly discipline, to solve the problems raised by AI. Its goals must be more modest—beginning, for example, with the attempt to label AI-assisted or AI-generated texts as adaptations or non-adaptations and accepting the implications of either label. What adaptation studies, like adaptations themselves, is best equipped to do is to play with these problems in a way that is as serious as the ways proposed by Jenkins, Bogost, and Chang. No single text can exhaust the possibilities of adaptive play, but a surprisingly comprehensive introduction to these possibilities can be found in *Barbie*.

The very first sequence of Greta Gerwig's movie dramatizes the many layers of play it will introduce. Even as the Warner Bros. logo is followed by the Mattel logo, the soundtrack presents a quiet breeze, echoing the opening sounds of Stanley Kubrick's 1968 sci-fi epic *2001: A Space Odyssey*. The unlikely link between the two films is confirmed by the visuals of the opening sequence, which show several girls playing with baby dolls as Helen Mirren's voiceover announces that girls have long played with baby dolls, but the unavailability of any non-baby dolls obliged them to pretend to be their mothers, which "can be fun. At least for a while. Ask your mother." As the opening notes of Richard Strauss's tone poem *Also sprach Zarathustra*—the signature tune of Kubrick's sequence—are heard, the girls look up to see the gigantic figure of Barbie (Margot Robbie) looming over them, smiling and posing in a black-and-white swimsuit. Rousing themselves from their awe-struck astonishment, the girls begin to smash their baby dolls, imitating the apes in *2001*, the music from *Zarathustra* continuing until a flash cut replaces one of the dolls tossed high into the air with the film's main title, sending up the self-seriousness of Kubrick's similar cut from a tossed bone to a spaceship even as it closely imitates it. The sudden appearance of this title indicates that the film will be about play (it will feature many characters who play roles by playing with toys); that it will play with sequences from earlier canonical films (it will go on to reference many other films and will include brief sequences from Francis Ford Coppola's 1972 gangster epic *The Godfather* and the BBC's 1995 television miniseries *Pride and Prejudice*); and that it will play constantly with its own subjects, characters, conventions, and affordances.

This last kind of play, the most distinctive in the film, is confirmed by its playful exposition of Barbieland, a pastel utopia marked everywhere by glowing smiles, pink outfits and backdrops, and female power. The President of Barbieland is Barbie. So too are all nine justices of the Supreme Court and all recent winners of the Nobel Prize. As Stereotypical Barbie drives down the street in her pink convertible after awakening to yet another perfect morning, she calls out to all the other Barbies, from crossing guards to construction workers, "Hi, Barbie!" and they all answer, "Hi, Barbie!"; though her greetings to Ken (Ryan Gosling), who hangs on her every word and glance, are considerably more perfunctory. Such a world gives its title character—or, more precisely and playfully, the most prominent version of its many title characters—every reason to be happy: as Lizzo sings while a glowing Barbie looks out at the audience through an empty frame: "If that was really a mirror, you'd see a perfect smile."

Figure 6.1 The title character of the 2023 film *Barbie* (Margot Robbie) beams out at the world through the frame of her nonexistent mirror on the last perfect morning she will experience for quite a while

It soon becomes apparent, however, that the film's self-reflexive playfulness has a darker side. The morning after Barbie suddenly silences her latest Girl's Night party by asking, "You guys ever think about dying?", she awakens still groggy and bleary-eyed, as if she had a bad hangover. Worse, everything in her normal routine goes wrong. Her toast pops out burned; her feet—originally arched, like those of Mattel's toy, to conform to her high-heeled shoes—have become mysteriously flat and big-toed; and instead of floating from the top floor of her Barbie Dreamhouse to the street below, she plunges down in a freefall. Clearly, something has happened to disrupt Barbie's fond wish that every day be exactly the same as the day before. Urged by the other Barbies, who recoil from her condition with cries of "Flat feet!", to consult Weird Barbie (Kate McKinnon)—a marginalized seer whose face and body have been distorted by the many times the girl who owned her banged her against the ground—she learns that her intimations of mortality have

> opened a portal, and now there is a rift in the continuum that is the mem-
> brane between Barbieland and the Real World, and if you want to be
> Stereotypical Barbie perfect again, then, baby girl, you gotta go fix it …
> You have to go the Real World, and you have to find the girl who's been
> playing with you.

When Barbie replies incredulously, "Playing with me?", Weird Barbie explains, "We're all being played with, babe," adding: "Her thoughts and feeling and humanness are interfering with your dollness. The two of you are becoming inextricably intertwined." In the world of *Barbie*, every kind of play—from playing with dolls to self-reflexive winks at the audience—is connected to every other kind, and those connections have serious implications, for the ways that Barbie's owner is playing with her are having dire effects on Barbieland.

As it turns out, those implications cut both ways, for Barbie's own reactions—and the odyssey to the Real World she reluctantly undertakes at the insistence of Weird Barbie and in the company of Ken, who pops up unexpectedly from the rear seat of her convertible as she's singing to herself on the road—will have an impact on the Real World that both the Federal Bureau of Investigation, when it first learns of her incursion, and her corporate creators at Mattel are determined to minimize by capturing her in an adult-sized version of the display boxes Barbies were originally sold in and sending her back to Barbieland. After escaping, she soon learns that the thoughts of death that had upended life in Barbieland had come not from Sasha (Ariana Greenblatt), the tween who owned her but hadn't played with her for years, but from Sasha's mother Gloria (America Ferrara), a Mattel designer whose recent play sessions with Sasha's Barbie, intended to alleviate her loneliness and generate new ideas by bathing her in nostalgia for her own childhood, have instead led her to create designs for "Irrepressible Thoughts of Death Barbie, Full-Body Cellulite Barbie, Crippling Shame Barbie." As Gloria confesses to Barbie: "Maybe because I couldn't be like you, I ended up making you like me."

In the meantime, Ken—sent away by Barbie so that she can focus on identifying the owner who has infected her mind—has discovered the joys of patriarchy, which he identifies with male power, male bonding, and horses.

Able to return to Barbieland while Barbie and Gloria are arrested for charges of theft that are quickly dismissed, he wastes no time in turning Barbieland into Kendom, whose capital seems to be the Ken Mojo Dojo Casa House. Although Ryan Gosling's Ken is too self-effacing to be truly threatening, the menace his newfound patriarchal temperament brings to Barbieland is truly existential, beginning with the replacement of the four Barbies on Barbieland's version of Mount Rushmore with four horses and extending to recasting President Barbie as a bartender, members of the Supreme Court as cheerleaders, and all the other Barbies as equally subservient roles which they accept unquestioningly because they have been brainwashed.

Stereotypical Barbie—whose recent adventures in the Real World, which have raised her consciousness even as they have crushed her once-cheerful spirit, have rendered her immune to this brainwashing—works with Gloria, Sasha, and Weird Barbie to distract the Kens, snatch the brainwashed Barbies one at a time, and restore their sense of empowerment by deprogramming them. Together the reunited Barbies hatch an improbable plot to turn the Kens against each other by arousing their jealousy, distracting them from voting on the male-friendly changes to the constitution of Barbieland they have proposed long enough for the Barbies to vote affirming the original constitution.

This happy ending resolves the conflict the film's plot has posed between Barbieland and Real World patriarchy but unmasks the deeper challenge of pulling off an ending that isn't reducible to the vote "in favor of making Barbieland Barbieland." It becomes easier for Barbie to win over a contrite Ken once he confesses that "when I found out the patriarchy wasn't all about horses, I lost interest anyway." But she keeps resisting the conventionally romantic couple's ending Ken is seeking, rejecting the implication that they would make the ideal couple but telling him, "Maybe it's Barbie, and it's Ken." Is the only way to banish male superiority to vote in favor of female superiority? The film plays with several possible answers to this question. President Barbie refuses the request of the Mattel CEO (Will Ferrell) to go back to the way things were before. Responding to the President's offer to appoint a Ken to a circuit court but not the Supreme Court, Mirren archly announces in voiceover: "Well, the Kens have to start somewhere. And one day the Kens will have as much power and influence in Barbieland as women have in the Real World." The film's thematic resolution must wait for a final quiet conversation between Barbie and Ruth Handler (Rhea Perlman), her original designer and creator, who replies to her anguished sense that "I'm not sure I have an ending" and "I don't feel like Barbie anymore" first by suggesting, "Maybe you're Self-Effacing Barbie?", then by warning her of the real limitations of the humanity she seeks. But Barbie's determination to embrace the humanity Ruth gently insists she can discover within herself centers the film's promise of resolution on her own identity, not the fate of the war between patriarchy and feminism.

Barbie's discovery and acceptance of her humanity, with all its limitations—beginning, ironically, with the awareness of mortality that set the film's plot in motion by rocking her world—is adroitly capped by the film's punchline: Barbie's visit to her gynecologist. Ultimately, Barbie doesn't need agency to adapt; that agency is reserved for the children and audience members who play with her, since play is the purest and most inventive form of adaptation. As Justin Chang noted in reviewing the film for the *Los Angeles Times*:

> Gerwig has conceived 'Barbie' as a bubble-gum emulsion of silliness and sophistication, a picture that both promotes and deconstructs its own brand. It doesn't just mean to renew the endless "Barbie: good or bad?" debate. It wants to *enact* that debate, to vigorously argue both positions for the better part of two fast-moving, furiously multitasking hours.
>
> (J. Chang)

Barbie could fairly be described as adaptation on steroids. It proposes and manages different ways of thinking about the many kinds of texts that invite play, different motives for playing, different consequences of playing, and a wide range of relations between playing with someone, playing against someone, playing a role, playing yourself, playing at something, and the kind of playing around we call "free play." For this reason, it is not a copout but a fulfillment that the film's real goal is not to resolve the sociopolitical conflicts that have emerged in Barbieland in ideologically definitive terms but to use the rift in the continuum between the real and imaginary worlds—the worlds of Barbie the doll, Barbie the character, *Barbie* the movie, and the audience—to raise the audience's consciousness even as they are playfully entertained in ways only an ingeniously multilayered adaptation could entertain them.

Questions

- How does your experience of *Barbie* change when you watch it for a second or a tenth time? How does it compare to other adaptations in that respect?
- One common reaction of many filmgoers to problematic fictional characters is to adapt them to the real world by psychoanalyzing them and offering therapies or cures for their problems, as Jonathan Decker and Seawright do in the YouTube series *Cinema Therapy*. How valuable do you find this approach to *Barbie*, or to other movies?
- Given the dangers of interactive adaptations, is your participation worth it, or are there certain boundaries you wouldn't cross in entering their storyworlds?
- What do interactive engagements allow or reveal about adaptations that other engagements don't?

References

Bogost, Ian. "The Rhetoric of Video Games." *The Ecology of Games: Connecting Truth, Games, and Learning.* Edited by Katie Salen. MIT P, 2008, pp. 117–40.

Buell, Lawrence. *The Environmental Imagination: Thoreau, Nature Writing, and the Formation of American Culture.* Belknap/Harvard UP, 1995.

Burke, Kenneth. *A Rhetoric of Motives.* 1950; rpt. U of California P, 1969.

Burke, Liam. "Cosplay as Vernacular Adaptation: The Argument for Adaptation Scholarship in Media and Cultural Studies." *Continuum*, Oct. 5, 2021, DOI: 10.1080/10304312.2021.1965958.

Chang, Alenda Y. *Playing Nature: Ecology in Video Games.* U of Minnesota P, 2019.

Chang, Justin. "Review: With Barbie in Pink and Gosling in Mink, 'Barbie' (Wink-Wink) Will Make You Think." *Los Angeles Times*, July 18, 2023, https://www.lati mes.com/entertainment-arts/movies/story/2023-07-18/barbie-review-margot-rob bie-greta-gerwig-mattel.

Coggeshall, Elizabeth. "Abandon Hope All Ye Who Attend This Session: Adaptation, Quotation, and Memetic Logic." Presentation at the South Atlantic Modern Language Association conference, November 2022.

Elliott, Kamilla. "Doing Adaptation: The Adaptation as Critic." *Teaching Adaptations.* Edited by Deborah Cartmell and Imelda Whelehan. Palgrave Macmillan, 2014.

Gee, James Paul. *What Video Games Have to Teach Us about Learning and Literacy.* Revised and updated ed. Palgrave Macmillan, 2007.

Hutcheon, Linda, with Siobhan O'Flynn. *A Theory of Adaptation.* Second ed. Routledge, 2012.

Jenkins, Henry. *Convergence Culture: Where Old and New Media Collide.* New York University P, 2006.

Jenkins, Henry. "Acafandom and Beyond: Week Two, Part One," *Pop Junctions*, June 20, 2011, http://henryjenkins.org/blog/2011/06/acafandom_and_beyond_w eek_two.html.

Jenkins, Henry, with Ravi Purushotma, Margaret Weigel, Katie Clinton, and Alice J Robison. *Confronting the Challenges of Participatory Culture: Media Education for the 21st Century.* MIT P, 2009.

Meikle, Kyle. "Adaptation and Interactivity." *The Oxford Book of Adaptation Studies.* Edited by Thomas Leitch. Oxford UP, 2017, pp. 542–56.

Meikle, Kyle. *Adaptations in the Franchise Era, 2001–2016.* Bloomsbury Academic, 2019.

O'Flynn, Siobhan. "Epilogue." Linda Hutcheon, with Siobhan O'Flynn, *A Theory of Adaptation*, second ed. Routledge, 2012, pp. 179–206.

Schober, Regina. "Adaptation as Connection: A Network Theoretical Approach to Convergence, Participation, and Co-Production." *Adaptation in the Age of Media Convergence.* Edited by Johannes Fehrle and Werner Schäfke-Zell. Amsterdam UP, 2019, pp. 31–56.

Thornley, Davinia. "Introduction: Scripting Real Lives." *True Event Adaptation: Scripting Real Lives.* Edited by Davinia Thornley. Palgrave Macmillan, 2018.

Toffler, Alvin. *The Third Wave.* William Morrow, 1980.

Zimmerman, Eric. "Narrative, Interactivity, Play, and Games: Four Naughty Concepts in Need of Discipline." *First Person: New Media as Story, Performance, and Game.* Edited by Noah Wardrip-Fruin and Pat Harrigan. MIT P, 2004, pp. 154–64.

Index

Note: *Italic* page numbers indicate figures.

For Product Safety Concerns and Information please contact our EU
representative GPSR@taylorandfrancis.com
Taylor & Francis Verlag GmbH, Kaufingerstraße 24, 80331 München, Germany